ALSO BY ALEKSANDAR HEMON

The Book of My Lives

Love and Obstacles

The Lazarus Project

Nowhere Man

The Question of Bruno

The **MAKING** of **ZOMBIE** **WARS**

The MAKING of ZOMBIE WARS

ALEKSANDAR HEMON

Farrar, Straus and Giroux   New York

Farrar, Straus and Giroux
18 West 18th Street, New York 10011

Copyright © 2015 by Aleksandar Hemon
Printed in the United States of America
First edition, 2015

Library of Congress Cataloging-in-Publication Data
Hemon, Aleksandar, 1964–
    The making of zombie wars / Aleksandar Hemon. — First
edition.
        pages   cm
    ISBN 978-0-374-20341-2 (hardback) — ISBN 978-0-374-71253-2
(e-book)
    1. Screenwriters—Fiction.   I. Title.

PS3608.E48 M35 2015
814'.6—dc23
                                                    2014043832

Designed by Abby Kagan

Farrar, Straus and Giroux books may be purchased for educational, business,
or promotional use. For information on bulk purchases, please contact the
Macmillan Corporate and Premium Sales Department at 1-800-221-7945,
extension 5442, or write to specialmarkets@macmillan.com.

www.fsgbooks.com
www.twitter.com/fsgbooks • www.facebook.com/fsgbooks

1   3   5   7   9   10   8   6   4   2

The mind can neither imagine anything, nor recollect past things, except while the body endures.

—BARUCH DE SPINOZA

When I was coming up, it was a dangerous world and you knew exactly who they were. It was us versus them and it was clear who them was. Today, we're not so sure who the they are, but we know they're there.

—GEORGE W. BUSH

The MAKING of ZOMBIE WARS

Script Idea #2: *An elderly contract killer with a heart condition is forced to go into retirement after he failed at his last hit. It's his only miss, so when he has a chance to redo it and restore his perfect record, he cannot say no, even if he's risking a heart attack. But then he falls in love with the target's teenage daughter.* Title: The Last Heart

Script Idea #7: *A blind man and a blind woman, attracted to each other by smell. On their first date, they find themselves at a murder scene and catch the killer's particular scent. Nobody believes them, and the perfumed killer is now pursuing them.* Title: Where Do We Go from Nowhere

Script Idea #12: *DJ Spinoza is a misfit no one understands: not his schoolmates, not his friends, not his teachers. His one dream is to DJ at his prom night and blow all those assholes away. After his radical DJ-ing results in a disastrous party at the place of the girl (Rise) he aims to hook up with, he ends up castigated. What will it take to make everyone dance and Rise fall for him?* Title: Spinning Out of Control

Now, what could I do with the boy? Joshua asked himself.
All human feelings are derived from pleasure, pain, and desire—but most important, Spin could say to Rise, from the beat. And what if he said nothing? What if he was the strong, silent type? Why this and not that? Writing is nothing if not carrying the hopeless, backbreaking burden of decisions devoid of consequences.

Afternoon at the Coffee Shoppe slipped into evening just as Joshua's caffeination reached the heights of the Rwandan plantations where his beverage originated. Hence he was burning to surf the web for Rwanda, learn some interesting facts about other cultures and allow his current creative dilemmas to resolve themselves. Back in the day, before the worldwide web of temptation, there used to be that thing called inspiration. Then the spirit was perpetually displaced by trivia and vanity search. Mercifully, there was no Internet access at the Coffee Shoppe.

Hence Joshua opened up a file with another script in perpetual development (Title: *The Snakeman Blues*), in which a comic-book geek and a retired superhero (the Snakeman), ungainfully employed as a public-school English teacher, team up to fight the evil mayor of Chicago. Joshua was incapable of deciding whether the Snakeman would die at the end or live to go back to teaching—a truly heroic activity in the city of Chicago—and if so, whether he would do so in his human or his serpentine form. The happy ending was corny, while the death was depressing, and Joshua could think of nothing in between. Besides, how exactly would a reptile fight the Chicago Police Department and the devious mayor?

Too hypoglycemic to type a word, which would then perhaps lead to the next word, he could perceive only the blank space below what he'd written last. (Snakeman: Don't! Let's take care of the boss first.) Baruch the Spinner was right: infinity exhausts all reality. But finitude does it too, almost. Joshua stared at the crosswalk outside the Coffee Shoppe where nothing was happening, until he discovered some comfort in devising wisecracks for some imaginary audience at some future dinner party: How is a *shoppe* different from a shop? Did the Wife of Bath drink soy milk chai lattes? Are the Middle English–speaking baristas commonly stricken with black death, et cetera?

He was about to open a new file to log all the shoppe cracks when a pack of ROTC cadets appeared on the Olive Street horizon in fatefully slow motion, reminding him of that long shot in *Lawrence of Arabia* where in the flat-line desert a speck grows into a horseman. The cadets forded the street fake-punching one another, slapping shaven necks, no worry in their lives, save the fear of being expelled from the pack. And then he saw them in the desert, thickly coated in dust, tongue-hanging thirsty on their way to a battle where they would mature and/or heroically die, the nefarious natives offering them contaminated piss-warm water in beaten tin cups. The cadets couldn't begin to conceive of their sandstorming future; they couldn't as much as pity themselves in advance. In fact, they could see little beyond their imminent meal, beyond acting out their childish toughness, beyond playacting hand-to-hand combat at lunch break. He who has a mind capable of a great many things has a body whose greatest part is eternal, wrote Baruch. And out of the sad ROTC mindlessness the scene from *Dawn of the Dead* was recollected in which zombies tottered in circles around a depopulated shopping mall unable to forget their life before their undeath, their infected brains still retaining the remnants of their happy Christmas memories. A chubby cadet sensed the intensity of Joshua's inspired gaze and, as the rest of the corps trundled on to the next-door sandwich shop, stopped to grin at him from the other side of the window. His face was wide, his cheeks flushed, his front teeth of uneven sizes like a skyline, his eyes lit up with the arrogant innocence of youth. In a blissful blink, Joshua saw the narrative landscape neatly laid down before him: all the endless possibilities, all the overhead and wide shots, all the graceful character trajectories blazing across the spectacular firmament, all the expanse conducive to a love interest—all Joshua had to do was stroll through that Edenic symmetry and write it down. This time, he was determined, his vision would not decompose in the computer's memory with the skeletons of his other ideas; he opened, right then and there, a new Final Draft file and created the title page to stare at it:

Zombie Wars
by Joshua Levin
Chicago, March 31, 2003

Whereupon he stared at it.

Alas, unless you're the Lord himself, creation cannot be willed: Joshua needed to eat something before embarking upon it, and hence stood in line behind an overtattooed prick who couldn't decide between banana and pumpkin bread, while the barista in a Che Guevara hat (yet presumably fluent in Middle fucking English) looked on indifferently. The impasse allowed Joshua to imagine a zombie biting into the prick's neck tattoos, blood splashing the ready lattes, turning them pink, the zombie oblivious to the hysterically hissing espresso machine. The revolutionary-Chaucerian barista, artistically striving for the perfect foam, took an eternity to steam the milk for Joshua's cappuccino, giving enough time for the zombie apocalypse to smoothly exhaust its cataclysmic reality and sink to the bottom of Joshua's mind. Back at his shaky table, he sat munching on carrot bread until he reached a Zen-worthy level of caffeine-crash blankness. He closed the file, then the program, and then, finally, his computer, to put it in his bag, to sleep.

Substantial portions of Joshua's life had been wasted before, leaving no trace of trauma or regret. But the pressing problem on this particular Monday was that he needed to turn in some pages to his Screenwriting II workshop(pe?), which was to be conducted that night at Graham's place for the first time. The Birkenstock cocksuckers from the Film Collective were bloodsuckers as well, per Graham, taking a shameless cut of the class fee without bothering to provide enough toilet paper. He'd been paying for it out of his pocket, until he'd concluded that his faithful workshoppers could just as well wipe their asses at his humble abode, while he could keep all the money for himself.

The pageless Joshua, equipped only with the vaguest zombie memories, was thus ensconced in a purple beanbag on Graham's living-room floor. Pretzels and a spacious plastic bottle of defizzed Diet Coke crowded the coffee table. With his testicles squeezed by his twisted underwear, Joshua avoided all eye contact with the beflanelled Dillon, who was outlining some idea of his, hip-deep in the faded, sunken futon. Bega was there too, hunched at the desk in a Motörhead T-shirt, contemplating the splendorously lit Wrigley Field in Graham's window. The baseball crowd emitted a home-run roar and Bega grunted wistfully, his thick, unneatly parted gray hair conspicuously rhyming with the grayish shrub on his face. Graham interrupted Dillon's rambling to make a point by sharing a pertinent section from the script he'd just completed.

" 'Blessed be the amateurs!' " Graham spoke in the bloated voice of one of his cardboard characters. "'The triers, the failers, the shit-swimmers! Let us praise those who dream big and achieve nothing, those undaunted by impossibilities, entrapped by possibilities! They are the dung beetles of the American Dream, the unsung little fertilizers of American soil.'"

Graham rubbed his thumb pensively against his cleft chin as he looked up at his audience for their reaction: Dillon was looming over an open notebook in his lap, writing something down furiously; Bega nodded, chewing his Bic pen to pieces; Joshua was fixated on Graham, but only because his very balls were swelling in the painful squeeze. Addressing the problem required standing up and shoving his hand into his pants to free his testicles from the grip of his underwear. He was not ready for such a commitment, so he endured. The mind can imagine nothing except while the body endures.

"Just so you don't wonder what happens," Graham continued, "my boy goes on to make it big. He's gonna bottom out at the end of Act Two, but then comes back in Act Three, winning a Golden Globe."

Joshua tried to reach for his backpack, but the pain in his groin made him gasp and sit back. Graham's living room was overwhelmed with paperbacks—on the shelves, on the floor, on the windowsills—all of them dusty and invested in the magic of film and the science of screenwriting. The only wall without books featured a gigantic poster for *The Godfather: Part II*, Al Pacino looming over them like Jesus in an altarpiece.

"This is all based on a true story, gentlemen. Hollywood big shots lined up all the way to the Hills to have a diet soda with me, but I wasn't gonna let them fuck me! No, sir!" Graham flashed his middle finger to the erstwhile line of big shots. "Feel free to fuck yourselves, you bunch of Weinsteins!"

Graham rocked back and forth, Hasid-like, as he ranted, his bald crown reddening patchily like a lava lamp. Bega seemed to enjoy the rant, as he abandoned the Bic mastication for a hearty laugh. Meanwhile, Joshua rolled out of the beanbag to stand up, grimacing in the pain overriding Graham's anti-Semitic insinuations.

"Point is," Graham continued, "you're willing to learn, and that's undoubtedly fucking great. So, Dillon, to be perfectly and productively honest, that's far from the smartest idea I've ever heard. But we're gonna work on it all day long and we're gonna make it good."

Dillon wrote something down, then turned the page to write some more. Joshua finally pulled down his pants to release his balls, in the process of which his navel-eye blinked at everyone from a tuft of hair.

"What in hell are you doing?" Graham asked.

"Inadvertent self-wedgie," Joshua explained.

Graham clapped his hands, startling Dillon. "Do you hear that, Dillon? Inadvertent self-wedgie! Write that down! That's what you want your characters to say, not some anodyne bullshit about corporate greed."

The pleasure of untwisting his balls was compounded by Graham's praise, so Joshua felt entitled to make Dillon scoot over so he could sit down on the futon. He examined the night outside: the sparkle of the ball game all over Wrigleyville; the lit El train struggling along the Sheridan curve; the Lake Shore skyscrapers on the horizon; the endless darkness beyond. Bega shook his hair over the desk, as if trying to get something out of it. Could it be lice?

Joshua had been in Screenwriting I with Bega; they'd never talked much beyond exchanging remarks on their inchoate scripts. Bega would always project mean superiority while mocking the inane plots in the pages of other workshoppers. His plots would not be much better, but he'd protect himself by withholding their resolutions, claiming he wanted to keep the workshoppers involved.

"Is there such a thing as an advertent self-wedgie?" Dillon asked.

"There are all kinds of wedgies. Let a thousand flowers bloom," Graham said. "What happens next?"

Dillon consulted his notebook. There was no writing in its pages, Joshua noticed, only doodled arabesques.

"They're like in the desert," Dillon said, "and there are like all these things. He like stops by the fear booth and these like guys ask him what his fears are and he says, it's like sharks and waves, and these like guys come out dressed as his worst fears and like follow him around. And then he takes 'shrooms with the goth girl, and they go on the most fantastic trip of their like life, and then he decides not to go on to LA for the job and like live with the goth girl in the desert community."

Graham watched him intently, conceptualizing the fear booth and the guys dressed as sharks and waves. "That's gonna cost a lot of money," he said.

Evidently, money had never crossed Dillon's mind—he wrote *money* in an empty space left between the arabesques, then underlined it twice.

"Fact: you need no money to write a script, but you need oodles to make a movie. Fact: you will have to beg for money, part of the job." Graham began rocking again. "And the Weinsteins will unleash their twenty-two-year-old dipshit suckerfish to skim your life's work in one lazy afternoon. Then they'll throw at you the piddly coin they spend monthly on their chest depilation and expect you to work with that. You need to know you're nothing to them! You're a zero! Absolute fucking nothing! Zero!"

Bega laughed again—Graham's hatred of the Weinsteins seemed to amuse him to no end. Joshua's chest constricted with a gasp of guilt—he should counter the slight, but couldn't. Dillon blinked in what must have been panic at the blotches floating across the expanses of Graham's cranium. He then returned to the safety of doodling: at phenomenal speed he was now turning spirals into tornadoes, which in the upper half of the page biblically connected with dark-ness. On the opposite, tornado-free page, there was a scene featuring stick people with speech bubbles over their O-heads, one of them grasping an oval surfboard with his stick hand. *Zombie Wars*, Joshua thought. Where do we go from nowhere?

"The good news is that if you could get a hunky male star to be the surfer dude you might be able to find some dough," Graham said, having steadied himself. "Maybe that, what's his name, Hartnett?"

"I think you should make this dude more of real person," Bega said. It was surprising to hear him talk—he'd been laughing on the fringes all night. "He should be normal, little bit of philosopher, maybe loser. Like Josh here."

In Screenwriting I, Bega had wittily and deservedly, Joshua thought, picked on a Peruvian whose drafts had featured Inca gods fighting sea monsters. This time Joshua said: "Me? How did I come into this?"

From a distance, they all examined Joshua, the survivor of an inadvertent self-wedgie: the body of a lightweight wrestler who'd quit wrestling after middle school; the droopy eyes that, in a more flattering light, could appear contemplatively sorrowful; the slight overbite that often made him look unduly perplexed.

"To be perfectly honest, finding hunkiness in Joshua is a challenge," Graham said. "I'm just kidding."

Dillon laughed, relieved that Graham was off his back, and embarked upon drawing houses with smoke-spewing chimneys. Crematoria? Was it a subliminal—or, fuck it, liminal—way for Dillon to align himself with Graham's latent anti-Semitism? Even before the crematoria tableau, Joshua firmly believed that Dillon's chubbiness was born of devotion to obscure nineties bands, which required a uniform: flannel shirt, Costello glasses, expensive trucker hat. And who comes from LA to take screenwriting workshops in Chicago? He probably came here to *like live* for free with his grandmother. Mrs. Alzheimer, née Loaded.

"Now that he brought your ass up, Josh," Graham says, "whaddya got? Fresh, stunning work? A roller-coaster ride of violence and sex?"

Bega leaned forward to hear Joshua, his eyebrows' grays now shimmering under the desk light.

"I don't think I have pages. But I do think I have a new idea," Joshua said. "The working title is *Zombie Wars*."

"What happened to DJ Spinoza?" Graham asked.

"I need to figure some things out. I can't hear the music yet."

"And what about your teacher superhero?"

"He can wait his turn," Joshua said. "The world is full of superheroes."

"Sure it is," Graham said, "as it's just about to run out of zombies."

Dillon snickered. Joshua imagined smacking him with the back of his hand. That boy could be a tasty snack for a zombie. Bega nodded, as though approving of Joshua's vision.

"Okay," Graham said, with exaggerated patience, "let's pretend you don't change your mind every week. Let's pretend we don't give a flying fuck. Okay. What matters is how good in the room you are. So: pitch me the damn thing! I'm your fat Weinstein. Make me fall in love with you and your story! Sell me *Zombie Wars*! I got what you need! I got no brains, but I got oodles of money!"

Joshua inhaled. He imagined a fat Weinstein behind an intimidating desk, glowering at him; he also considered getting up and leaving, never to see Graham or endure his knee-jerk bigotry, never to write another line of dialogue. There was a solid case to be made for a screenwriting career entirely organized around avoiding the Weinsteins as well as for a life arranged around the absence of hope and ambition. But Bega was looking at Joshua as though burning to hear what he had to say, and Joshua exhaled. Anything whatever can be the accidental cause of hope or fear.

"Okay. Okay: The American government has a secret program to turn immigrants into slaves," he improvised. "The government creates a virus to turn them into zombies who work in factories, chained to the production line."

Now they all watched him with apparent interest. Dillon stopped doodling; the blotches on Graham's forehead merged into a solid vermilion field; Bega nodded at Joshua again, approving of the immigrant aspect. It was difficult to make stuff up in the limelight of their attention, but he'd leapt up and now had no choice but to fall.

"Things go wrong," Joshua said. "Things go terribly wrong."

"They would," Graham said.

"And virus spreads?" Bega asked. "Not just immigrants are infected?"

"Yeah," Joshua said. "The virus definitely spreads. Anybody can get infected."

"Who's gonna stay alive?" Graham asked. "Any ladies?"

"Not sure," Joshua said. "Probably. Some will pop up as I work on it."

"The virus spreads, then what?" Dillon asked.

"Well," Joshua said, slowly, to bide his time. "Well, the government sends out the military. To wipe them all out. The army guys just shoot them in the head and blow them up and have fun. It would be a bloodbath, if zombies actually bled. But there are so many undead immigrants that soldiers turn into zombies too, and they start killing everybody, not just foreigners. Things get crazy, killers and zombies everywhere, chaos, no one to trust, nowhere to go. It's a nightmare."

It all just came out, without effort or thinking. It felt like lying, only better, because he couldn't be caught, and he couldn't be caught because there was nothing to verify it against. Immersed in the flow of bullshit, they had no reason, or time, not to believe him.

"But there is an army doctor, Major Klopstock, who believes he can beat the virus. Major Klopstock works on a vaccine—"

"Wait a minute," Graham said. "What kind of a name is that? Major Klopstock? Are you kidding me? Might as well call him Major Crapshit."

"I actually like Klopstock," Joshua said. "Klopstock could be a main hero. Why not?"

"Do you really think Bruce Willis would agree to be named Klopstock? You could never pay him enough for that. Think of something else."

This was a chance for Joshua to confront Graham and defend Major Klopstock's implied Jewishness. On the other hand, the character was not quite alive yet, nor was Joshua married to the name; and strictly speaking, Graham hadn't actually mentioned his Jewishness. This was neither the time nor the place.

"Okay: Major Something Else gives the vaccine to himself," Joshua went on. "At first we don't know if he'll make it or become a kind of zombie himself."

"And then what?" Dillon asked.

"And then struggle ensues," Joshua said. "That's what the story is about. The major's struggle."

"Struggle is good. Outside the name issue, it's a start,"

Graham said. "Maybe the army can also fight some, like, terrorist zombies, blowing themselves up like crazy. It's a good time to be thinking about all that, given that we're just about to tear a new hole in the ass of Iraq."

"I didn't actually think of that," Joshua said.

"It could be fun, believe me. We unleash the zombie army at the camelfuckers and then it all flies off the handle and our undead boys come back to feed on our flesh. I think that's pretty fucking good. Don't you think it's good? Let me pat myself on the back!"

Graham patted himself on the back.

"I don't know," Joshua said. "I don't want it to be too political."

"Why not?" Bega offered. "Look at situation now. Muslim enemies everywhere, every movie, everything on television, everybody happy to invade. Everything is political. Everybody is political."

"Hey, they took our towers down," Graham said. "Revenge is a dish best served with carpet bombing."

"Saddam had nothing to do with towers," Bega said. "No connection."

"People say we did it ourselves," Dillon said, "so that we could like attack Iraq and take their like oil."

The red patch flared up on Graham's forehead, but then he chose to say nothing and the blotch disintegrated.

"I'd love to bullshit for a living, my friends," he said instead, "but right now you're paying me oodles to help you with your screenwriting. You got ten minutes, Vega, if you want to talk about your stuff."

"I'm just saying," Dillon said.

"*Bega*," Bega said. "I am Bega. As I was before."

"Whatever. *Vega. Bega.* You can call yourself Klopstock for all I care. Let a thousand flowers bloom," Graham said. "Whaddya got? Pages?"

"No pages. Pages I have when I know everything."

Bega rubbed his face vigorously with both hands and then scratched his skull, ruffling his hair, possibly releasing some lice. He grinned as if experiencing a spasm. Something was always happening on his face, some flow of tricky mental states ever visible.

"It's basically love story," Bega said. "Man is from Sarajevo. He was happy there. He was young, he had rock group, had women. War came. He is refugee now. He goes to Germany. They are Nazis there. He works like security in disco, plays his guitar only for his soul. He drinks, remembers Sarajevo, writes blues songs. Comes 1997, Nazis throw him out. He goes back to Sarajevo, but nothing is same. Heartbreak."

"Yeah, yeah . . . We heard that the last time. Got something beyond that?"

"Can I smoke?" Bega asked.

"Can you smoke? Can you *smoke*? Hell no!" Graham said. "With all due respect."

"Okay," Bega said, licking his lips. "Man has no more friends in Sarajevo. Half of his group is dead, other half everywhere. Women have husbands. Everybody talks about the war all the time. He says, Fuck it! and goes to America—country of Dylan and Nirvana and best basketball. But he lost his soul. And American women are all feminists—"

"Ain't that the truth," Graham said.

"—and he works in store that sells guitars. One day mother and daughter come in. Mother is pretty but daughter is fantastic. He plays a beautiful song for them from Sarajevo. Daughter falls in love with him. It is like in love novels, but mother calls police. He is stalker, she says, because she's jealous."

"How old is the daughter?" Dillon asked.

Bega failed to hear him. At some point his gaze drifted toward the *Godfather: Part II* poster and he spoke as if pitching his story to Saint Pacino himself.

"But then mother dies from pills for depression. Daughter thinks he killed her. Police thinks it's him too. Newspapers think it's him. He has to prove it's not him. He's just immigrant, but his picture is everywhere. All America hates him. Big problem."

"Is there a killer?" Joshua asked, returning the favor of attention.

"Maybe husband," Bega said. "Maybe not."

"That's pretty good," Graham said. "Immigrant detective, that's pretty cool. Like, you are illegal, but you have to go around to figure things out. I would be careful about the detective clichés, though. And also grammar."

"Maybe the daughter can help clear his name," Joshua said. "I'm a little concerned about the ending."

"American movies always have happy ending," Bega said. "Life is tragedy: you're born, you live, you die."

"This could be like a European art-house movie. Which would be good because you could show tits," Graham said, pausing to picture the tits. "Anyway, we gotta go. Next time, I'd like to see some pages. Things change when you have pages. It all becomes real."

"Real is real good," Dillon said.

Joshua walked out into the thick lightlessness of Grace Street and was just about to unlock his bike when, somewhat noirishly, Bega lit up his cigarette and called to him, exhaling smoke from the restored darkness: "We go for beer? I'll give you ride." Joshua trawled his mind for an excuse to decline. An arbitrary vision of Bega twisting his arm behind his back presented itself, but then he didn't want to be scared nor did he want to look scared. Bega regarded him with a smirk that might have been a derisive smile, or just a long expression of expectation. Dillon walked out and stood before them, beaming a friendship offer. They both ignored it. "Have like a good night, guys," Dillon finally said, and got into his rust-eaten vehicle, kept together by stickers expressing someone else's thoughts: *If you want peace, work for justice* and such. If Joshua had to put one sticker on his car (which he didn't have) it would be: *Whatever is, is either in itself or in the other.* Who on the street would ever understand what that meant? That's exactly what would be so cool about it.

"All right, let's go for a drink," he said.

Bega was at home, he informed Joshua proudly, at the Westmoreland; he practically lived there, everyone knew him. But there was no one there to know him tonight, as the Westmoreland was desolate: a derelict jukebox in the corner; the Cubs game on TV high above the bar; a drunken couple drool-coating each other's faces over a far table. It was one of those Chicago watering holes that proudly wore the badge of neglect on their tattered sleeves, reeking of yeast and sawdust. Here, the Westmoreland pronounced, livers have been pickled, marriages destroyed, guts disgorged. Joshua took the stool next to Bega, who rearranged a cluster of beer bottles on the bar as though solving a chess problem. The bartender came over wordlessly (Bega: "Hey, Paco!"), stuck his

fingers in the rearranged bottles, and nodded barely percep-
tibly to indicate he was available for orders.

"Whiskey," Bega said. "And Bud."

"What kind of wine do you have?" Joshua asked.

"Red," Paco said. "White."

"I'd like a glass of red," Joshua submitted. Paco's face
expressed nothing, but Joshua was sure he could detect contempt in his eyes for his unbecoming fussiness.

"I was thinking, Josh," Bega said. "Why America now
must have superheroes? Why can't you just have normal heroes? John Wayne was not good enough, now you must have
Batman? What do you think?"

"Actually, Batman is not a superhero, strictly speaking,"
Joshua said. "He's kind of an insanely entitled capitalist
with a lot of gadgets. He has no superpower, he just works
out like crazy."

Paco brought drinks: Joshua's red wine was in a martini
glass. Ordering wine in this place was not unlike ordering
milk—he was fortunate there were no real (or any) men at
the bar to mock his pussiness. If you want peace, get a Bud-
weiser. He stared at the wine; he'd have to drink it now, even
if fully expecting vinegar.

"John Wayne would throw few punches, break bad furniture, and settle moral argument," Bega went on, downing
his bourbon shot between *moral* and *argument*. "These days,
you can't do nothing without special effects."

The Cubs were losing by ten runs in the eighth inning,
but Paco was transfixed, his head tilted back so far it seemed
it might break off and clatter onto the floor. It was hard to
tell whether he was expecting a miracle or he'd entered some
kind of trance where the difference between victory and defeat was void. On the side of his neck he had a perfectly

perfect goiter, glowing under the dim lights like a commercial for cancer. In *My Darling Clementine*, Henry Fonda asked the bartender at the saloon: "Have you ever been in love?" and he said: "I've always been a bartender."

"In Sarajevo I knew one fat kid," Bega said, washing the whiskey down with beer, waving to Paco to request more. "Fat kids were rare, not like here, so bullies loved him, loved to beat him. Once he came up with crazy story: he saw spaceship through his window in the middle of night and aliens gave him superpower. After that, he says, he can lift cars and destroy buildings, so bullies make secret organization against him. They are after him, always ready to attack. One day, he points at one building and tells us: They're watching me right now. We look, there is nothing. But he is not afraid anymore."

"That's a great story," Josh said. "That could be a great screenplay." Bega dismissed the compliment with a flick of his hand. In addition to smoke and cologne, he exuded shapeless contempt for weakness. It was quite possible that he'd been a fat kid who eventually tormented other kids; or a bully who turned fat—his girth was still impressive.

The Cubs had finally lost their game by twelve runs. All the players looked absurdly inept, as though they were expressly drafted to be humiliated, entrepreneurs in the industry of losing. Paco scratched his goiter and it wiggled a bit under the skin, like a mature fetus. Script Idea #11: *A gay pitcher sells his soul to the devil to play in the World Series. The price: he has to turn straight.* Title: *At the Bat.* Joshua took a gulp of his wine and it burned his interiority. It was worse than vinegar, it was like dry-cleaned brine, the taste of rough-edged authenticity: by reality and perfection I understand the same thing. Paco pointed the remote at the TV and switched to the news: George W. Bush spoke to the camera, his face so decisively earnest that it was clear he was lying, his button eyes lit up with amateurish subterfuge. Only truly great men can be adept at shameless lying, Joshua thought. This dude was straining to the point of snapping.

"Tell me why is that," Bega said, "last eight presidents have simple names: Johnson, Nixon, Ford, Carter, Reagan, Clinton, two with Bush. You used to have Washington, Roosevelt, and Eisenhower, and then something happened. You can't elect your president with complicated name anymore. Idiot voters have to be able to spell fucking name."

Joshua gave thought to the hypothesis but the authentic wine ruthlessly interfered with the thought, which subsequently dissolved like a body in acid. Bega swallowed another shot, then washed it down with beer. What Joshua could not understand was why Bega cared at all. Why would he bother to parse these matters American? Joshua himself didn't care. Americans would never worry about the names of other countries' presidents. That's what's great about this country. Bega surely was enough of an American now to stop giving a fuck.

"Dukakis," Joshua said.

"Correct," Bega said. "No chance."

On the TV, a retired, Humpty Dumpty–shaped general was now pointing—with an actual pointer—at the map of Iraq. It was clear that he thought it was all going swimmingly, his pointer flying all over the map, as if he were caning it.

"Rumsfeld—a snowball in hell," Joshua said.

"Don't know about that," Bega said. "Only two syllables. He could do it."

"You're right."

Bega offered his beer for another chin-chin, as if to confirm the achieved mutual understanding, and Joshua raised his brine martini glass to meet it.

Men think, also drink, bond. Deliver lengthy soliloquies built of improvised conviction, incomplete sentences. They touch the biceps of their fellow man, punch his shoulder affectionately; a few bruises—why not?—the marks of shared manhood, of alcohol-enhanced circulation. Men confide, lust rhetorically, copulate hypothetically with women of unacknowledged fantasy. Men outline their life stories and philosophies, relive ball games, take good care not to care visibly about anything. Fuck, they say, a fucking lot. Men don't even have to be from the same country as their fellow man.

Paco kept delivering the booze while the two men huddled close. Snout to snout, they shared with each other their identifying obsessions and favorites: *The Wild Bunch* (Yes! Bega: "Last western ever."); Led Zeppelin (Yes!); drinking (they chin-chinned); Dylan (Josh could not stand the whiny voice); women (Bega lecherously licked his lips); *Conan the Barbarian*, the movie (Josh: "Isn't it a touch fascist?"); Radiohead (Bega retching); Pantera (Josh had never heard of them), et cetera. Bega sketched in a beer puddle on the bar a map of Bosnia and the bellicose Balkans, deploying cigarette butts for national capitals. Proudly, he proclaimed: "We surf catastrophe!" as Josh refrained from inquiring who exactly the *we* was. For his part, Josh listed the relevant points in his drama-deprived life: his Wilmette childhood, tolerable except for his parents' divorce; a complete set of grandparents, all Florida-based Holocaust survivors, Nana Elsa his favorite; college years at Northwestern, three miles away from his parents' home, majoring in film studies, minoring in philosophy. And Spinoza was *da man*, the first secular Jew in history. "My man Baruch predicted movies in the seventeenth fucking century!" Josh spoke excitedly. "He said: 'The more an image is joined with other images, the more often it flourishes.'" Nana Elsa loved old movies and watched them with Josh—"Good movies are like wine," Nana used to say, "they need to mature." "Not like this shit," Josh said and downed his swill.

Whereupon he proceeded to paint the picture of his hot Japanese-American girlfriend, his beautiful Zen mistress, with the lovely name of Kimiko, Bega's eyes widening. Josh went on to paint, if with a less colorful palette, his teaching English as a second language to a bunch of Russians and other immigrants at a Jewish vocational school. He watercolored, so to speak, his laptop as brimming with script ideas, none close to being actualized. He finally sketched a bright future in which he would sell a script for a bucket of coin, quit his job, and move in with Kimmy, who had at least once, by her own confession, participated in a threesome.

Actually, there could never be any reason to believe that there would be a future, Bega retorted. We end up expecting it only because we do not know how not to imagine it. It's a human deficiency, constantly plotting some kind of future— and from that deficiency comes cinema. Unless you're watching a movie, it is crazy to expect that the present will continue happening—any moment could be the last moment. In lieu of evidence for his claim, Bega subsequently offered the incoherent highlights of what he referred to as his previous life: his two years in the film academy while working on what he called Top List of Surrealists; the fantastically beautiful women of Sarajevo; the orgiastic euphoria on the eve of the war disaster; the drinking, the drugs, the end of it. Finally the war foreclosing and canceling the future while everybody believed that good life would go on forever. "So here I am!" Bega said and downed his shot.

Another round of drinks; more talk; more images on the TV of our troops in Baghdad; the euphoric broadcasters; Paco dipping beer mugs in a foam cloud in the sink; the jukebox playing a plaintive song; the couple stumbling over to fuck in the bathroom stalls; everything as it should be, because it could not be otherwise. Reality and perfection are definitely the same fucking thing.

Another round and Bega and Josh were arguing over what might qualify one for the title of a survivor. Bega adamantly denied it to Josh, unconditionally claiming it for himself. Joshua was by now too drunk to win the argument, even if he descended from an estimable dynasty of survivors, and was presently in the midst of surviving the acid in his glass.

On the positive side, the two men were equal in their inebriation, which led to a unanimous consensus: they were drunk like foxes. "Fuck it!" they chin-chinningly proclaimed. "Fuck the fucking future!"

INT. NORIKO'S BATHROOM — NIGHT

Captain Enrique takes off his Marine uniform, exposing his tattooed biceps and chest. Noriko in-
vites him to join her in the shower. He does,
followed closely by Linda. The three of them have
intense sex, Captain Enrique's dog tags steadily
rattling.

Suddenly, a zombie rips the curtain off the rod
and bites into the man, who has a map of Mexico on
his chest, taking out a chunk of his shoulder. As
Noriko and Linda scream in horror, Captain Enrique
grabs the showerhead and pummels the unrelenting
zombie. Fighting for his life, he tears off the
zombie's ear, then an arm. The undead keeps biting
into his arm. Bleeding profusely, Captain Enrique
finally succumbs. The zombie feasts on his body as
Noriko and Linda lose their voices screaming. Soon
we hear only their HOPELESS PLEADING.

John Wayne goes to Sarajevo. They feed him, they get him drunk, they show him around. There's this, there's that, this is where World War One started, here's an old mosque. But John Wayne is walking funny, and he finally says: Man, I really gotta piss. They take him to a public toilet. He goes, comes back, his cowboy hat soaked with piss, boots full of it. What happened? they ask him. Well, John Wayne says, I walk into the men's room and all these guys are at the urinals and they scream: John Wayne! and they all turn to me with their dicks in their hands.

Bega had started grunting with laughter, swinging his torso in the driver's seat to replicate the urinary lash, the plush dice bobbing with his movement. He'd clapped his hands following the punch line, his mouth open so wide for the roar that Joshua could see his tonsils. It was still funny: walking toward Magnolia after Bega dropped him off, Joshua kept chuckling to himself. So immersed in a vision of regaling someone with the joke was he that only as he stopped by Kimiko's place did he realize his bike remained locked up outside Graham's.

He considered stopping by to see Kimmy before sleep. The glow in her bedroom window suggested she was reading. Kee-mee-ko. He relished the sound of her name, shaped exactly like her: the long legs, the curved hips, the long hair.

He liked her confidence, the peace with which she made decisions. She was a child psychologist, specializing in divorce trauma. Also, molestation trauma. She'd been married once before, right out of college, to a self-professed guy named Haskell Something the Third. She mentioned him rarely, but whenever she did she referred to him as the Third. *The Third liked three things: his Porsche, lacrosse, and Newt Gingrich.* She never explained the role of the Third in her life, as though the marriage happened to someone else. She analyzed others, but not herself. She read Harry Potter because it helped her better understand her little patients better. She always referred to the kids as little patients.

Joshua adored the way she laughed: she constricted her mouth, shook her head, then snorted, then exploded. He wanted to serenade her with the John Wayne joke, so he dialed her number from the street: perhaps she would invite him up for a triple-header of laughter, BJ, and full intercourse. But the network was down and his calls were repeatedly dropped and then her light went out. He would've rung her doorbell if it wasn't for his fear of her finding the joke stupid. Moreover, the piss aspect of the joke put extra pressure on his buckling bladder, which now insisted that he quicken his step. That made something down there hurt. Could that be his prostate? By the time he reached his door, merely two blocks down Magnolia, his bladder was bulging to the point of bursting. The mind strives to imagine those things that increase the body's power. Say, urination.

He hastily unlocked his front door, dropped the keys and the phone on the table under the cracked mirror, and hurried on to the bathroom. Before he reached it, he noticed the billowing curtains in the living room; he heard the tiny peals of oriental chimes. He was almost sure he hadn't left any windows open—it was, after all, the end of March. A deep memory of the way late-night ninjas sensed presences was consequently activated and like a ninja he did tiptoe. All flimsy skin and hollow bones, Joshua was practically weightless: he cast no shadow; the floor did not creak. The living room was empty, but dust balls led him, levitating, to his bedroom.

No deep movie memory was available to help him decide what to do if indeed there was someone in the bedroom. Hence he became instantly paralyzed when he discovered a man kneeling on the floor, weeping with his face buried in what was, without a shred of a doubt, a pair of Joshua's boxer shorts patterned with stars and stripes. He'd dropped the shorts in the dirty-laundry basket this morning, and there was indeed the wicker basket, pitilessly knocked over, and there was the rest of his dirty underwear lined up on the floor for some perverse inspection. The man's ponytail was tightly pulled back, fluttering in concert with his sobs; he wore a sleeveless denim jacket, so that the tattoo of an eagle with the earth in its talons was blazingly visible on his sinewy biceps. I know this man, Joshua realized—for a fleeting micromoment, the realization was soothing.

"Stagger! What the fuck are you doing?"

Stagger leapt to his feet and charged toward the open window, managing to wipe away his tears with Joshua's underwear, as if the actual problem were that he'd been caught crying. He batted the billowing curtains apart and slipped out like a true ninja and the former marine that he was. Stagger, it might be pertinent to mention, was Joshua's landlord and downstairs neighbor.

The room was cold as a morgue. His prostate hurt like hell, but Joshua sat down on his bed, puffing out vapor, and stared at the boxer shorts array on the floor as if it contained a message that needed to be urgently decoded. His heart was galloping toward a heart attack, his brain away from comprehension. He let out a primally inarticulate scream at the still-billowing curtains and went over to shut the window. He kicked up the boxer shorts arrangement. The heart was pounding, the prostate collapse imminent, but Joshua lay down on the bed to look up at the motionlessly indifferent ceiling fan.

A siren wailed down the street, reminding Joshua that time sometimes did flow forward on its way to consequences. He did wish the police to come by, but that was all he was going to do about it. In the mind there is no free will, but the mind is determined to will this or that by a cause that is also determined by another, and this again by another, and so on to infinity. He would've watched the ceiling to infinity, had his bladder not started leaking.

When the going gets tough, the tough might find comfort in the smallest of pleasures: Joshua's urine stream was thick and steady with relief.

When Joshua had signed the lease the previous summer, Stagger had appeared as stolid and reliable, his cut-off denim jacket notwithstanding, as one would expect from a marine who'd proudly served his country. But soon after moving in, Joshua could occasionally hear Guns N' Roses blasting from downstairs, accompanied by the sound of things being smashed and Stagger's screaming "Watch it bring you to your knees" and such in unison with Axl Rose. More than once, the party would go on for an entire night. The following morning Stagger would come up to apologize and ascribe his appetite for destruction to his alleged Desert Storm trauma. It made him act crazy, he'd said. It hadn't always been clear to Joshua whether that was a concealed threat or a way to invite pity and forgiveness. Either way, Joshua hoped his continued understanding would keep the rent low. As a way of additional reconciliation, Stagger had offered to show him his samurai sword, so sharp, he'd said, it could slice a running dog in half and both halves would still jump at the same time to catch the Frisbee.

He was moving out of this fucking place, Joshua decided, come the weekend. He should have already moved out for the Guns N' Roses abuse alone. Above the toilet hung an inexplicable reproduction of a foxhunt painting: red coats and black bubble caps and tall horses and a few clouds bumbling forth over a composed Victorian landscape. Joshua heard his front door clicking, whereupon something shifted in the corner where the fox was frozen in her escape, her future forever foreclosed. The voice Joshua instantly identified as Stagger's said: "What's going on in here?"

In a lightning move, Joshua turned, swinging the dick in his trembling hand to spray—from right to left—the upright toilet seat, the toilet paper roll next to it, *A Spinoza Reader*, and a basket full of magazines, until he—still emitting spurts onto his own thigh—faced Stagger, who stood akimbo under the hallway light, his face calm and composed to the sharp point of insanity.

"Everything okay, Jonjo?" Stagger lowered his gaze to grin at Joshua's trickling dick.

Joshua broke out of the bathroom, bouncing off Stagger's flank to fly through the front door, conveniently unclosed. He raced down the stairs, not stopping until he found himself in the middle of Magnolia, where he finally returned his penis to its natural habitat. His groin and pant legs were completely wet, his left hand sticky with panic and urine. With his right one he groped for his cell phone to call the police (another siren wailed up Clark), only to recall the very motion of dropping the keys and the phone on the front-hall table. He rolled up into a squatting pose of pain, but then unrolled like a fern in sped-up footage, because a cab hit the brakes not to run him over. The cabbie, grim as a nightmare, stepped out of the car and said: "Hey, man!"—and Joshua, his mind loosened by the combination of alcohol and Stagger, retorted: "Hay is for horses!"

Naturally, Joshua wished he could reverse the flow of time and make everything the way it had been before he found Stagger sobbing into his filthy underwear. But the before was no longer available, nor would it ever be, while the after was mercilessly launched between the glad *ding* of Kimiko's bell and its despondent *dong*. It was well past midnight, so that when she came down to open the door and look unpleasantly surprised, he was wise enough to appear apologetic. Bushy welcomed him by rubbing his fat-cat ass against his ankle. My fair girlfriend is innocently sleeping, Joshua thought. What would love be without mutually assured oblivion?

Bushy would not quit and Joshua picked him up. He stroked the cat pantingly telling Kimmy what had happened, minus the details of self-urination, though her smirk indicated that she might've found his odor disagreeable. She wore a large Chicago Fire T-shirt, its hem touching her knees. It was a man's shirt.

"What are you going to do?" she asked.

"What can I do? He's my landlord. I can't go back there. He lives on the first floor."

"You could call the police," she said. She was beautiful,

even if her calmness could be interpreted as indifference. He was aware, of course, that the reasonable course of action would indeed be to call the police. But he couldn't bear the thought of the CPD, ever happy to go gun crazy, confronting the batshit Stagger. Going back was also impossible. Stagger might be trashing his place, for all he knew, wearing Jonjo's underwear on his head to the soundtrack of "Welcome to the Jungle," armed with his Desert Storm trauma and samurai sword.

"What do you want to do?" Kimmy asked again. What he wanted to do was nothing, every day, all day long, until the glacier of time ground everything back into its smooth shape. The force by which a man perseveres in existing is limited, and infinitely surpassed by the power of external causes. He wanted to press up against Kimmy's warm, soft back and stay there until things sorted themselves out. Music was coming from her bedroom—she liked to read and fall asleep listening to Bach's cello suites. Everything about her was gentle and sovereign. There was always a self-evident reason for whatever she did, even if he seldom knew what it was.

There was a reason for the shirt she was wearing as well. His groin and inner thighs were now beginning to itch. The Fire-shirt hem was fondling her knees.

"I think," Joshua said, "I need to take a shower right now."

"Whatever you want," Kimmy said. He wanted her to embrace his bepissed body, to kiss him, slipping her tongue into his mouth, to approve of him as he was, to take him unconditionally. It didn't seem likely at that moment. Bushy suddenly swung his declawed paw at Joshua's face, missing his eyeball by a missing claw. Joshua dropped him on the floor to trot toward the promise of food.

"Is that your shirt?" he asked.

"No," she said. Why would she wear a soccer shirt? Foreigners wear soccer gear, particularly foreign men. He waited for her follow-up elucidation, but she stayed silent, as if daring him to ask whose shirt it was. He wasn't so much jealous as he wanted Kimiko to confess that she experienced lust independent of him—the thought of her sovereign lechery turned him on, because it frightened him. He wouldn't have admitted it, but one of the reasons he was attracted to her was that he couldn't read her.

"I might need something clean to wear," Joshua said. She glanced out the window at a dark back alley, then pulled the shirt over her head and handed it to Joshua, exhibiting her beautiful, lithe body: the perky breasts, the smiley navel, the curly crotch. In the parlance of child psychology, the shirt would be a transitional object.

In the shower, tired though he was, he acquired a hard-on prompted by the fantasy of Kimmy grabbing the buttocks of a man in the Fire shirt who gradually attained an impromptu shape: he was Kimmy's fellow therapist; he was a soccer player, therefore tattooed and tall and not Jewish; he was probably Latino, thus automatically adept at fucking on the sly or in threesome formation. Brushing his teeth with Kimmy's wet toothbrush, Joshua examined his face in the mirror: narrow; his eyes too big and sunken; an archipelago of zits stretching below a dandruff-peppered peninsula of hair; the overbite reliably overbiting. He speculated about the man's name: Hector, Fidel, Enrique. Enrique was the name. Enrique the Fucker.

Joshua put his clothes into the washer and considered searching the dirty laundry basket for other man-sized clothes. The Kimmy-scented Fire T-shirt reached his mid-crotch. Somehow, inexplicably, she wanted him. At least that was what she'd said the first time they'd hooked up. She could have any other man, a squadron of Enriques, but she wanted him. He'd asked her to tell him what it was in him that attracted her, but she never wanted to talk about it. Only once did she say: "I love the way you think without thinking," and he hadn't dared to ask whether she would like him more if he thought *with* thinking, or, perhaps, if he didn't think at all. He'd asked her instead if she loved his naked body, and she'd rolled on top of him. Only later would he realize that the subsequent coitus allowed her to avoid answering. It was all terribly disconcerting, as he thought (without thinking) that she could at any time look at him and realize her mistake. This relationship: the fanciest item in Joshua's fear booth.

When he slipped into bed next to her, Bach was off and she was hugging Bushy. Joshua inched toward her and pressed his dick, at attention again, into her lower backside like a gun. She smelled of lavender.

"Kimmy!" he whispered. "Kimmy!"

She did not move. He held her at dickpoint for another moment, in the hope she would change her mind and roll over to him, and confirm that, as of tonight, she chose to let her lust loose upon him.

"I have two little patients tomorrow morning," she whispered.

Joshua repositioned to look up at the ceiling. They seldom had sex before sleep—when she was done with the day, she immediately directed her attention to the next one. Sometimes he managed to wedge himself into her schedule and solicit a random fuck. The ceiling fan was moving above in the dark, like a killer drone. A Harry Potter book lay like a brick on the nightstand.

But then Kimmy released Bushy, rolled over to him, and placed her dainty hand on his undainty cock.

"What about the little patients?" whimpered Joshua.

"They'll be fine," Kimmy said, "they're just spoiled little brats." She moved her hand in all the right directions, and, as Enrique bled to death in the shower, Joshua submitted himself to the pleasures of being the chosen one.

She'd left for work when he woke up. A world of unavoidable actions presented itself to Joshua. First, the least painful: he transferred his damp clothes to the dryer. Then he went back into the bedroom to rummage through Kimmy's life: his current status as the chosen one demanded further confirmation.

Kimmy had many fashionable pieces of clothing in her closet: tasteful dresses, delicate blouses, silky stockings, most of which he'd never laid eyes on in the seven months they'd been dating. When did she wear those things? She was from elsewhere, and not just because she was Asian; it was because beyond her appearances there was the unknown. He had never met anyone from her work, least of all Enrique; her family was forever in California. Linda notwithstanding, all of her friends were in New York or Los Angeles. She had a much older sister she hadn't spoken to in months; she had thoughts she never expressed. He moved on to her dresser drawer: her ascetic running gear, her lacy bras, her diminutive underwear. He pressed his nose into the scentful pair of her porn-red panties—she always kept bags of dry lavender in her drawers. From the depths of the duvet, Bushy watched him inspecting Kimmy's jewelry. Joshua was just about to feel creepily stupid when in the far corner of her bottom drawer he discovered, still in its original packaging, a shiny cock ring.

"A cock ring?" he exclaimed to Bushy, who blinked back listlessly at him. The packaging claimed the ring diameter was two inches. Was it a present for him? Or was it for Enrique? Regrettably, he was not sure what his cock's diameter was, though he liked to think of it as respectably thick. The human mind does not involve adequate knowledge of the parts composing the human body. Joshua continued the search, somewhat heedlessly, until he discovered a pair of handcuffs. These were not in their original packaging; they were rattly, with a key in the lock; they appeared to have been used. Did she handcuff the Third? Didn't seem like something Enrique would be into. Maybe he handcuffed her. He'd had no idea Kimmy would be into this kind of thing— she never discussed her desires. Their copulation was usually uncomplicated, if enjoyable: simple penetration and uncontorted positions—the wholesome bread and butter of American sex practices. Most of the time she had her eyes closed, even as she was coming; it had more than once occurred to him that at such moments she was fantasizing about someone or something else. He wanted to enter the domain where her fantasies were part of the resplendently horny landscape. She never responded to Joshua's cautious inquiries, never confessed to any fantasies, but here they were shining in his hand now, the fantasies. He imagined her handcuffing him to the bed, his face down; his dick peeked out from under the Fire shirt. Script Idea #29: *A man wakes up to find out that he's a captive sex slave of a depraved rich woman he'd met at a cocaine party. His only chance: to make her fall in love with him. Struggle ensues.*

The phones rang all over the house and Joshua, startled,

quickly put the handcuffs and cock ring back in their places. The ringing abruptly stopped, but now there was hysterical buzzing coming from the dryer.

None of his clothes were fully dry, but he still put them on. His flannel shirt was tight in the shoulders; his denim pants were pinching his groin; even his socks' heels slipped down his Achilles tendon. The clothes belonged to the before, and he had no attire for the after.

INT. SCHOOL — DAWN

Major Klopstock sneaks across a baseball diamond,
pushes a lawn mower aside to uncover a small, broken window. He slips through it into the basement.
He moves gingerly down the hallway, unlocking and
locking doors. Children's drawings on the walls; a
few little coats still on the hooks. He's armed with
a twelve-gauge; a cluster of hand grenades and a
pair of handcuffs hang off his belt. The final door
opens into a small, dark lab. He turns on a lamp
over a workbench with vials and petri dishes. A
shabby mattress lies in the corner — this is Major
Klopstock's only home. He leans the twelve-gauge
against the wall.

Major K puts away the hand grenades, and then out
of his backpack pulls a zombie head: a small hole
above the left eye, the eyes wide open. He puts on
a mask and rubber gloves. Carefully, he cuts off
the top of the head with a circular saw, scoops out
some brain, puts it in a few petri dishes. He pours
some solution over the samples and puts the rest

of the head in the fridge, which hosts a collection of heads, all of their eyes wide open.

He sits down and writes in his notebook.

                    MAJOR KLOPSTOCK
                        (v.o.)
        Intermittent life on North Side. Saw Dr.
        Goldman, roaming with a herd of the undead.
        Everyone alive is in hiding. Somebody needs
        to figure out why this is happening to
        figure out how it will end. Good news: found
        an army truck full of goodies up in
        Andersonville. Going downtown tomorrow. The
        moon waxing crescent. Goodnight stars.
        Goodnight air. Goodnight noises everywhere.

The samples in the petri dishes bubble up and spill
over.

There were seven students in Joshua's Level 5 ESL class, and they sat there facing him like a jury that had already reached its grim verdict. In the far back row, as far from Joshua's dubious authority as they could get, sat Captain Ponomarenko and his rotund wife, Larissa. Captain Ponomarenko had been an officer of the KGB, unhappily decommissioned by the collapse of the USSR, and still resented the fact that America, the land of limp imbeciles—amply represented by Teacher Josh—somehow managed to win the Cold War. He steadily aimed his barbed questions and contemptuous scowls at Teacher Josh, while the fair and larded Larissa endorsed whatever her husband was hatefully thinking. Presently they were convinced that Teacher Josh was personally and primarily responsible for the ongoing invasion of Iraq. They brought up the whole mess in nearly every class, and not at all because they cared about the Iraqis, let alone democracy or justice, but rather to expose the eternal rottenness of America's imperialist soul. Accordingly, Joshua had become adept at changing the subject and pushing the class toward discussing the challenges they would face while acquiring, say, a fish tank.

Then there was a pair of heavily postmenopausal *matry-oshki* who could not possibly care less about invadable distant lands or English grammar or anything at all save for the intimidating presence of black people in their new country. The ladies never offered any thoughts, stories, or opinions that failed to reiterate their belief that African Americans were inherently criminal. The squatter of the two, Yekaterina, had been blessed with having once heard of *one black* stealing a car door off its hinges, which provided her with a conversation topic for the rest of her natural life.

There was Fyodor, an ex–rocket scientist prone to randomly quoting Dostoyevsky in Russian, who had demanded that Joshua help him translate an old VHS player manual; expertly egged on by Captain Soviet, he'd taken Joshua's claim that VHS was obsolete at the beginning of the new millennium as yet another instance of blind American selfishness.

Then there was Varya, who, it had recently turned out, was iffily progressing through brutal chemotherapy. She'd been coming to class wearing a variable head scarf and sat always silent under the colorful map of Israel, all of which had misled Teacher Josh into thinking she was Orthodox. Only after he'd forced the class into one of those role-playing exercises whereby Captain Ponomarenko had become the doctor and Varya the patient had it come out that she'd been battling advanced ovarian cancer. Since Teacher Josh could formulate no appropriate response to the immense fact of cancer, he would consequently find himself providing the medical vocabulary for the entire female genital area. He clumsily sketched a lily-shaped vagina on the board, discovering along the way that he was entirely oblivious to many of its parts, and could not remember the words for others. The evil Ponomarenkos had kept nudging each other and chuckling, either at his ignorance or at his embarrassment—likely both.

The only bright light in all that post–Cold War darkness was Ana, she of the downcast eyes. A Bosnian in her late thirties, Ana was his best student by a long shot, not least because she kept away from the collective contempt of the whispering Russians, congenitally infected with Soviet malice. She used to study medicine, she'd said, adding a few small parts to the vagina floor plan, including a clitoris most impressively rendered as a large dot. She'd done it so unabashedly that Joshua thought up a pun—*anabashedly*—which often came to him whenever he laid eyes on her. And she was easy on the eyes too: she was partial to knee-length skirts and cleavage-enhancing décolletage, her heels high enough to be sexy, never high enough to be slutty. Her fashion style, however, seemed wholly incongruous with the indelible sorrow she constantly radiated, which Joshua found as compelling as her curves.

One day he'd given his students an assignment to write about their respective hometowns and read them aloud: the Ponomarenkos were from Vitebsk, a town barely worthy of a lazy paragraph; the Moscow *matryoshki* drew a poor picture of the magnificent monuments built by the tsars and Bolsheviks; Varya was from Kazakhstan and wrote about the radiant and radioactive beauty of the desert. But Ana, raising her sea-green eyes to meet Joshua's, read her composition mournfully, recalling the *normal life* back in Sarajevo, her hometown, before the war: people greeted one another on the street; the youth danced all night; there was a linden tree smelling sweetly and quaintly right under her window. He understood that her hot attire did not signify promiscuity—contrary to the consensual interpretation of the other male teachers—but a kind of nostalgia: this was what she used to wear when she was happy, when she used to live the *normal life*. She simply could not let go, just as Captain Soviet could not let go of his Cold War bullshit, or Varya of her cancer. All bodies agree in certain things.

The thing was that Joshua wasn't expected, let alone required, to teach female anatomy in his class, or indeed anything at all that could have significant application in his students' lives. The ambition of his employers at the PRT Institute's ESL program was to train the students to pass the mandatory state tests, which made the institute eligible for the funds needed to issue educational visas to Jews arriving from the former Soviet Union. The presence of other refugees— say, Bosnians—provided a convenient veneer for the noble scam the institute was perpetrating: the whole operation was really a front for a resettlement program, a leftover from the heroic Operation Exodus times. Joshua had no problem with anything that helped his people get the hell out of the Cossack lands, he'd assured his puny, frightfully balding boss, Mr. Strauss, who'd summoned him to his office to demand, softly and unequivocally, that he stay away from the vagina and similar genitals and stick to grammar, useless though it may be. "We," Mr. Strauss said, patiently picking his point out of the depths of his nostril, "have larger roles to play."

That particular Tuesday class was devoted to the elusive mysteries of the future perfect, a tense that in its dull clunkiness was bound to get on the nerves of Captain USSR and his troops. Bravely, Joshua consulted the textbook (*Let's Go, America!* 5) and wrote an example on the chalkboard: *By*

the time I am seventy-five I will have had my knees replaced.
Facing the wall of contempt, he underlined *I will have had*
with an unnecessary flourish. "This is the future perfect.
It's used for an action that will be completed by a defined
point in the future," he recited, slicing up the sentence into
its bits, pretty much running out of the things he cared to
say about it.

Yet Ana was leaning forward, her eyes lit up as though
she really cared how the idiotic tense worked. The rest
watched him blandly, counting the minutes—in Russian, no
doubt—to the break. Joshua conjugated the verb by erasing
I and writing *you*, then crasing *you* and writing *he/she/it*.
He read it all aloud, while considering the possibility that
Ana might be focusing on him. He disliked his emaciated,
bony frame (his father had once told him he had the body of
a fanatic), his large feet, his overbite, and his pencil-shading
facial hair, which made him look dark-skinned. He could
never entirely reconcile the strange fact of Kimiko's attrac-
tion with what he saw in the mirror. At best, it was related to
her natural stoicism, as if Joshua were a kind of bonsai tree
she trimmed and watered lovingly. "I enjoy being with you"
was her preferred mode of expressing her affection. At
worst, she kept him around so he could make her feel better
when she needed it, a winning combination of a pet and a
dildo. Somewhere along the range between the best and the
worst, there was the possibility of her deep love. When we
love a thing like ourselves, we strive, as far as we can, to bring
it about that it loves us in return.

Now then, what could Ana be seeing in Joshua?

Back at the Westmoreland, Bega had ardently flaunted
his own un-Americanness, complete with *experience* unat-
tainable to the likes of Joshua. Whatever troubles Joshua

had gone through to end up on the stool next to Bega were nothing compared with war and displacement and survival and all that heavy stuff. Bega had kept using the phrase *life problems*, which Joshua had previously been inclined to interpret as *the problems inherent in being alive*. According to Bega, however, even if there were different kinds and degrees of such problems, all of them could be reduced to the simple difference between being alive and staying alive. "There are people who just live and there are people who just survive," Bega had said. "Americans live, we survive." It'd all been told jokingly and back-slappingly, of course, and Joshua had laughed it up in drunkenness, but it had been undeniable that, as far as Bega had been concerned, Joshua's life was too good to be good enough and that he could never attain the noble title of survivor. Joshua had submitted his survivor grandparents along with thousands of years of anti-Semitic oppression, to claim some legitimacy, but Bega would have none of it—Joshua's fundamental Americanness was all that really mattered. "Your life," Bega had told him, "is warm blanket."

But here was a random Tuesday when Joshua's best student, a beautiful woman clearly belonging to the elect Bosnian survivor tribe, appeared interested in him, despite—or perhaps because of?—his warm-blanketness. The magnifying glass of her gaze burned the back of his neck as he was trying to come up with examples of the future perfect less moronic than *Let's Go, America! 5* offered. All he could think of was *By the time the world ends we will all have lived*, but he did not wish to put that up on the chalkboard, lest he look too pretentious, clearing the way for an argument with Captain Stalin. Nonetheless, his waffling was quickly punished.

"Teacher Josh," Larissa asked, "why you cannot say, 'I will replace my knees'?"

"You could," Joshua responded. "But it's much better this way."

"What is correct?" Captain P needed to know, testily banging at his notebook with a pencil, as if beating a dissident with a shovel handle. "One must be correct. Not two."

Joshua could hear the rustle of Ana's stockings as she crossed her legs. At the Westmoreland, he'd drunkenly spun into claiming that necessity reigned in the world, a natural and therefore moral order was in place, only for Bega to reassert that Josh's moral system consisted of a little bit of right and a little bit of wrong and a lot of reasonably comfortable—if the order was such, you didn't have to do much, and it rhymed too. "Survivors have no time to dillydally," Bega had said. Perhaps he hadn't used that exact phrase; *dilly-dally* would be a strange idiom for a foreigner to use.

"Both could be correct," Joshua said. "It kind of depends on the sentence."

Captain Ponomarenko nodded, slowly, as if all of his expectations of Teacher Josh's failure had once again been met. If it hadn't been for the continued deafening rustle of Ana's stockings, if her perfume had not suddenly floated his way—jasmine was certainly present—Joshua would've dared to further pursue his moot grammatical point. But he could sense that an insurrection was brewing, the Russians soon to be fully mobilized by Captain USSR's susurrous slurs, so he called a break. The students went out to the hallway to stand in a discontented circle where Joshua and his warm-blanket ineptitude would doubtless be the preferred topic. And sure enough, there was an immediate quick fire of derisive laughter. Script Idea #38: *A bizarrely rich Russian oligarch hires an American detective to find out what happened to his parents, who were once upon a time arrested by Communists as American spies; as the mystery deepens, the detective pairs up with a beautiful Russian woman; they discover that the Soviets sold the parents' organs on the underground market; the oligarch wants the organs in order to clone his parents; adventures follow.*

Teacher Josh closed the door and embarked upon wiping the chalkboard, sneezing occasionally. The vagaries of the future perfect and Ana's presence had allowed him to forget temporarily that he'd had to escape from his place and now stayed with Kimmy, the woman who hoarded cock rings and handcuffs. Erasing the future perfect from the board, he couldn't escape what had happened. He didn't hear Ana come in.

"Teacher Josh," she said. He turned around and immediately noticed that her nipples were hard. Looking into her eyes, sea green as they were, required effort.

"Can I talk with you?" She even spoke in a rustly, deep voice.

"Yes," he said. "You may."

"There is party," she said. A dimple in her left cheek appeared and disappeared without anything else in her face changing.

"A party," Joshua said.

"Saturday in the evening."

"Saturday evening."

"What?"

She was confused and glanced, possibly out of habit, at the blank board. He regretted his condescension, but then it allowed him to spend time looking at her: at her carmine lips, at her jawline, at her perfect nose, at the dimple mirage.

"You can say: Saturday evening," he said.

"Okay. Saturday evening there is a party," she said. "Many friends, many Bosnians. Also students from here."

"What is the party for?" Joshua asked. She had the habit of readjusting her bra by pulling up the straps and straightening her shoulders. Her breasts leapt up like happy little animals.

"It is my birthday."

"Well, happy birthday! May I ask how old you are?"

"If you want to know, you must come."

"To your party?"

"To my party."

The implicit requirements of the committed relationship Joshua was pursuing with Kimiko assumed spending Saturday nights together for the purposes of intimacy. It should've been easy for him to say no to Ana. He didn't even need to explain.

"I don't know," he said. "It might be hard."

He was conscious of avoiding mention of Kimmy to Ana, conscious that he was thereby involved in negotiations.

"On Saturday you will have had fun," she said, and the dimple doubled—both of her cheeks were adorned with one—because she pursed her lips slightly, for an instant. It could've been just a twitch, certainly unconscious, or she could've been innocently proud of being clever, but to Joshua it looked like a conspiratorial signal, a hint of a kiss. He wasted the time he should've used to say no in an attempt to swallow a huge lump in his throat: at first it went down, but then it came back up tumescent. Ana, however, used that time to write down her phone number in the margin of *Let's Go, America! 5*. She shouldn't have done it, she shouldn't have so brazenly violated the good book. Her insouciance was sexy.

Captain Ponomarenko must have mocked Teacher Josh again, because choral laughter echoed out in the hallway. Joshua fixed his gaze on the map of Israel on the far wall, pretending to be reviewing in his head his Friday schedule. The lump bobbed in his throat. Was she flirting with him? Or leaving the door temptingly ajar for him to walk through? He could see Jerusalem, the largest dot on the map.

"I'll see what I can do."

"There will be music," she said. "It will have been fun."

"It will be fun," he corrected.

"Yes, it will be lot of fun."

Joshua swallowed the lump, and this time it didn't come back up, settling in his stomach as a steel ball. Ana took her seat, smiling coyly at him, as if they were now bound by a shared secret. Captain P walked in and grinned, recognizing in his infinite KGB wisdom a potentially illicit exchange.

"Teacher Josh," Captain Ponomarenko said. "Happy First April!"

Ah, Joshua, the ever lost boy! He'd never been properly seduced before. Back in college, doing Jägermeister shots until all the inhibitions were sufficiently suppressed had been the main format for his carnal negotiations. More recently, his relationship with Kimiko had progressed unnoticeably from quick friendship to sleeping together. As far as Joshua could remember, there had been few seductive signals exchanged between them prior to commitment, little flirtation, no arousingly ambiguous suggestions. Eight months earlier, they'd spent a long weekend in Linda's vast Door County cottage, their rooms the only two in the basement. He'd been pursuing Linda, and hence accepted her invitation to Wisconsin thinking that she might finally end up being responsive, or at least horny. But the sleeping arrangement suggested that Linda had set them up so as to deflect him. Everyone had driven up on Friday evening; on Saturday Kimmy would eat sausage links off his breakfast plate, dip her bun in his yolk, as Linda grinned approvingly; in the afternoon, Kimmy would snuggle up to him on the sheepskin by the fireplace. On Sunday night she'd sneak into his room and slip into his bed equipped with a condom. They'd drive back to Chicago together on Monday, making plans for the following weekend, devoid of Linda, just the two of them—they would go to see *My Big Fat Greek Wedding*. Thus they had coupled. They never mentioned Linda.

Riding a bus back (home?) to Kimiko's after class, he parsed the exchange with Ana, analyzing all the expressions of her conspicuous interest, which in turn became an elaborate fantasy, featuring his hand crawling up the inside of Ana's thigh and into her wet depths, touching the dot she'd drawn so vividly. So possessed was he with the possibility of Ana's seducing him that he walked past Kimiko's to Stagger's place, managing to stop himself just before touching the front door handle. He went back up Magnolia, hoping that Kimiko would not be home, or that she'd be at least asleep, so he could regain his bearings. But she was home, watching *The Daily Show*, curled up on the sofa under a very small Wisconsin-made quilt.

INT. RESTAURANT — DAY

Restaurant patrons devour their food, indifferent to their surroundings. DOUG (42) looks out the window. We cannot see his face but he wears a leather jacket over suit and tie. Outside, the sky is gray. Doug drinks his wine, refills the glass, absentmindedly watching a plastic bag flutter down a desolate street. An army convoy ROARS by, an occasional shot is heard, along with wailing sirens. Nobody pays any attention to what is going on outside, except for Doug. He lights a cigarette. By the way he inhales, it's clear that it's an oh-fuck-it! one, his first after a long time.

The kitchen door swings open and a waiter, evidently zombified, stumbles out, his white jacket stained with blood and brains. The waiter heads toward Doug, who gets up, toppling over the wine bottle, and retreats in horror.

                    DOUG
     No! No! God! No!

He flicks the cigarette at the waiter. The waiter corners him, then bites into his face. Blood spurts out of the hole where Doug's nose used to be. All the other patrons are petrified, only to lurch out of their seats and rush out the door. BOY (9) screams:

                        BOY
            Flesheaters! Flesheaters!

The waiter feeds on Doug's brain. An explosion destroys the restaurant, blowing the plastic bag away.

Joshua hated sleeping, but waking up was worse. Night- mares were not the problem: he never really had any. Nobody ever bothered to chase him in his dreams; he never plunged from a tall building to wake up just before exploding like a pomegranate, nor did he ever experience even the vaguest presence of death. There was little violence, only occasional vanilla sex, his dreams damp rather than wet, his subconscious a Wilmette where he was forever sleepily immortal. Still, he would wake up sweating, his heart thumping. What caused his torment was that the dreams were inconclusive; they did not so much end abruptly as they whimpered their lame way into his wakeful state; the absence of notable transition was the troubling thing. Baruch thought that whatever is, is either in itself or in the other. Well, Joshua's dreams were neither one nor the other.

Some weeks before, he'd found himself enmeshed in a dream conundrum of laundry separation: he couldn't decide whether his long johns were to be put on the underwear pile or the pants pile. When he'd woken up, furious and still undecided, he'd stuffed all his long johns in a garbage bag with the intention of getting rid of them. Just as he'd been about to drop the bag into the gaping mouth of a malodorous black bin, a flurry had descended from the gray heights to linger before his nose, reminding him that Chicago winters were ruthless and long.

The terrible inconclusiveness seriously impeded his will to rise. As soon as the dream residues dissolved into full oblivion, a terrible doubt would start forming, weighing on his intestines, concentrating in globs in his muscles, so that he kept tossing in search of a position comfortable enough for snoozing. The painful doubt would swell like a balloon, steadily squeezing out of his head all that he'd seemed to have accomplished or thought up theretofore.

This morning, all of the love for Kimmy, painstakingly accrued, all of their earned closeness, was transformed into a sense of entrapment, enhanced by her sleeping quietly, romantically next to him, a warm pile of a stranger's flesh. He pretended to sleep until Kimmy left for work, leaving an indentation on the pillow and a single long, whorled hair. Therein was a trace of the woman he was supposed to love; he had all the reasons to love her; he'd bragged about her to others: his Zen mistress, brash, self-sufficient, and prone to kinkiness (yet to be fully exploited). But he now found comfort in her absence; he liked the idea of her, but her presence—sometimes, presently—made him want to be alone. A desire that arises from joy is stronger, other things being equal, than one that arises from sadness.

Then there was the Stagger incident, the fact that he'd had to escape from his apartment, hadn't dared to call the police, and had entirely failed to be sufficiently aggressive and angry. A better man would kick Stagger's ass, hurt him terribly. Revenge is a dish best served with carpet bombing. But what Joshua wanted was for all of it to simply resolve itself, as it undoubtedly would, without his having to do anything radical. Somehow, someday, it must be resolved.

And then there was the continuous fiasco of his writing. Once upon a time, Joshua had read *Portnoy's Complaint* and figured he too could write novels—it hadn't seemed overly taxing, all one had to do was be unsparingly honest. Then he'd read *Goodbye, Columbus* and thought he could write short stories instead. He would write only one, about a seventeen-year-old so urgently intent on deflowerment that he saved money and hired an escort, who then refused to sleep with him because she didn't believe he was old enough. He'd entitled it "The Age of Consent" and it'd kept being awful, no rewrite improving it one bit, because he repeatedly changed his mind about what happened: in one version, the escort blew the hero; in the other, she blew his brains out; in the terminal revision, they embarked upon furniture-crashing sex just as Joshua dropped his pen. But he'd thought the dialogue was bearable, and he'd been trying to write scripts since. The problem, however, was that he could never figure out how to establish the necessary determinism of the plot: characters would do this or that, while neither his will nor his talent was ever strong enough to compel them to follow their goddamn trajectory. When the mind imagines its own lack of power, it is saddened by it.

In the ten years he'd been doing it, none of the handful of scripts he'd finished had ever got close to being read, let alone optioned, by any film people; none had gone far in any of the screenwriting contests he'd entered, while the unfinished scripts were almost certain to remain unfinished. He had files upon files of script ideas in his computer, but none of them developed or stood any chance of development: most of them died within the first draft of the first scene, unable to take off and come anywhere near a self-sustaining plot. He took screenwriting workshops, which were exactly like going to the gym: he never got stronger, never felt any better, just more tired; but if he didn't work out, he'd turn frighteningly obese and die from a stroke.

He got up, the doubt now a shadow hovering at his shoulder while he brushed his teeth, muttering nasty things into his ear, deriding the weakness in his face, the limpness in his muscles, the someone else's Fire shirt he was wearing. Then it followed him to the kitchen, where it maliciously moved the cup as he was pouring coffee into it, so he was forced to spend an eternity wiping the counter, everything in him sagging into a sludge of despair. The coffee Kimmy had made wasn't strong enough, yet there was no other coffee to be drunk. Perhaps anything at all could be the accidental cause of hope, but this morning there wasn't much of anything.

And there was nowhere to go. He took up a position on the sofa to work on his screenwriting, nothing else left to do. Bushy curled up at his feet and turned up his purring rotor, uninterested in Joshua's struggles. The doubt was radiating unhealthy light from the laptop screen as he decided to give *Zombie Wars* another try. He opened the file, wrote the slug line: *INT. WRIGLEY FIELD—NIGHT*. Now what?

Before Joshua could immerse himself in correlating the Cubs and the apocalypse, the distracting memory of Ana presented itself to him, detail by detail: the curve of her neck as she leaned to grace the margin of *Let's Go, America!* 5 with her phone number; the momentary pursing of her lips and the double dimple; her smell: jasmine and sweet sweat; her short, boyish hair, likely hennaed; her legs crossed, dangling her shoe on her big toe. Soon the infinitely rewarding universe of Internet porn was beckoning him—but the DSL cord was far beyond the horizon of his will and, even if he could get off the sofa, self-abuse would relieve neither his doubt nor his longing. There was no remedy for the unsettling fact that Ana, along with all the other women of the world, was elsewhere, and he was here. Right here, conceiving a zombie pitcher repeatedly dropping the ball, sprawled on the sofa in the living room of his newish life: the yoga mat in the umbrella spittoon; the polished pseudotropical plants in the corners; the inedible multicolor pasta in the tall jars; the pictures of Kimmy's numerous family scattered on the bookshelves; the books about amazing animal friendships and Japanese-American internment camps on the coffee table; and upstairs, in the corner of a deep drawer reeking of lavender, a treasure chest of titillating sex toys.

Bushy transitioned to the windowsill to look out at Magnolia, where leafless tree crowns scrambled the morning light, where bicycles with training wheels lingered on the porches, Andersonville dreaming itself up. A large mailman pushed a bundle through the front door mail slot, waving and smiling through the window at Joshua, who waved back at him. Joshua couldn't hear anything, but he had plenty of reasons to believe that all the birds out there were atwitter.

The phone rang from atop the stack of coffee-table books and he picked it up unthinkingly, as if he were at home.

"Hey, Jonjo man!" Stagger said. "What's brewing?"

"Stagger? Are you out of your fucking mind?" It was self-evidently a rhetorical question. "How did you get this number?"

"You left your cell phone here, buddy. It looks like the only people you ever call other than Mom Wilmette and Bernie Dad are Kimiko Cell and Kimiko M. Home. What does M. stand for?"

"It stands for motherfucker, you crazy motherfucker!" Joshua slammed the phone down on the coffee table and stood up as if it had just bitten him. When it rang again he stared at it with blinding hatred, until the answering machine in the kitchen turned on.

"Jonjo, Jonjo . . . A friend less loyal than me wouldn't put up with such language." Stagger's nasal tone was of someone affecting indifference.

"Fuck you!" said Joshua to the answering machine.

"But you might care to know that an Ana called to ask about—"

Joshua rushed to the kitchen to pick up the phone, slipping on the floor in his tube socks.

"Who called?"

"Your student Ana. The good Lord knows I am no expert on ladies' feelings, but it seems pretty clear to me she'd be more than happy to lick your balls."

Fumblingly, Joshua pressed all the buttons on the answering machine to stop it from recording. Bushy leapt on the counter to bear witness to this suspicious behavior.

"It seems she'd really like you to come to her party. She invited me too by the way. I'm gonna have to consult my calendar."

A flutter wing touched Joshua's heart: he envisioned Ana at the party, and himself leaning into the curve of her neck to speak over the noise. The dimples, the warmth of her skin, the jasmine smell.

"Are you going, Jonjo? She really needs to know. You should call her."

Finally, the machine beeped and stopped recording.

"You have my cell phone, you maniac!"

"Maniac though I may be, you can have your phone anytime you want. In fact, you can shove it up your ass like a freaking gerbil!" Stagger screamed and the line went dead. Down on his knees, Joshua banged his head against the kitchen cabinet where Kimmy kept her select Tupperware. Doubt banged back from the inside. Script Idea #48: *A man with terminal cancer decides to exact revenge on all those who wronged him, including his landlord and the doctor who diagnosed him late. Title:* Road to Gehinnam.

The phone rang again. Joshua stood up and shooed Bushy away.

"I beg your pardon," Stagger said. "That was not professional."

"I need my phone back. And my keys."

"The door of your home is always open to you."

"I don't think I'm comfortable after what happened the other night."

"What happened the other night?"

"Come on, Stagger! It's really hard for me not to think that you're a lunatic."

"If this here lunatic wanted to hurt you, he would just walk up Magnolia and hurt you," Stagger said. "I know where Kimiko Motherfucker Home lives. I walk my dog past her house every day."

"What dog? You don't have a dog!"

"Metaphorically speaking."

Desperate, Joshua opened the fridge door and looked inside: there was a six-pack of beer tucked in the back.

"I tell you what," Stagger said. "I'm about to go to a game, so I'll leave the phone and the keys on Kimiko Motherfucker's porch. I won't even get in. You don't have to invite me in or even offer me beer. How's that for generosity and kindness?"

Kimmy never drank beer. Joshua never drank beer. He didn't even know if Kimmy knew that.

"I'm really uncomfortable with that. I'd much prefer if you just went and fucked yourself."

"All right then, Jonjo boy. I'll drop your stuff off and then I'm gonna go and fuck myself," Stagger said and hung up.

Joshua stood frozen in disbelief; when he moved to return to the sofa a sharp pain in his back stopped him in his tracks. The thought of Stagger at Kimmy's door was terrifying. He would have to do something about it: call the police, stab him in the eyes, protect his domain and his woman. Or he could just get himself temporarily situated elsewhere, on the off chance that Stagger might get his insanity under control.

The phone rang again. Furiously, Joshua picked it up and growled into it:

"What the fuck is wrong with you?"

"That is not a way to show proper respect to your big sister, Jackie," Janet said. Many years ago, she'd carefully picked a name that would inflict the most torment upon him and had started calling him "Jackie" in front of his friends and girlfriends. Everybody had names for him; it drove him crazy, and Janet was perfectly aware of it.

"What can I do for you, Jan?"

"First of all, are you okay?"

"I'm fine."

"I called your cell number and your landlord picked up. He seems like a very nice man."

"He's a gentleman and a scholar, all right. You have no idea."

"Have you moved in with Ms. Cio-Cio San?"

"It's none of your business, Janet."

"She is not good for you, Jackie, because she's too good for you."

"None of your business, Janet."

"If you have no other place to live, you can live with me. I have plenty of space. You'll have to live like an adult, though. Respect, responsibilities, things like that."

"I'd rather live in a dog crate. What can I do for you?"

"Lunch with *maman et moi*."

"I'm really busy."

"With what?"

"With being really busy."

"We're meeting at Marcel's."

"That's fancy."

"My treat. Unlimited wine intake too, to help you along with being really busy."

"What time?"

"God, I can always count on you being a slut, Jackie."

Janet had a mailing list, and her little brother was on it, so whenever she managed to offload an obscenely priced Gold Coast condo onto some rich fool, Joshua would receive a postcard featuring Janet—her hair Photoshopped for extra blondness, her grin expressing the full range of the positive-thinking pathology—and a banner that read: JANET DID IT AGAIN!! The extra exclamation mark was the dagger, the infuriating extra touch of heedless superiority. He'd repeatedly begged her to take him off the list, but she never had and probably never would.

Joshua showed up at Marcel's Cork Room in an aerodynamic bike helmet, fluorescent yellow shirt, and enhanced-crotch bike shorts. His initial intention had been to go get his bicycle, still locked by Graham's, before lunch. But the plan was changed after Stagger had dropped off his phone and keys on the porch, and Joshua had had to interrupt erasing the recorded exchange re: Ana to check the cell phone call log, since calling his marine buddies in Iraq from Joshua's phone was not beyond Stagger. Ana had called him a few times, and he'd listened to her tantalizingly brief messages, unable to summon any gumption to call her back. Her voice sounded throaty, the voice of a woman with spunk and depth.

He expected some pleasure from embarrassing Janet by showing up in his bike shorts, his balls bulging squeezily, at her fancy downtown French restaurant, where Armani-clad men guzzled vintage wine while devouring hundred-dollar steak frites. But Janet did it again: she was there already in full-blown yoga attire, complete with tight-ass sweat pants. Moreover, the restaurant was empty, except for Marcel at the bar, nursing his pastis, watching despondently the U.S. troops on the TV churning up sandstorms on their way to Baghdad. Noah, Joshua's insufferable little nephew, was there as well, lining up chairs to make a convoy of trucks. Why wasn't he in school? Marcel glared over at the unstoppable Noah, evidently tempted to say something. But he didn't, because he couldn't—Janet practically kept his Cork Room in business, closing many of her multimillion-dollar real estate deals with the wine from a shelf Marcel kept only for her.

Mom was contemplating her arugula, brooding over her duck breast. She was unhappy, and more so than usual. She wore a Native American necklace matching her feather earrings, her hair blown into a rigid shape. Joshua leaned in to kiss her cheek but was wise enough not to ask what was up. He saw her tumid ankles, the swelling crawling up her shins toward her knees, her burst capillaries like a tattoo of the Amazon and its tributaries. Once upon a time, he'd fallen asleep with his head in her lap, as she'd stroked the hair away from his temples. Once upon a time he'd watched her with pride as she leapt from a springboard, bending perfectly in midair to slip into the pool as into a glove.

Janet was staring at the TV over the bar—the intrepid invaders were mesmerizing.

"Marccl says he's bleeding money because people are angry at the French for not joining the party in Iraq," she whispered. "I'm as patriotic as the next guy, but I draw the line at boycotting wine. What are we fighting for if I can't have my Bordeaux?"

Joshua filled up his glass with 1983 Château Margaux and rinsed his palate with it. If there was a perfect thing in the world, it was Château Margaux '83, and no coalition of the willing could drive a wedge between them. He'd had his first wine in 1983: he was almost thirteen, Bernie had left an open bottle on the table; not even his vomiting later could dampen the memory of that first-kiss experience. He imagined sharing a bottle with Ana, her lips claret, teaching her to sniff it, to feel it on her palate, teaching her the tasting vocabulary. Noah slid into the chair next to Joshua and matter-of-factly said: "Camelfuckers."

"Watch your language, young man," Janet said sans conviction.

"Camelfuckers," Noah repeated.

"Secret word, Noah! We don't use it in front of other people. We talked about secret words, didn't we?"

Mom looked up at Noah, then at Joshua, and rolled her eyes—this was some kind of signal to him, but he could not decode it. She'd moved to a downtown condo after the Wilmette house had been sold as part of the divorce settlement; she'd wanted to be able to walk to theaters and museums and Symphony Center; to date and have lunches with her fellow ballast board members. But lately she left her condo only to go to her hairdresser or book club. Janet was worried that she was depressed and developing an addiction to sleeping pills. Janet worried meant Janet called Joshua to complain.

"How's your father?" Mother asked him.

"Rachel!" Janet said. She'd started calling her Rachel after she'd had Noah, the title of Mother now available to her as well.

"I don't know," Joshua said. "Haven't talked to Bernie for a while."

Janet was shaking her head to indicate her disapproval and worry. The Levins were a family whose communication system was founded on decoding secret words and silences. What was not actually uttered was always what mattered more. It was like poor-man's psychoanalysis, except they were not particularly poor. The first time he'd taken Kimmy to a family dinner she'd quickly recognized, smart as she was, that they'd been reading her and talking about her in the Levin code. Moreover, Mother had randomly rolled her eyes; Janet had kept topping off Kimmy's wineglass, intent on getting her loose and tipsy; Doug had ogled her shamelessly. What would the Levins say about Ana?

"He's on a cruise," Janet said. "I told you that."

"With his big-tits babe?"

"Rachel! She's older than you."

"Where did they go, Joshua?" Mother said. "Where are they cruising?"

"Mom, please," Joshua said. "I don't know."

"Israel," Mother said. "The Holy blasted Land."

"Wasn't there another suicide bombing there last week?" Janet asked.

"He probably didn't even leave the cruise ship," Joshua said.

"He probably didn't even leave her tits," Mother said.

"Tits," Noah said, smashing the top of his crème brûlée with a spoon.

"Secret word, Noah!" Janet said. "Could you cut it out, Rachel, please?"

"I hope they're booked on the *Titanic*," Mother said. "I hope she ends up holding his hand as he turns to ice, like that boy in the movie."

"Tits," Noah said.

"All right, you're in time-out, young mister," Janet said.

Time-out meant that Noah was afforded more time to plan another irritating thing to do or say. It was clear from his impish grin that his mind was now thinly stretched between *camelfuckers* and *tits*. What is it with boys? How do they slide into fucked-upness so quickly, with such natural ease? Joshua refilled his glass with Château Margaux then put the bottle down. Janet pointedly picked it up to add wine to Mother's and her glasses, as Marcel hurried over to snatch the bottle from Janet's hand.

"Merci bien, monsieur!" she said with a courtly nod, thereby pretty much exhausting her French vocabulary. She'd convinced Doug to marry her in Paris; neither of them could understand what the official had been saying, so they hadn't answered properly when she'd asked them if they'd take each other for better or for worse, or whatever they said in France. It'd been a running joke between Doug and Jan that they were not sure they'd been married. Doug, priapic

as he was, had certainly behaved as if they were merely good friends from high school.

"De rien, madame!" Marcel bowed and smiled. It was not beyond Janet to appropriate Marcel for retributive intercourse, Joshua realized. Marcel walked away, bouncing on the balls of his feet, like an Olympic diver.

"So," Janet said. "Seder at my place."

"When is it?" Joshua asked.

"When is it!? You're a real bad Jew, Jackie," Janet said.

"Okay, but when is your Seder?"

"April sixteenth. You've got two weeks to Jew up."

"Reading from the same script every year, thanking the Lord for getting our ass out of the situation he put us in in the first place—that's not my idea of a good time."

"God will smite you."

"God doesn't give a damn about me."

"He sheds his wrath upon the nations that do not recognize him, and on the kingdoms *and* individuals that will not proclaim his name. I'd be careful."

"Whatever."

"And it's a good story too," Janet said.

"Cameltits," Noah said, proud of his cleverness. He was Doug's son all right. Janet grabbed him above his elbow and pulled him away from the table. She dragged him into the women's bathroom, as he wailed like the little patient he was. Perhaps it was true that everything was Oedipal with boys. Perhaps Papa Freud was in fact right.

"You haven't heard this from me, but Jan and Doug are separated," Mother said. "He sent Janet an e-mail from Dubai, except it was meant for some other woman and was describing his crotch."

"His crotch? You mean his penis?"

"Don't ask me for details, Joshua, for God's sake. I'm your mother."

"So where's he now?"

"Maybe still in Dubai. Or in some downtown hotel with a hooker. Dead, as far as Jan's concerned."

"Are they going to get divorced?"

"Jan's mad more than ever before."

"Is she okay?"

"She's very mad."

"Poor Doug. She'll destroy him," Joshua said, and immediately realized that he shouldn't have.

"Poor Doug?" his mother growled, actually showing her incisors, but before she could say more Janet came back with Noah. His blond hair now was wet and pasted to his skull, with a neat straight line down the middle.

"Now," Janet said, emptying the Château Margaux into her glass, lifting the bottle to ask Marcel for more. "Now we're going to enjoy this goddamn lunch."

INT. HOSPITAL — DAY

Major Klopstock, gun in hand, sneaks up the back
stairs, barely lit by the streaks of sunlight from
obscure windows and cracks. Every once in a while,
he checks to see what floor he's on. The undead LOW
in distant hospital spaces. When he reaches the
25th floor, he carefully opens the door to look
down the dark hallway, where all the lights are
out. It appears to be zombie-free. He turns on his
flashlight: it's the neurosurgery floor. He moves
soundlessly, pressing his back against the wall.
He knows his way around that labyrinth. He opens a
door to look in, but has to duck quickly as he
spots a zombie munching on a brain from a glass
jar. The undead one is too busy to notice Major K,
who moves on.

Major K rummages through a file cabinet, looking
for something in particular, throwing down what he
has no use for. In the corner, he sees a small fire
extinguisher. He puts it in his backpack.

As Major K is about to enter the nurses' room, he
hears a CRASH inside. He turns off the flashlight
and presses his back against the wall, then crawls
along it to look in through a small window. He sees
a flashing move, too fast for a zombie — someone
ducks behind a stack of boxes. He raises his gun
and cocks it. He looks again, and this time spots
an elbow of a living human sticking out, then an
eye peeking from behind the box. There is GROANING
in the hallway, then more zombies roaming. He
pushes the door open and slips in, pointing the
gun at CANCER PATIENT (37), bald, skinny, and wearing a hospital gown.

MAJOR KLOPSTOCK
(whispering)
Do not make a sound!

She shakes her head and stays silent. She shifts
her gaze to look at something behind Major K.
Still pointing his gun at her, he turns to see
NURSE (55) and a chubby BOY (12), both shivering in
fear. There is a FOREIGNER (40) kneeling next to
them, holding a cell phone, from which a cord
stretches to an outlet.

FOREIGNER
Power out.

MAJOR K
Everything's out.

Ana lived way out in Lincolnwood, in a building that
looked like a depressing dorm, what with its dun color and
standard-issue windows, but was called the Ambassador.
She buzzed him in, but didn't tell him her apartment number.
On his way up, Joshua pressed his ear against suspect doors,
each of which offered the sounds of myriad lives: a radio gib-
bering in an obscure language; Mexican oompah-oompah
music; a desperate, barking dog; the hum of an empty space.
Ana's place was up on the Ambassador's top floor. There
was a crowd of shoes in front of the door, lit dispiritingly by
the skylight. Some were lined up, some thrown together:
men's shoes, wide and deep and brown; Chuck Taylors; fine
Italian leather shoes. There were women's high heels too,
and flat ballet shoes and even flower-patterned rain boots.
Visions of the Holocaust shoe heaps came to Joshua and in
their wake a memory of Nana Elsa's Florida plastic flip-
flops, conforming to her bunions perfectly. She'd had them
for at least fifteen years and wouldn't hear of getting rid of
them. In fact, she never got rid of any of her shoes; Papa Elie
disposed of them behind her back, so she never let her pre-
cious flip-flops out of sight. She wanted to be buried with
those flip-flops. Nothing exists from whose nature some ef-
fect does not follow.

Joshua took his tennis shoes off and placed them at a distance from all the others. Then it occurred to him that that might be interpreted as his being a snob, and moved them a little closer, but still not touching any other shoes. He walked in, somewhat embarrassed by his white tube socks—his grandmother's grandson, he too had a hard time getting rid of things. A teenage girl walked out of the bathroom, her purple shirt severely tucked into a pair of latex-tight jeans. She considered Joshua and said, "Hi!" with a ladylike nod. "Hi!" Joshua nodded back. She was lanky, her long mane brushing her skinny, half-pubescent behind. She had narrow, awkward-looking feet and a constellation of pimples on her chin, but she seemed to be at ease with herself. You could tell she was Ana's daughter: the same green eyes, the same long neck, the same, if unripe, sadness.

"I'm outta here," she said. "You kids have loads of fun."

Her English was purely American, no accent whatsoever. Should she not have a Bosnian accent? She slipped past Joshua, picked her shoes off the pile, and scuttered down the stairs. In Joshua's memory of his adolescence, there was no need to worry about the ease: he'd spent much of his teenagehood watching old movies in the basement, thus escaping the ubiquitous unease.

In the center of the dining room there was a long table, thick with plates of food and bottles of booze. Everyone crowded around it, teeming like wildflowers, no space between the chairs. On the far side of the table, Captain Ponomarenko and his faithful wife drowned in a sofa, their chins nearly touching the edge of the table. Bega was there too, fully present in his Bad Brains T-shirt, Corona in hand, pontificating to a woman slowly backing away as he leaned into her to make his indisputable points. What was he doing there? Had she invited people Joshua knew? Why would she do that? She had invited Stagger too—or so he'd claimed—to this party. Terrified, Joshua scanned the room. Apart from his students and Bega, everyone was comfortingly anonymous. He waved wordlessly at everyone, which everyone ignored. He stood at the door, waiting for something to happen and determine what he should do next. Eventually, he turned to go elsewhere and there was Ana behind him, her short hair so freshly hennaed as to approach purple, matching nicely her sky-blue summer dress and her cleavage beaded with sweat. She had a tray of thin-sliced meat in her hands.

"Teacher Josh," she said. "Super to see you."

She wiggled past him and he had an urge to grab her and keep her by his side. Her face was flushed, and Joshua determined he should be hot as well: he wiped the imaginary sweat off his forehead with his hand, and everyone laughed. "I'm Joshua," he said, but no one bothered to introduce themselves. Bega finally raised his beer to greet him then poured all of it into his mouth.

"What are you doing here?" Joshua ventured to ask.

"Bosnia is small world," Bega said. "And world is small Bosnia. And I live close."

The rest of the guests raised their glasses, except for Captain Ponomarenko and Larissa, who hailed him with an ungenerous stare, as if his arrival irreversibly spoiled the reigning harmony. Ana joked in her language with the people at the table and everybody neighed with laughter looking at him. They all appeared Eastern European, but he could not determine what exactly it was that made them so. The flat back of male heads, perhaps. Or the dark circles around their eyes. Or the abundance of defiantly unhealthy food. Or the huddling around the table. On all other nights we eat either sitting up or leaning back; on this night we lean forward and giggle at strangers.

Ana put the platter down and returned to him. "What did you say to them?" he asked.

"You don't know if you don't learn Bosnian," she said and winked at him mischievously. "Let me show you where is the kitchen."

It wasn't clear why he needed to know where the kitchen was, but she touched him above the elbow to direct him and his biceps rubbed against her breasts. He could feel their fullness, their weighted maturity. Kimmy's breasts were small, somehow expressive of her control, as if she willfully prevented them from growing.

"So, you know Bega," Joshua said. "Small world."

"I know him. He lives close."

"Captain Ponomarenko and Larissa are here too. They hate the thought of me."

"Yes," she frankly confirmed. "But I like you." There was the momentary purse of her lips and a flash of the dimples before she smiled, rendering Captain USSR and his wife harmless and irrelevant. She bespoke the supreme authority of the governing hostess—everyone in her domain was going to be taken care of. Kimmy had a similar quality, but her domain was spare: he and Bushy were the only ones populating it. Ana pulled up her bra and Joshua compliantly followed her to the kitchen.

"You know Bega?" she asked.

"We're in the same screenwriting workshop."

"What is workshop?"

"Oh, we share our work with others and then talk shop about it."

"Nice," she said, in a way that suggested that she understood what he was talking about. Kimmy claimed that the workshop format had emerged at the same time as group therapy, but she hadn't experienced Graham's workshopping, which was as far from healing as can be.

In the small kitchen, there was a man taking up half of the space. A cleaver in hand, he was dismembering what appeared to be a whole lamb stretched on a plank, its eyes about to pop out in roasted surprise. Whenever the man brought the cleaver down, everything on the counter leapt up and the lamb raised its head. Barbed wire was tattooed in a circle around the man's neck, as if to keep his head and body segregated.

Ana said something to the man, and he revolved to give her an angry look, responding with a word that, to Joshua, sounded gutturally ugly. The man did not look at Joshua once, waving the cleaver around as he was getting wound up about something. Ana stood between Joshua and the door, blocking off the retreat route, so he looked around the kitchen with feigned interest: a calendar from a butcher shop on the wall; a cuckoo clock with weights and an unmoving pendulum; the spice rack, spiceless. He nodded, as if to show his admiration for the simple, human ambition of the kitchen. The Levin syndrome: always seeing himself from someone else's point of view, as if in a movie.

Finally, mercifully, Ana said: "This is Esko, my husband."

"Pleasure to meet you, Esko," Joshua said. "I'm Joshua."

Esko moved the cleaver from his right to his left hand, as if considering shaking Joshua's hand, still saying nothing. His jaw was wide and not only unshaven but layered with unshavenness; a big, blackish wart protruded from the depths of his hirsute cheek. Joshua understood at first glance that Esko disliked him.

"I'm Ana's English teacher," he said, unnecessarily.

"Good," the man said and returned the cleaver to his right hand. A scene presented itself to Joshua: Esko grabbing his right hand, carelessly offered for a shake, then swinging the cleaver and slicing it off, the blood spraying the kitchen walls. Instead, Esko went back to dismembering the lamb, the splinters of meat flying about excitedly.

"My husband was born in boat," she said.

"Oh really?" Joshua said. "That's fascinating."

"That's what we say in Bosnia when somebody doesn't know how to be nice."

"That's okay," Joshua said. All of his utterances felt wrong, as if English suddenly were a language foreign to him. Esko placed the lamb's head on the board, complete with its grotesquely googly eyes, and split it in two with one powerful blow. He picked up a piece of the brain with the cleaver and licked it off the blade. Born in an abattoir, more likely.

"It is not okay. He was not really born in boat. He is from good city family."

She was upset, he realized.

"He is my second husband," she said, which Joshua elected to understand as *not my first choice*. She was grinding her teeth, snorting instead of breathing. He had an urge to put his arms around her and squeeze her hard, just to see how strong she was. She made choices: she was strong. But there were no dimples in sight.

"I like your place," Joshua said, helplessly.

"Go look around," she said.

He slipped past her out into the hallway, but there was little to look at. He could hear Ana speaking to Esko with restrained fury, riddled with hard Eastern European consonants. Obediently, he opened the first door and it was the bathroom: towels, mirror, moldy dampness. He opened another one and it was their bedroom. The bed was unruly, as if sex had just been had in it; chairs covered with clothes; the smell of married bodies. A tower of books stood to one side, on top of which was *Let's Go, America! 5*. On the closet door handle, there were her bras, bundled like scalps. As a kid, Joshua had thoroughly searched his parents' bedroom whenever they'd gone away: he'd frisked his father's inside suit pockets, finding condoms; he'd looked through his mother's dresser drawer, dug through her bras and underwear; he'd gone through their documents: bills, bank statements, letters to lawyers. He'd kept tabs on them; he'd found out unmentionable things. He'd known well before Rachel that Bernie had been fucking Constance on the sly. He closed the door.

"It's crazy messy," Ana said, right behind him. There was only one more door to open: a handwritten sign on it said "Welcome to Hell!"

"Room of Alma. My daughter," Ana said, but she didn't open the door for him, and he didn't insist. What could've been in there? Script Idea #62: *A secret door in a teenager's closet leads to an alternate universe, where she is the heiress to a powerful empire, her life endangered by her evil stepfather.*

Ana placed him at the head of the table, so that everyone now regarded him with expectation, as if he were supposed to conduct a workshop, or affirm his authority by delivering a salutation of some sort. No authority, however, was affirmed except for Ana's, as she went around the table introducing all of her guests. Their names consisted entirely of unpronounceable sounds, therefore incomprehensible and impossible to remember. When she got to Bega, he said something that made her laugh.

"We go way back," Bega said in English and winked. The woman sitting next to Bega was Ana's boss, it turned out, and she was Russian. She had coal-black hair and biblically dark eyes, which made her appear very young. Joshua hadn't even known Ana worked but he refrained from inquiring. Everyone at the table was now quiet, still waiting for Joshua to say something, and he couldn't think of a single word to utter. Everything excellent is as difficult as it is rare.

In the meantime, Ana packed a plate and set it down before him. "Little bit of everything," she said. When Esko walked in with a pile of lamb on a platter, she picked a boneless piece for Joshua and dropped it on his plate, to which everyone responded with an appreciative "oooh."

"What do you want to drink?" Bega asked. "There is everything."

"I like wine," Joshua said, before he saw what was on the table. There was little doubt he looked like a snob.

And thus he drank some overoxidized wine and it was vile, but people talked at him and he could not fend off their foreign blather without alcohol, and he drank a lot of it, oxidation be damned. Ana was seated next to him, their thighs rubbing. It seemed that she was looking for ways to touch him surreptitiously, and mind he did not. She refilled his glass with the dreadful wine, while she sipped Johnnie Walker. Esko came in occasionally to bring more food or another bottle of booze, but he pretty much spent the evening in the kitchen. There was a cloud over his head, and everyone quieted down whenever he came by. "He doesn't like parties," Ana told Joshua by way of explanation. "Because he doesn't like people."

"Earth is populated with reasons not to like people."

"He is wild man."

"I think I ran into your daughter on my way in," Joshua said, mainly to change the subject.

"Yes, Alma. I am worry about her," Ana said. "Drugs, sex, crazy people. I don't know her friends, where is she going. I think we maybe must go back to Sarajevo."

"She'll be fine," Joshua said. "Teenagers have a lot of energy."

"Energy is not good for mother," Ana said. "Mother gets tired."

Joshua arranged an empathetic face to signal he understood. The arrangement required raised eyebrows and lips rolled in; he could feel his forehead muscles straining. The easiest thing would be just to hug her or hold her hand. Kimmy liked to snuggle up and put her head on the side of his chest to listen to his heartbeat; he often worried she could smell his armpit.

"You are too young to get tired."

She laughed: "How old you think I am?"

"Thirty," Joshua ventured. Thirty-five or thirty-seven, really, maybe even forty, but he knew better than to say it.

She pressed her hands against her cheeks and said: "I can kiss you for that."

Bega was ranting forcefully about something in Bosnian, occasionally sitting up to loom over the table, while everyone except Ana's boss and the Ponomarenkos convulsed in laughter. Joshua's plate defeated him with its demanding foreignness—apart from lamb, bread, and tomatoes, he did not know what any of those things were. Some were yummy, some bitter, all confusing in their combination of unfamiliar tastes.

"What am I eating?" he asked her. She pointed at things and named them in Bosnian and he kept trying to repeat the words. There was no hope—Bosnian sounded like Hebrew spoken by someone with a debilitating speech impediment—but he enjoyed watching her mouth. The lips that could make those sounds must be very soft. Those lips were certainly not forty, but younger, much younger.

Their naming game kept them apart from the rest of the table. Joshua could see Bega glancing over, even in the middle of his performance, and he made sure his body was at an angle in relation to hers that prevented their circle from completely closing. He considered calling Kimmy and reporting as if from a far-off land about all this: the strange language, the strange food, the strange people—all this, that is, except Ana's body. In any case, as far as Kimmy was concerned, he was at the movies, watching *Touch of Evil* yet again. His throat narrowed around the returning lump; he took in her jasmine smell and her overmanicured nails (Kimmy gnawed on hers) and watched the veins on her hand and her long fingers and imagined kissing it all. No one can desire to be blessed, to act well and to live well, unless at the same time he desires to be, to act, and to live, that is, to actually exist. Whenever Ana's husband reappeared, Joshua tried for eye contact with him, so as to exhibit his honesty and innocence, thereby covering up his humming desire. *I can kiss you for that*, she'd said.

———

Right after Ana blew out the candle—her lips immaculately pouted—on the chocolate happy-birthday cake, the Ponomarenkos left, then some other consonant clusters departed, and then Joshua had to stand up to let Ana's boss out. Her name was Zosya, he found as she thrust her limp, cold hand into his. She owned a chocolate shop and was Jewish, Ana told him, as if those two things were connected. Joshua showed interest, but couldn't go as far as to own up to his Jewishness—somehow it demanded complicated, fine-tuned qualifications—though he did own up to liking chocolate. Ana walked her out and Joshua could see Zosya stroking her cheek before kissing it goodbye. Now there was more space at the table, and when Ana came back she sat a little farther from Joshua.

Bega seemed to have started a new story. He spoke slowly at first, taking sips from another Corona, but then he sped up and raised his voice until he was shouting, banging the table with his hand. The more commandingly he talked, the more his audience laughed. The skinny, gray-haired man at the far end fell off his chair laughing, and was now on his knees, holding his stomach. Ana was clapping her hands as she laughed, throwing her head back, thrusting her bosom out.

"What is he talking about?" Joshua asked her. He deployed a nonspecific grin so as to participate in the general merriment, waiting for her to regain composure, but Ana could not stop laughing. Finally, she said, still chuckling:

"Very hard to translate."

"Come on," Joshua pleaded.

She looked at him as if trying to decide whether he was worth the effort. *I can kiss you for that.* Joshua held his breath. All the dubious flirting, all the body positioning, all the surreptitious touches—the reality and the value of it seemed to depend presently on whether she would try to translate the joke.

"Come on," he said.

"Maybe," she said, "maybe it will not be funny."

"Let's just give it a shot," he said.

"Okay," she said. Bega stopped talking. The skinny man got off the floor and reclined in his chair. They all wanted to see how Ana would do, how Joshua would react to her translation.

"One old man in Bosnia," Ana said. "He liked his mobitel—"

"Cell phone," Bega said.

"—cell phone so much," Ana continued, "that he asked his son to go to grave with it when he dies. So old man dies and his son respect his wish. But his grandson steals SIM card—"

"Cell phone chip," Bega said.

Shut up! Joshua thought.

"—before funeral and puts it in his phone. So they put him in the ground, they cover him with earth."

Bega and the others seemed rapt—they kept nodding in approval, encouraging her. Joshua was all ready to laugh, so eager for the rendition to work out. Ana giggled and took a nervous sip of Johnnie Walker.

"But grandson sends text to his father. Text comes, it looks like it comes from old man and it says: I arrived to other world. His son goes crazy! Text from other world!"

Joshua chortled, hoping this was not it. Ana seemed out of breath, as if she had been running. This was not unlike an exam for her; she had stage fright. He had seen it before: her stuttering, the rise at the end of a difficult word, as if she was reaching for it, the thought in her eyes as she parsed the possibilities, her dramatic breath intake. He realized he was attracted to her striving, to her struggle to survive. *I can kiss you for that.*

"But then"—Ana inhaled and exhaled—"best friend of old man dies. His name is Fikret and he has funeral. Before the funeral, grandson sends text message to his father: Please send phone charger with Fikret."

Everyone laughed, but nowhere near as much as when they heard it in Bosnian. The skinny man certainly didn't fall off the chair. Joshua laughed too, but his laughter was devoid of the abandon he'd witnessed in the Bosnians. Ana didn't laugh at all; she just shrugged, as if to say that she'd done her best and it wasn't her fault. She finished her glass of whiskey.

"Hard to translate," the skinny man said.

They sat in silence for a while. When Bega restarted the conversation in Bosnian, it was serene, as if the mistranslated joke had reminded them how sad and displaced they really were. History: the first time a joke, the second time a badly translated joke. Joshua was now the only one in the room not speaking the language, but he could not leave, as if that would violate the sacred impenetrability of Bega's words. A woman with dyed-blond hair and a chest armor of necklaces listened for a while and then started crying, pressing her face against the skinny man's shoulder to sob mutely. Ana saw it, but said nothing, nor did she offer to translate for Joshua. It was not unlike watching a movie: he was simultaneously there and absent; present, but not responsible for any of it. Ana was sitting close to him again and he could feel the warmth of the thigh, the deep vibrations of her flesh, the hum of her blood on its way to her heart.

"So what you are speaking is the Bosnian language, then," Joshua said, just to keep her engaged, away from Bega's lamentations.

"It has many names. I call it Bosnian, sometimes I don't like to argue so I say 'our language.' I much more like to speak English, not complicated."

"You speak English well," Joshua said.

"I need to speak better to find better job," she said. "I don't want to work in chocolate shop whole life."

Their faces were turned to each other conspiratorially. He smelled her alcoholic breath and he could see himself moving deeper into her space to plant his lips on hers. Kimmy's mouth was sweet, but almost never alcoholic. Alcoholic breath turned him on: *I must kiss you for that.* As if reading his mind, she leaned back, just in time for her husband to walk in and sit across from Bega. They knocked their beer bottles together and drank.

"Your boss seems nice," Joshua said.

"Very nice," Ana said. "But she likes to touch me. She stands by me, touches me and says: 'Oopsie daisy.'"

"Why does she touch you?"

Ana straightened her back, pushing out her chest, and circled her hand around her breasts, *anabashedly*.

"Here," she said.

The unswallowable lump was back.

"So what do you do about that?"

"I ask her: 'Why you touch me like that?' And she says: 'I must make love to you.'"

"That's illegal," Joshua said. "That's sexual harassment."

"She is beautiful woman. Maybe many years ago. But now . . ."

She flung her hand in the direction of Esko, who looked

over at them with a cloudy frown of oblivion. Joshua downed his glass of wine and licked the dregs off his lips. It was time to go.

"What do you think I must do?" Ana asked him.

"About what?"

"About Zosya."

"What do I think? Frankly, I can't think right now," Joshua said.

He refilled his glass and had some more wine, which had a distinct bouquet of Palmolive dish detergent.

"I don't know what to do," Ana said.

Joshua leaned to whisper into her ear: "Do it."

She looked at him in shock, glanced at Esko. "What?"

"Do it," Joshua whispered, this time barely audibly.

Her cheeks trembled as she smiled, and back they were— the great dimples of Ana.

"I'm kidding," Joshua said, and she chuckled, knowing he meant it.

For a long while he could not find the keyhole on the bike lock, and then pedaled listlessly on the sidewalk because he was too drunk. More precisely, he was aroused and didn't want to go home, where Kimmy was asleep. The simple fact of his present life was that he was lusting for Ana. *I can kiss you for that*, she said to him. *Do it*, he said to her. He drunkenly recognized that the lust was part of something bigger, of a craving to pursue pleasure unreasonably, beyond the right and wrong, to go as far as his body took him. In the body there is no absolute, or free, will, but the body is determined to desire this or that by a cause that is also determined by another, and this again by another, and so on to infinity. She had brought her body to him, she carried it over here all the way from elsewhere. Why shouldn't he dive into it? She should sleep with her boss. He should sleep with her. And, if need be, the boss too. Or whoever else he desired to sleep with. Man must fend off the void with his dick. Why should he go home to be a good boyfriend? The dead end of the Levin syndrome: wanting people to see him as good and loyal, precisely because he was neither good nor loyal. All he had to do was stop caring. Kimmy had her handcuffs and cock rings. What did he have, other than a false, worthless claim to decency? Why should he not be who he really was? Why pretend? *Do it!*

He decided to stop by a bar for a nightcap and then some. Fuck this, he thought, by the end of this night I'll have been laid. *I can kiss you for that.* He'd never in his life been picked up by a woman in a bar—or any other place—but tonight he felt that he could finally have the shameless gumption to let it happen. *I don't know what to do*, she'd said. Here I am, Joshua thought, prepared and ardent, allied and present. The Westmoreland was around the corner, but there was no chance that he could find there any women worthy of copulation, and even if he could, they were likely to be more desperate than him. *Maybe many years ago*, Ana said. He envisioned the young Ana kissing Zosya, Zosya undressing her; nipples; moaning; the whole shebang. He who recollects a thing by which he was once pleased desires to possess it in the same circumstances as when he first was pleased by it. He who was never pleased is doomed to an eternal hard-on.

He biked down Clark, stopping to peek through the windows of various bars, looking for women. Only gay bars were full; the heterosexual joints were empty—the heteros massively committed to watching television with their falsely monogamous spouses. He recalled that a cute, potentially promiscuous bartender worked at Charlie's Ale House, but when he looked in, there was nobody, not even a bartender. In case of a zombie apocalypse, would people fuck more, or less, or at all? What if the zombie hunger were not visceral but carnal? He should look more into zombie porn. If they'd already come up with a flick called *Weapons of Ass Destruction*, there had to be a *Night of the Fucking Dead*.

To the Westmoreland it was, then. Down Clark Street people moved in units of desire and negotiable friendship, under the neon lights promising pleasure and warmth against the Chicago chill. He left Clark to enter the side-street darkness at the end of which he found the Westmoreland, ever tucked inside a strip mall between a tire shop and a Curves front office. The bar was, naturally, vacant—time seemed to have stopped here, as Paco was in the same position, with the same goiter, watching the same TV, except this time it showed baseball highlights.

"Hey, Paco!" Joshua said. He would've loved it if Paco could remember him, but he didn't and it was likely that he never would. He nodded instead, bartenderly.

"Do you have any good Pinot Noir?" Joshua asked.

"No," Paco said, not a muscle on his face moving. "But the Jell-O shots are fantastic."

Joshua waited for some indication of Paco's seriousness level, but he was unbending: no indication was provided.

"I'd prefer some red wine," Joshua said.

There was a time when he could conceive of a life that would permit him to wake up happy in the morning. Such a life was now beyond the reach of his imagination, nor could he remember what it would've exactly looked like. Still, it was fair to say that the minimum requirement for a truly enjoyable existence would be unbridled promiscuity. There is that great moment in *Goldfinger* when the leader of the fantastically blond crew of female flyers tells James Bond: "I'm Pussy Galore," and he says: "I must be dreaming!"

Right now, it didn't look good, the life. What doesn't kill you makes you horny. Paco delivered the wine and said, "Three dollars," at which point Joshua patted his pockets to find out that his wallet was absent.

"I can't find my wallet," he told Paco, expecting understanding or forgiveness. But Paco kept staring at him, the goiter throbbing with judgment. Whereupon he took the wine bottle, unscrewed the top, and poured the wine back into the bottle. He then returned to the same position to watch the TV.

Joshua retraced his bike ride back to Ana's place, stopping by the same still-empty bars, scanning the pavement in the hope of spotting the wallet, the coil of his lust unshuffling along the way. There was nothing to be found other than cigarette butts and shreds of coupon sheets and broken bottles and a few used condoms. He stopped at the light and, more out of need to distract himself from worry than out of a sense of responsibility, he checked his phone and discovered he had eight calls and five messages from Kimiko, and there was one from his father. He listened to Kimmy's first message: she just wanted him to call back and let her know when he'd be coming home. Now it was nearly midnight and she must be sleeping. He called and hung up after one ring. If someone imagines that someone loves him, and does not believe he has given any cause for it, he should love in return.

Leaning on his bike in front of the Ambassador, he looked up in search of Ana's window. Only one was lit up, and he decided, based on nothing at all, that it belonged to her. He looked at buzzers, searching for her last name, which he could not pronounce, even if she'd pronounced it for him in class nearly every time. There were names that looked Bosnian in that the consonants were randomly distributed, but he could not be sure. He called the number in his cell. It rang, then the answering service picked up. Her voice was clear and bright and lovely. He left a message to a vision of her in a nightgown, barefoot, warm.

He loitered outside until someone walked out of the building with an ancient, sick beagle and gave him a glance of suspicion. Rather than slipping in through the glacially closing door, he decided to walk around the neighborhood and wait for Ana's call.

The rows of houses were dark; here and there a light was on. A dog barked in some backyard. The swings stood still on porches. Who lived here? He could spend his entire life in Chicago—in this very neighborhood—without ever learning anything about the people who lived at 4509 West Estes. The unknown lives, the dark matter of the city. *Message comes, I arrived to the other world.* Except, in front of a dark house, he saw a red car with a pair of plush dice hanging from the rearview mirror. It was Bega's car.

His phone rang. It wasn't Kimmy.

"Hello, Ana," he said with the gentlest of his seductive voices.

"Teacher Josh," she whispered, "you find your wallet?"

"No," Joshua said.

"This is not good time," Ana said. Esko yelled in the background. "I look for it and I call you. Or I see you on Monday. Goodnight."

And then she hung up. What if Monday never came? Joshua thought. Script Idea #72: *The last day on Earth as it approaches a voracious black hole. Title:* The Last Fucking Time.

INT. THE AMBASSADOR — NIGHT

A group of men under the leadership of Major Klopstock moves through darkness, carving it with their
flashlights. CADET (20) and GOITER (59) with a
shotgun follow in Major K's wake. They enter an
open, vast space with high ceilings. They hear
ECHOES OF WATER SPLASHING, and then the flashlights
reveal a pool full of floating zombies in army
uniforms. Most of them are bloated and fully dead.
Some are broken open, like pomegranates. A few of
them are on their backs, moving feebly, but it's
clear they're done for. The men stand in silence
at the pool's edge. The water is murky with pus and
blood.

                    GOITER
            (scratching his goiter)
        I wouldn't wanna swim in that fucking pool.

                    CADET
        This used to be our guys. Now they're
        mindless killers.

MAJOR K

They're harmless in the water. They don't
sink, but they soak up water until they
burst like balloons.

A floating zombie slightly moves its hand, as if
trying to swim. Goiter shoots it in the face. The
head explodes into smithereens. The shot ECHOES.
Cadet joins in, as do other men. They shoot like
crazy. The waves make other corpses bob in the pool.
Major K tries to interrupt the shooting.

MAJOR K

Cut it out! Cut it out!

But the men enjoy the free-for-all too much to
stop. Finally, Major K rips the gun out of Cadet's
hand and smacks him. Everyone stops shooting. Major
K stares them down angrily. The silence is even
more oppressive. Except now they can hear ECHOES
of a cell phone RINGING somewhere in the building.
The ring tone is "Welcome to the Jungle." They exchange glances, grip their weapons, and move in
the direction of the sound.

Joshua needed his wallet and thus had a legitimate excuse to call Ana. He was shivering on the porch steps—it was a cold day, clouds on the western horizon getting lined up for a rain assault—because he was reluctant to call her from Kimmy's house, as though his illicit desires were less so outdoors. He was going to claim urgency; he wasn't going to tell her he'd canceled his credit cards because, well, he wasn't exactly sure who those people at her place had been, nor could he trust Esko. Ana's answering machine picked up but he left no message. He put the phone back in his pocket, but then took it out immediately because it appeared to be vibrating, which it wasn't.

Cackling squirrels chased one another up and down the trees. There was a pretty spotted pointer across the street, for some reason pointing at Joshua; the young man on the other end of the leash bent over to pick up a clump of shit. Joshua felt in his chest the emptiness commonly accompanying the sense that he was wasting his life and that all this—this porch, this body, this mind, this Monday—was part of a self-generating delusion, his own private *Matrix*. What if he woke up one day, after a night of unsettling dreams, and realized he was transformed into a giant, chitinous failure? If one day someone were to write his biography (*The Fall of*

Joshua Levin), this morning might end up being the turning plot point, the moment of his demotion to the middlest of ages, of his realization that the spoor of his meaningful existence was as scant as that of memorable sexual experience. He called Ana again, and this time Esko picked up, his guttural grumble befuddling Joshua, who hung up instantly.

Bernie honked from his ferry-sized white Cadillac. In addition to the glaring absence of sun, Bernie's shades were not age-appropriate at all: the frames were too narrow for his sagging face; there was fake-diamond glitter on the sides; and the lenses were far too dark even for a bright summer day, suggesting glaucoma rather than senior coolness. The shades were most likely Constance's present, just like the flannel shirt he was wearing with his sleeves rolled up, like a campaigning congressman feigning to be the American people. Constance bought things for Bernie Levin that made him appear younger (a razor-looking cell phone, many-geared bicycle, surfboard), thereby constantly setting up Bern (as she called him) for some kind of age-based failure. The next thing on her list was a spiffy car. She wanted him to get something smaller and sportier than his enormous Cadillac, which Joshua was presently entering and which would've smelled like a pine-scented taxicab if it wasn't for the reek of Bernie's rampant paradentosis.

"Where are we going?" Joshua asked testily. Once he'd watched a nature documentary in which young chimps would strut around the uninterested older males making contemptuous chimp faces; and then, one day, they would dare for the first time to smack the elders.

"I don't know," his father said. "Aren't we having lunch?"

"It's too early," Joshua said.

"It's never too early for being too late."

Joshua was no strutting chimp, but Bernie annoyed him simply for doing what aged fathers did: asking *Where are you?* as soon as Joshua picked up, still confounded by the concept of the cell phone; always worrying about money, ever a Holocaust descendant; celebrating his Jewish heritage by imparting incomprehensible stories about obscure relatives; driving like a terrified lunatic, flying over speed bumps, hitting the brakes arbitrarily; insisting that he wasn't as old as he was, even if he was nowhere near as young as Connie wanted him to be. And then there were the anthological non sequiturs, whose frequency kept increasing since he'd retired and sold his dental office. The previous time Joshua had seen him, just before he took off for the cruise, Bernie proclaimed—over dinner, out of the blue, Connie squeezing his hand as if to show her forgiveness and understanding for his dementia—"the future of the world is in a bag of dog poop, because that's where the bacteria that can eat plastic will evolve." After he'd retired into a life of magazine subscriptions and cruises, he had more than enough time to think inconsequentially. It's never too early for being too late? What the hell did that mean?

"I've got to go to my screenwriting workshop later," Joshua said.

"You'll be fine," Bernie said. "Let's go to the lake."

Whereupon he made a U-turn right in the middle of Broadway, cars honking furiously in their wake.

"How's your movie stuff going?" Bernie asked. He didn't really want to know, as he didn't really care. *Your movie stuff* meant that, as far as he was concerned, it was all just plain indulgent.

"Swimmingly."

"What are you working on now?"

All that screenwriting and film business was, as Bernie had once eloquently put it, "smoke up the ass." It certainly didn't help that Joshua never sold anything, never earned a dime with his writing; nor did it help that, for Bernie, Saul Bellow was the be all and end all of narrative art, truer than the truth itself, pretty close to displacing Moses as the greatest Jew of all time. Not least because Bernie had met him more than once at various dinner parties.

"It's called *Zombie Wars*," Joshua said, spitefully.

Bernie made another turn and now they were driving down the parking lot along the lake; the expanse of the Wilson Street beach opened up in the distance like a prairie. He kept tapping on the brake as if it were a bass-drum pedal, so that they kept lurching forward. There was nobody around, except for an occasional man sitting alone in a car. Joshua knew it was a daytime pick-up spot for cruising men, but he didn't mention it to Bernie, sure he'd have no idea. Bernie parked two spots down from a man who tried to make eye contact to determine if he was going to get lucky with a threesome. The man looked exactly like Dick Cheney: pale and bald, egg-shaped head, rimless glasses, the detached gaze of a sociopath.

"What's it about?" Bernie asked. Another annoying thing: relentless questions. He never let Joshua be silent, quick to counter his reticence with an onslaught of inquiries. It was love, but maddening still. It was also fear of being left out of his children's lives: it had started after the divorce, after the routine of biweekly visits with him had been established. The waves crested far out on the lake and kept coming; the Wilson Street beach was desolate, except for a silhouette throwing something to a very speedy dog, maybe a greyhound.

"It's about zombies. And wars," Joshua said.

"Let me ask you a question: how do they turn into zombies? Medically speaking. That's never been clear to me."

"In my script they're infected with a virus."

"What virus?"

"It's a virus, it doesn't have a name. It's a zombie virus."

"Okay. But if you know it's a virus, shouldn't you have a name for it? You know, something like H1Z3 or something."

"It's called zombie virus."

"Zombie virus. I get it."

The water was brown-gray; the mud at its bottom had been disturbed. For Chicago, the lake was merely decoration: nobody lived on it or off it; if it somehow were drained, the city would just pave it for parking all the way to Michigan. Script Idea #79: *A brutal storm releases a sunken sailboat from the bottom of the lake, and the body of a young man is found. Nobody in the small town knows who it is, as no one has been missing. Who was he? What happened to him?*

The moment of quiet was evanescent, as Bernie was whipping up more questions in his head. Like all senescent Republicans, Levin the elder believed in leadership, which started with identifying the essence of the problem.

"But where does it come from, that virus? From a cat scratch? Or are there monkey zombies? Or bird zombies? Did the virus jump species?"

A car pulled up next to Cheney's. The man in it was young, wearing a suit, blond as Hitlerjugend. He and Cheney rolled down their windows, conducted their negotiations, and were gone in a blink. A little bit of lunchtime dicksucking never hurt nobody. Joshua envied the ease with which homosexuals arrived at their common interest in sex. The sad fact of life was that there were no cruising spots for heterosexual men. If there were, Joshua would be parked somewhere every day of his life, willing to sleep with any woman generous enough to pull up alongside him.

"Maybe it's not a virus, but some kind of cancer," Bernie said. "I'm just thinking aloud."

"Let's not think," Joshua hissed. "Let's go to Charlie's Ale House. I'm hungry."

Charlie's Ale House was a long way away, with a lot of stop signs for Bernie to force the Cadillac into a great leap forward. The way he leaned into the steering wheel, the way he looked over it, as if over the fence—it just drove Joshua crazy. People honked at them from behind at every traffic light. And then, for reasons unknown, Bernie took the residential streets, quaint and porchy and lousy with speed bumps, riding them like waves. Joshua was getting nauseated.

"Your grandfather had a cousin back in Bukovina," Bernie said.

Goddamn, Joshua thought.

"Chaim was his name, I believe, and one day he stopped believing in God. The family saw that something was wrong, they took him to the rabbi. The rabbi took one look at Chaim and said: 'My child, you will not die until you regain your faith.' So he kept not believing. Once he was drowning and people jumped in to help him and he yelled: 'I'm fine! I'm fine! I don't believe in God.' And he swam to the shore."

It took him a few times to park right in front of Charlie's, never interrupting his narration, bumping into the car behind.

"Then the Germans rounded up everyone in the village, crammed them in a house to burn them all alive. But he ran out of the burning house, screaming: 'I don't believe in God! I don't believe in God!' He lived, everyone else died."

Joshua was unbuckled, ready to get out, but there was no getting out until the story was over. He watched Bernie's eyebrows—two pointy tufts of hair—as they oscillated in harmony with his narrative excitement.

"So then after the war he made it to Israel and there he had a family and then a stroke, so went into a coma. But he couldn't die. He could be still alive, for all I know. He might stay comatose forever. God is patient."

"Nice story," Joshua said. "What's your point?"

"Maybe it's not the virus. Maybe it's that zombies lost faith."

"You are something, Bernie!" Joshua said. "Zombies are self-hating Jews? If you don't stand with Israel, you are one of the living dead? Is that what you're saying?"

Bernie shrugged in the manner that was part of his annoying repertoire: slanting his head to the side, scrunching his shoulders, his face signaling, *Maybe I know nothing, but I'm just saying*—the shtetl shrug.

"It's just a virus, all right?" Joshua said. "It's a convention. Suspension of disbelief. Those who care about the story accept that it's a virus, they don't question the goddamn virus. It's like these weapons of mass destruction—Saddam has them because he's Saddam. If there are zombies there is a virus. The zombie virus. That's it. Can we drop the fucking virus?"

Bernie read the menu, squinting—another annoying thing— and moving his glasses up and down his curled-up nose to zoom in and out. Joshua knew that what he hated about the moments like this would end up being precisely what he missed about his father when he was gone—his irritating tics would be converted into heart-wrenching recollections. For instance, Bernie liked to announce his nutritional choices, as though everybody was on the edge of their seats to find out whether he intended to take salad or not.

"I'll have some soup," he informed Joshua. "And also lamb. What are you going to have?"

"I don't know yet," Joshua said. "I misplaced my wallet. So you're buying."

"Okay, I'm buying, no problem. Get whatever you want," Bernie said. "Have a steak if you want. Two steaks. You're pale. You look like a zombie."

The cute, big-eyed waitress was working today—her name tag read Kelly—and just her twinklesome smile was worth the lengthy digestion of the slop available at Charlie's Ale House. As Joshua watched her walk over to them, he tried to think of some clever, flirtatious thing to say to her. But she was far too fast a walker, and when she pulled out her notepad, he just ordered a glass of rosé and a grilled cheese, while his father ordered soup (with extra crackers), lamb (rare), salad, and bread pudding. On the TV above the bar, there was Bush the beady-eyed president, ever stuck in the middle of incomprehension. Cheney, fresh from cocksucking, stood right next to him like a maleficent step-father.

"How was the cruise?" Joshua asked.

"Israel really is a promised land," he said. Normally, Bernie looked bronze after returning from a cruise, but today he looked waxy.

"Did you stop anywhere else?"

"Oh, some sunny islands. I wasn't feeling too well until we got to Haifa. Constance loved it!"

"And how's Constance?"

"Great! Her boobs grow with age," Bernie said, shaking

his head in appalling admiration. "When she's in the double Ds, I'll be double dead."

Kelly brought soup and Bernie emptied five little bags of crackers into the bowl. Will I be like this when I grow old? Joshua wondered. Will I turn into a man who eats as if hurrying to finish before the food is snatched away? Bernie cradled the bowl with his left hand, looming over it. He learned that from his parents, it was a habit they'd acquired in the camp. You had to eat quickly and there was no talking while food was being disposed of. Bernie slurped a few spoonfuls, but then stopped to clear his throat, as if about to say something important.

"How's your mother?" he inquired.

"She seems fine," Joshua said. "She asked about you too."

"Did you tell her Connie and I went on a cruise?"

"She knew. She was hoping you were cruising on the *Titanic*."

Bernie chortled: "A funny girl, she is, your mother."

Kelly brought the rest of their lunch on a big tray, holding it high, so Joshua could see her nicely shaped biceps. Now that the food had arrived, the conversation was over for a while: Bernie cut into the lamb and it bled. Joshua watched Kelly swing her hips, slipping with ease between chairs, turning to push the kitchen door with her back. Women's presence in the world, Joshua realized, reliably provided torment for him, for his fatigued, unyielding flesh. He couldn't eat; he just sipped his rosé, far too dry, watching Bernie torture his undead meat. Normally, his father looked down on the plate while eating, as if any eye contact would slow down his chewing, his fists clenched around the knife and fork on either side of the plate, never letting them down. But this time he moved his jaw fitfully, glancing up at Joshua only to return his gaze to the lamb, presently swimming in its own blood. He stabbed a green bean, brought it to his mouth but didn't take it. A single tear snowballed down his left cheek.

"Oh, man!" Joshua whimpered. He hadn't anticipated this; this was supposed to be a routine Monday lunch with his father. "What is it now?"

"I don't feel well," his father said. "I haven't been feeling well."

Joshua had once watched Bush the Elder address the nation from the Oval Office. He was about to send our troops to some godforsaken place and highfalutin drivel was required to placate further the already indifferent American people. He was front-lit, the better to deliver the platitudes, so the Oval Office window behind him looked unreal, like a painted set. But then, in the middle of presidential bullshit, Joshua sensed a slight motion behind Bush and spotted a tree leaf falling, twirling through the frame of the backdrop window, which hence became real. The deciduous leaf suddenly made Bush look terribly old, and getting older by the instant. Mr. President was going to die and no troop deployment could ever stop that.

"What's up, Bernie?"

Father pushed the bean across his plate, creating little blood waves.

"Nothing. Nothing really." He put his fork down first, then his knife. Now he was unarmed. "It's just that Constance was at a mall and some fat old geezer was throwing a penny into the fountain and just collapsed. He was so big they couldn't get him out of the fountain. They had to bring in a forklift."

"Did he die?" Joshua asked.

"I have no idea. If he didn't, he will. Either way, Connie

came back home to tell me she couldn't stand to watch me perish. I assured her I wasn't going to keel over anytime soon. She has a life coach now. She's discovered she wants to live in Florida year-round. She wants to spend the rest of her life suntanning. She wants a new life, she says. The fact is, I don't have much of it left."

"Sturdy guys like you don't keel over so easily, Bernie," Joshua said. "You'll be like Chaim. We'll have to take you out to the woods, tie you to a tree, and leave you there for the wolves."

Bernie wasn't quite convinced. He finally put the blood-soaked bean into his mouth and chewed it listlessly. With another overloaded tray, Kelly flew out the swinging kitchen doors, as if about to break into song and dance. It was an entirely wrong time for her to be so young and merry. Script Idea #85: *A mob informer, knowing that his lunch partners will take him out after dessert to clip him in a forest preserve, leaves a million-dollar cocaine package as a tip for the pretty waitress. She is forced to go on the run from the mob. Title:* To Insure Promptness.

"I was taking so much Viagra, I was at constant risk of a heart attack," Bernie said. "Lately I've been just eating her, and losing my breath at that."

"Way too much information, Dad! You talking to me like that is too weird." Joshua pushed his plate away. "Did something happen in Israel? Did you even go on a cruise?"

Bernie pressed the napkin into his face and shook his head. Joshua considered getting up and coming around the table to rub his back. Instead, he put his hand on his father's forearm—his skin felt cold and clammy.

"Bernie! Goddamn it!" Joshua said. "Dad! Don't."

His father whimpered and sighed. He wiped his tears with his bloodstained napkin and stopped crying. Young and innocent, Kelly arrived with a pitcher of ice water.

"How are we doing?" she asked blithely, topping off their glasses.

"Fantastic!" Bernie said, wiping his mouth. "And I think I'm ready for my bread pudding."

Joshua promised he'd pay back the two hundred dollars Bernie loaned him, but they both knew it would never happen. Outside Charlie's Ale House, standing by the cruise-ship-sized Cadillac, they hugged, slapping each other's back masculinely.

"We don't spend enough time together," Bernie said. "I like talking to you."

"I like talking to you too."

"I don't know enough about your life. What you want, what you do. One day you left home and became a stranger."

No, Joshua thought, one day Bernie left home and became a stranger. But this was no time for settling truth debts.

"I'm no stranger. I tell you stuff. I'm teaching, writing, hanging out. A simple life," Joshua said. "And you'll be okay. You're a tough Hebrew, hard as a nail."

"Sure. The Levins are survivors," he said and squeezed Joshua's face between his big palms, kissing his forehead, like the patriarch he wasn't.

The car beeped and its doors unlocked, as in a dream. One leg inside, Bernie asked: "How's Kimmy?"

"Fine," Joshua said.

"Don't screw that up. She's a catch."

Normally, Bernie would lean out of the window and wave at Joshua before he'd drive away, doing it exaggeratedly, as if he were about to go on a cross-country trip. Joshua waited for him to do so, unable to let go without the ritual, like a kid before sleep. But Bernie was taking his time playing with his phone and Joshua watched his hunched back, pathetically diminutive behind the wheel. On their family trips he'd loomed large, driving with blatant, if undeserved, confidence, complete with shouting along with the music from the radio and cursing at other drivers. "How's it that I can remember things that took place fifty years ago," Bernie had once asked him, "and I can't remember what I did this morning?"

Joshua was the first one at Graham's place, so he lingered alone in the living room, browsing the bookshelves. He picked up *The Climax: The Art of Resolving Conflict* and flipped through it. *Rule #24: Not every revelation deserves screen time*, he read. His phone buzzed with a message in his pocket. He decided that, today, if it came to that, he would point out the anti-Semitic implications of Graham's anti-Weinstein rants. Enough was enough. He sensed that his newfangled decisiveness had something to do with his father—if need be, Joshua could be a tough Jew too.

Graham walked in with the same pretzels and soda bottles from last week. It was as though he were just plugging the products: no one ever ate pretzels; no one drank whatever was in the bottles, it may well have been dyed toilet-bowl water. *Rule #33: Tension must pay off, otherwise it's torture.* Joshua, gearing up for a hypothetical fight, glared at him without a greeting.

"I like your zombie stuff, Josh," Graham said unexpectedly, settling in his armchair. He instantly applied his thumb to his cleft chin, rubbing it with pleasure. Did he have a residual clit there? "I do think you have a few good ideas in that pumpkin of yours. I was thinking of putting you in touch with an agent guy I know. He's a bit of an insufferable prick, and most of his clients are actually actors. But he's always wanting to expand into screenwriters. And you might get to practice your pitching. What do you think?"

Rule #45: What you see is what you get. A flock of butterflies fluttered up in Joshua's stomach. "I think that's great," he said. The phone buzzed again. He put the book away and sat down. Other than *Zombie Wars*, he couldn't remember any of his other ideas at that moment. Saint Pacino watched over him benevolently. An agent, even of Graham's breed, was something. Once again the phone buzzed, and then buzzed one more time.

"Are you going to look at that phone?" Graham asked. "It's really annoying." Joshua checked his phone. *Rule #50: Plot don't stop.* The message was from Bernie.

Spaking of hard, has check up, the message read. *Some leevel too higg. Ha anotjer tes. My prstte Prostate like roc. Hello cancer. Don tell Jan Rachel. Lov ypu.*

Joshua's first thought was: Bernie learned how to text. He then waited for another thought, but it was slow in coming.

"Why you want to have zombies?" Bega asked. "Do you have good reason? Or is it just because Hollywood?"

This time around, Bega's T-shirt had a Ford logo, except it read *Fuck* instead of *Ford*.

"Well, there's something about people just turning into

consuming organisms," Joshua said. "So that the living appear more human in contrast. They love, they suffer."

"Who?" Dillon asked.

"The humans."

"Have you seen *28 Days Later*?" Dillon asked.

"No," Joshua said. "It hasn't come out in the U.S. yet."

"Joshua watches only old movies," Bega said. "For him good movies are like wine, they need to become old. Everything after *Star Wars* is shit. He doesn't want to be influenced by shit."

Joshua must've stated this to Bega back at the Westmoreland, but he couldn't quite recall it. Still, the mocking tone hurt.

"I hate all of the Star Wars movies. Particularly *Star Wars*," Joshua clarified defiantly.

Dillon assembled his face into an expression of unmitigated shock and offered it to Joshua.

"The thing with zombies," Graham said, "is that they don't fuck."

"Really?" Dillon feigned shock again. "Like *really*?"

"Really," Joshua said. How does one become a Dillon?

"And they don't fuck," Graham continued, "because they have no functional bodies."

"They could fuck," Joshua said. "They could do anything I'd like them to do."

"Zombies are not real," Bega said. "When you see zombie in a movie you think: This is bullshit."

"The way I see it is they're the living dead," Joshua said. "Their human biology is not dead, it's just suspended, they're in a kind of a coma. So that their bodies are not necessarily dead. There's struggle inside them at the cellular level—good cells versus evil cells. That's why Major K is developing a vaccine for the virus. If it works, good beats evil, and they can just return to being human. It will be a little bit like resurrection."

"I always wondered how they digest the flesh they eat," Graham said. "I mean, how much of it can they actually eat? Do they get overstuffed? Do they crave fresh protein? Can they eat raw steak too? Do they shit?"

"Well, you do have to suspend some disbelief," Joshua said. "You have to accept that zombies are mythological creatures. Greek gods don't shit."

"Greek gods do fuck, though, as far as I know, and a lot," Graham said. "They are jealous, they do all kinds of wacky stuff to each other, they cheat on their wives, they change shapes. They don't just totter around howling."

"It's not about the zombies, it's about the living," Joshua said.

"But living don't do nothing in your story," Bega said. "They just kill lot of zombies. Good thing about zombies is you can kill million and nobody cares. You just shoot, they explode, nobody cares. It is for Americans to feel better about killing to make it easy."

"They're like terrorists," Dillon said.

"Maybe there is one zombie your hero cares about," Bega suggested. "Maybe he tries to save his wife or something."

"There's that family that Major Klopstock found," Joshua said. "He wants to save them."

"The name Klopstock is a bad idea, I promise you," Graham said. "He can have a Jewish name, but could he at least be Major Abraham or Major David or something? Actually, Major David is pretty good—as in David versus Goliath. Let me pat myself on the back!"

He reached for the spot between his shoulder blades. One day his joint will pop.

"I like Major Moses," Dillon said. "He takes them to the promised land."

"I don't want biblical names. I prefer Major Klopstock. It means nothing. I don't think it's even particularly Jewish. He's just an ordinary guy with an ordinary name," Joshua said.

"I don't think that Klopstock is an ordinary name anywhere outside Brooklyn," Graham said.

"Where is sadness?" Bega asked. "He lives in the world that is absolutely destroyed. He lost family. He lost his house, his city. Why is he not sad?"

"He is quite sad," Joshua said. "He just doesn't have time to stop and reflect upon it. Sadness will come after he survives."

"Fuck sadness, movies are not about being sad," Graham said, the red hand of excessive excitement emerging on his forehead. "Look anywhere around you, no sadness. Americans are proud people but we're not sad people. We're either deeply depressed or insanely happy. Either way, we don't care to see other people's misery. What we want to see is how to overcome the shit. We shall overcome! Overcome the shit! That kind of thing."

"But how do you overcome death?" Bega was getting upset. "That's why you have zombies. They are dead little bit so when you kill them you kill death."

"I think death is part of life," Dillon said.

"That's depressing," Graham said. "Who is going to watch a movie as depressing as that? You need to get a winner in there, Mr. Levin. Not the gentle Major Chickenstock. Someone who makes hard choices and goes for the kill if he needs to. People are losers, so they identify with the winner."

"But that is not real," Bega said.

"The real is for pussies," Graham raved, rocking. "People want better than real. I got plenty of real at work, where my boss is fucking me. Or at home where my real kids are really screaming their real heads off. If you want more real, go and live in Iraq. They got shitloads of real. They got so much real they blow themselves up with it all day long."

"I don't care about the real or the unreal," Joshua said. "I just want to tell a story."

"Exactly," Graham said. "Tell the fucking story."

EXT. A CHICAGO STREET — DAY

Major Klopstock opens his eyes and sees a herd of zombies surrounding him, GROANING and HOWLING. They include a few children in school uniforms, torn and bloodied. The circle narrows as the zombies advance. He has a twelve-gauge in his hand, a heavy bag on his shoulder. The zombies totter forward to reach for him. He blows a few zombie brains out, creating an opening in the circle big enough to escape. He moves toward the opening, shooting a couple more in the head. He shoves the zombie children out of his way, shooting continuously as they drop to the ground. He destroys all of them, but just as he's about to relax, one of the zombie kids on the ground grabs his ankle and tries to bite into it. Major K blows its head off, then wipes the mess off his shoes with its school uniform.

                    MAJOR K
         Bad boy! Bad boy!

Sears Tower is looming on the horizon. Above it a
helicopter hovers. The top of the tower explodes.

The basement classroom was empty, except for a faint fungal scent and the scrambled rows of school chairs. *Think, thought, thinker, thoughtful, thoughtless*, read the chalkboard, authored by some other teacher confounding his students in some other class. A word family: *think* and *thought* the spoiled, bickering children, *thinker* the drunk uncle doing who-knows-what in the small upstairs room, *thoughtful* and *thoughtless* the divorced parents.

And Bernie had goddamn prostate cancer. *My prstte Prostate like roc. Hello cancer.* Joshua had texted back: *Fuck! Sorry!* That was it. *Fuck* and *Sorry*, the Laurel and Hardy of filial empathy. What could he say? What was there to say? He was going to find something to say and then he was going to call Bernie and say it. Right now, however, he had to prepare for the class.

Ana startled him when she materialized in tall black boots, a knee-length red skirt, and a cloud-patterned shirt. She stood at a distance as if to allow him to take in the beautiful apparition.

"I have your wallet," she said. "I find your wallet."

Joshua waited for her to pull it out of her purse. His cards were canceled, but he had no driver's license, no PRT Institute ID, no wine-shoppe punch card with three more purchases before he could get a free bottle. Script Idea #88: *An American is mugged and pistol-whipped. When he wakes up, he discovers he was mistaken for an illegal immigrant and deported to Mexico. He has to find a way to come back home. Drug gangs, desert, border patrols, adventures, Conchita the illegally seductive immigrantess. Title:* The Pale Coyote.

But she didn't open her purse. Instead, she put it down on her chair and moved toward him until their thighs touched the opposite edges of the desk.

"Thank you," Joshua said. "Very much."

They faced each other across the desk as if about to break into an operatic duet.

"I don't have it now," she said. "I have it in my home. Esko find it."

There was a space for reasonable questions—"Why didn't you bring it?" or "Why didn't you call me back?"—but Joshua decided not to enter it. She glanced away and he knew that she was not telling him everything. The purse was tan fake leather; it slumped on the chair like a deflated heart, and just as full of secrets. Ana the mysterious immigrantess.

"Thank you very much," Joshua said. She gripped her elbow like John Wayne at the end of *The Searchers*. He imagined the tips of his fingers moving up her forearm and then up her biceps and then deeper into the vast, fragrant meadows of her body.

"I must give it to you first," she said. "And then you will own me."

Joshua was now leaning on the desk and it moved toward her an inch, with a screech.

"You mean to say, 'You will owe me,'" Joshua said. "I already do. I owe you."

"You owe me, yes," she said, with a smile. How would he describe those lips? They were far more than full, much better than thick. Lips, like clouds, forced clichés upon you. All the lips and clouds in the world had already been described.

"I will think of a way," Joshua said, "to return your kindness."

Captain Ponomarenko leaned back in his chair against the wall and spitefully shut his eyes. The class felt endless and devoid of meaning or purpose, like a Spielberg movie. Joshua kept pointing at the conjugation chart on the chalkboard, forcing the students to come up with their own ludicrous examples. "By the time I am sixty-five, I will have lived for very long time," Ana said and licked her lips. The desk had moved between them, as if his lust had telekinetic properties. "Beautiful, Ana," Joshua said, a bit too supportively. *You own me*, she'd said. It was possible that she knew what she was saying; it was possible it was an offer. Captain Prick, ever attuned to his enemy's fragility, asked: "Teacher Josh, maybe we go home early?" Not opening his eyes, he pronounced it as *errlyi*.

He gave in to Captain P without even pretending to think about it, not assigning any homework, which they never did anyway. By the time the world ends, everything will have happened; nothing will have happened just as well. We'll have soon run out of happening, and then there'll be nothing but being in a void. Very slowly, he picked up his papers off the desk so that he could furtively glance at Ana's knees and boots and her skirt, so that he could see her forearm and the dangling bracelet and her long, piano-player fingers. The lump was in its place, lodged firmly, ready to choke.

When he looked up, Ana was shutting the door, foreclosing all retreat routes. She stood in front of him, taking deep breaths.

"My heart hits very much," she said.

"Beats."

"My heart beats, Teacher Josh."

"Joshua," Joshua whispered, but only because all the wind was gone from his windpipe.

"Joshua," she repeated. "You want to touch it?" She took his hand and put it on her left breast. He could feel her heart, somewhere underneath the cloud pattern; she was alive all right. He plunged his mouth into the curve of her neck and pulled her stumblingly toward the Israel map. Their bodies knew what to do in such a situation, as they knew how to walk or open a door: his hand ran deftly under her blouse; she unfurled her tongue beyond the overbite, into his mouth; he released the saliva; she laid her long-fingered hand on his bulging crotch, raising her pelvis toward him, her moves determined and lustful, her pate rubbing against the Sea of Galilee. The lump was now throbbing inside his skull, exterminating the entire extended family of *think*.

But just as Joshua started pulling down her panties, just as he was to touch her famous clitoris, she gripped his wrist to stop him.

"What are you doing?" Joshua whimpered, bending over to ease the pain of severe erection.

"It's crazy. We're crazy," she said. "Esko is waiting for me."

"I don't want to know about Esko!" Joshua said. "Please don't talk about Esko."

Now he could hear the students lingering in the hallways, the din from a remote universe. She pulled up her panties, straightened out her skirt. She fixed her bra, buttoned up her shirt, and fixed her hair. The way women restore themselves—it was something that had always mesmerized Joshua: the care, the patience, the clear purpose. Ana did it with a composure that was well beyond Joshua's panic and comprehension.

"By the time I divorce him," Ana said, "I will not have loved him for long time."

She kissed his forehead lightly and slipped out of the classroom, back into the world overrun with Ponomarenkos and their ilk. Next year in goddamn Jerusalem! The map of Israel, vaguely vaginal as it was, made little sense: the sharp angles, the curlicues and straight lines that were supposed to be the borders. None of it made any sense. How many worlds could there be in the world? How many worlds would the cosmic asshole have gratuitously created? Joshua's hard-on was painful; he considered manually relieving himself right then and there.

But he didn't—the temporary victory of reason was a defeat of the body. The pent-up desire hence turned into groin tension and pain in the ass, not in the least figurative, auguring many prostate problems. The regrets and shame arrived promptly, as soon as the adrenaline levels dropped, as soon as he remembered that Bernie had never sailed in the waters of Israel, as soon as the dead-endness of it all became self-evident, as soon as he saw that door close behind Ana.

On a tightrope stretched between arousal and despair, Joshua crossed his inner abyss to reach the Westmoreland, which he recognized only as he was locking his bike in front of it. Bega was there, still in his *Fuck* T-shirt, perched on a stool, fitting so naturally into the dump landscape he might as well have been a piece of furniture. This time around, he had beer bottles on the bar organized in groups of three, perhaps in order to count them better—there were twelve of them. He was not surprised to see Joshua, nor was he particularly happy. There was, far too appropriate for the perpetual Westmoreland circumstances, a large, stopped clock over the mirror behind the bar. Paco was watching baseball again, somehow acknowledging Joshua without actually looking at him. His goiter seemed to be a little bigger and redder than a couple of days ago. It could've been the light, or it could've been that the tumor was growing rapidly.

"Why doesn't he take that thing out?" Joshua whispered to Bega as Paco attended to two thick-armed Northwestern frat boys, who must've adventurously descended into the city in pursuit of mindless fun. Both of them had their baseball hats backward, the better to announce their partying ambition, wearing shorts and flip-flops in early April, the month not quite cruel enough to them.

"What thing?" Bega asked.

"That thing on his neck. The goiter."

As Paco poured two double Jell-O shots for the frat boys, Bega looked at his goiter as if he'd never seen it before.

"*Goiter*. That's good word," Bega said. "Is it Jewish word?"

"Jewish word? You mean Yiddish? No, it's not a Yiddish word."

In truth, Joshua had no idea. Joshua inherited little Yiddish from his venerable ancestors, mainly what was already part of the English language, *mensch*, *schmuck*, and such. Paco's bulge could well be a *goyter*. What would *goyter* mean in Yiddish? Someone pretending to be *goy*? Nana Elsa used to curse her *goyrl*—her fate. Maybe *goyter* is *goyrl*'s sinister fiancé. Or was it the word for tumors, for what Bernie's prostate was turning into?

"Goiter," Bega said, with relish.

The frat boys emptied the shots into their gullets then slammed the glasses down on the bar dramatically, as if they'd just accomplished a brave and rare feat. Paco poured them another round. One day these wide-shouldered boys will be running mutual funds into the ground, loyally voting Republican, and supporting foreign wars while watching the Wildcats football games, their hands stuck into their sweatshorts.

"Goiter." Bega rolled it on his tongue like a sommelier.

"I just made out with Ana," Joshua said out of the blue, surprising himself. It could've been that he was hoping Bega, an elected representative of all the Bosnians residing in this particular universe, would understand and forgive him in one fell swoop, thereby quickly alleviating Joshua's nascent guilt; or it was that he wanted Bega to stop saying "goiter."

"I'm sure she's dying to fuck you," Bega submitted with what equally consisted of disgust and admiration. "Sincere congratulations!"

"I'm not interested," Josh said. "She's my student. And I have a girlfriend."

"Sure you do, Josh. But that is no problem if you play it right," Bega went on. "He is her second husband, but you must be careful. Esko went little crazy in war, now he's little bit fucked up."

"I don't want to think about Esko."

"Sure you don't," Bega said. "He drinks a lot. He does not get along with his stepdaughter."

"His stepdaughter? The girl is not his?"

"No. Her father was killed in the war."

"How do you know them?" Joshua asked. *Them*, he said.

"Oh, Bosnia is small world. I know lot of Bosnians," Bega said and winked. "Some better than others."

What was that wink supposed to mean? Know in what way?

"She has my wallet," Joshua said. "I lost it at the party."

Bega finished off his beer. "Goiter," he said.

"What?"

Bega raised his hand to call Paco over for another round. What they did at the Westmoreland was more than just drinking; they also longed for Paco and his attention. It was what other people went to holy temples for. Paco, for his part, was impervious to their prayers, ever looking up at the TV as at a celestial body. There must be a place in the world where there would be monks serving as bartenders, communing with spirits, mixing martinis to help you transcend your consciousness and fall facedown into enlightenment.

"Listen to me, I give you free advice: never, not even if they torture you, you must say anything to your girlfriend," Bega said. "If she has video of you having sex with Ana, you look her in eyes and say: 'That is not me!' Never guilty, always innocent."

"I just got carried away. It was a mistake. I have no intention of having sex with Ana," Joshua said. "Whatsoever."

"Whatsoever?"

"Whatsoever. She has a teenage daughter."

"She does."

The frat boys were high-fiving each other. They looked exactly as the ones Joshua remembered from his college days: the same arrogance acquired by way of torturous football drills; the same unblemished skin and well-organized bodies; the same victoriously sparkling eyes; the same unquestionable confidence in the arrival of the cozy future. There ought to be a scene in *Zombie Wars* where chesty fratboys are quartered by the undead. Paco finally came around to take an order.

"Red wine," Joshua said.

"No way," Bega said, ogling the goiter. "Give him Jack on the rocks. He's real man now."

Joshua was too busy examining the *goyter* to object. It looked just as it sounded: *goyter.* Bernie used to speak Yiddish growing up. Joshua must learn Yiddish. By the time I'm sixty-five, I'll have written unproducable scripts in unspeakable Yiddish. Bega was staring at the *goyter* too.

"What're you looking at?" Paco asked them testily.

"Goiter," Bega said. "We're looking at your goiter. Why you don't take it out."

"Take it out?" Paco the *goytermonk* said. "That's where I keep my spare head."

The Westmoreland Jacks should have rendered the Ana experience as distant as a medieval battle, yet Joshua spent much of his walk home (home?) searching for the exact way to convey the taste and texture of her lips: red licorice? tuna sashimi? a warm, split red-bean mochi ball? It was all wrong (why did only food come to mind?). He could not perfectly recollect the sensation, because his hands had been too busy exploring her skin and groin. He should've paid more attention to the lips—the stupid adolescent habit of always going for the deeper bases. He opened the front door like a burglar, hoping that, if Kimiko was sufficiently tranquilized by late-night television, he could slip into bed so that Ana and her lips would by the morning dissolve into the untroubling past.

But Kimmy was not tranquilized at all: a bottle of dreadfully Chilean wine was on the dining-room table, a Bach cello suite droned on, a candle sputtered with lavender-scented flames, some dead animal smelled appetizingly from the oven. There was going to be a sharing of thoughts.

"I would like to talk to you, Jo," Kimiko said, offering a place at the table as if it were a witness stand. She poured a full glass of wine for him and but a third for herself, and an arrow of fear whooshed into his chest to vibrate for a while: what if she was pregnant and about to announce it? She sat across from him; in the counterlight he could see the aura of her charged stray hairs. He'd begged Kimmy to let him watch her comb her long hair, but she never let him anywhere close to it, ever the empress of her domain.

"I've been thinking," Kimmy said, "and wondering: how is it that I've never read any of your writing?"

Joshua swallowed half of his glass. Interesting: a touch of Chapstick, ginger-ale nose, cat-hair finish. He couldn't remember the last time he actually enjoyed wine. Perhaps his nose was changing; perhaps his body was changing; perhaps an evil cell had already hatched in his groin.

"Well," he said. "I never thought you would care to see any of it. Most of it is not done anyway. Scripts change constantly. No living person has ever finished a script."

The truth was that he was too embarrassed to show any of it to her, fearing that she—she who combed her hair in privacy, who wrangled little patients daily—would instantly recognize the nonsensical silliness of, say, *The Ship of Doom*, featuring a killer on the loose who boarded a cruise ship on its way to the Caribbean, only to be recognized by Honey, the widow of a policeman he'd killed. All that in the thirty pages he'd written before he, wisely, quit. He longed to impress her, to show her he could think *with* thinking.

"I'm not admonishing you," Kimmy said. "I realize that we both need space. Which is okay. But I do care about what you do, about you."

She used to be on the archery team in college; she'd once almost made it to the Olympics. She could tie her hair in a knot on the top of her head and would never notice as it unraveled. She ran half-marathons, for the hell of it; she could run marathons anytime she wanted to. He downed the rest of his wine. The door of the fear booth flew wide open.

"This situation," Kimmy said, waving her hand as if everything around them indisputably constituted the *situation*, "might be a chance for us to take our relationship to a new level."

The part of Joshua that wasn't cowed wanted to ask her whether cock rings and handcuffs were commonly deployed at the new level. But that exact part of him had just unleashed itself upon Ana and then spent time doubled over with severe arousal and then some extra time feeling guilty about it all. Bushy walked in and abruptly rolled on his back to oversee the negotiations from the floor.

Her lease was up next month, Kimmy said, and they could sign a new one together. They would split the rent and he would pay her back half of the deposit she had already put up and *this*—she made another demonstrative circle, and the wine swirled again inside her glass—would be the home they share. The whorling moves were wholly disorienting, as if she were working to mesmerize him.

He applied the tip of his forefinger to his lips in a gesture of serious contemplation, and he could still smell Ana's skin on it. Kimmy noticed his empty glass and positioned the mouth of the bottle over it for him to approve replenishment. Joshua admired her determination, her ability to be perpetually goal-oriented—she was everything he wasn't, a smart woman included. If there had been such a thing as a perfect self-betterment instruction sheet, she would have checked off every item on the list. She was one hairbreadth away from self-completion.

"I don't want anything to change," she said. "I just want more of it."

Joshua nodded, and she emptied the bottle into his glass. Whatever beast was in the oven now reached the early stages of incineration. He'd thought that she knew more than he simply from being less disorganized; he'd believed she must be seeing in him something he had no access to. Perhaps it was his inchoate quality that she liked—he was incomplete: a Joshua without Joshua, a thinker without thinking. But if she couldn't tell that he was drunk after he'd groped another woman, if she couldn't see the sludge of lechery at the bottom of his alcohol-red eyes, then she couldn't anticipate the forms he would assume upon completion. Which is to say that Ms. Perfect wasn't that perfect, and Joshua stood a reasonable chance. They could, then, perhaps, manage to move on to the next level in the relationship game, the cock ring set to be the transitional object this time around. He would have to be responsible and productive, she would have to be forgiving and understanding; they could keep their secrets and work on the practicalities of common life. Ana would remain obscure in the before, while in the after he and Kimmy would be progressing toward the peaceful domain of grown-up commitment, whose denizens regularly read the Sunday *New York Times* before a brunch with friends and, if need be, nursed each other through grueling chemo. Here was Joshua, then, at the mouth of the fear booth; he could back out or step in. He offered her his glass for a chin-chin and she touched it with hers.

Joshua followed Kimmy upstairs and put his wineglass on the nightstand. But he never got to drink any more of it, as she expertly handcuffed him to the bedposts, then got on top of him. She bit his nipples; she sucked him while she fingered him to tickle the prostate—hopefully liquidating the evil cell—stopping as soon as she interpreted Joshua's shudder as the harbinger of ejaculation; she ignored the handcuffs cutting into his wrists. She uttered no word; after she came, she closed her eyes and closed they stayed. Bushy, perversely contorted on the dresser, licked his own asshole throughout the whole session.

Script Idea #69: *An S&M male porn star falls in love with a gentle poetry professor. When she is kidnapped by his jealous fan, he needs not only to save her but also to tell her the truth about his life. It turns out she loves to dominate. Title:* These Chains of Love.

EXT. NAVY PIER — NIGHT

Guarded by soldiers with night-vision goggles, a column of seven prisoners stumbles down the desolate Navy Pier. The prisoners' heads are covered with black hoods. Abandoned cruise ships, the Ferris wheel broken in half. The only sounds are the WAVES, the HOWLING of empty cruise ships, and WHIMPERING under the hoods. The soldiers have powerful guns but keep the prisoners in line with cattle prods, which cause sparks and make bodies twitch. They make them line up at the edge of the pier, facing the water. One of the prisoners tries to break away from the gang but is prodded back into line. Each of the soldiers points a gun at a hooded head.

                    PRISONER
              (with a foreign accent)
        I am not dead! I am not dead!

The soldiers fire. The flashing guns light up the exploding hoods.

                         SOLDIER
          Now you are!

The soldiers chuckle as the bodies SPLASH in the
water. On the horizon, smudges of dawn. All over
downtown Chicago flicker the pyres incinerating
zombie corpses.

The woman on the other side of Clark had Ana's shape, her gait. Joshua nearly got run over by a car as he crossed to enter her wake. He wasn't really sure it was Ana—the hair was different, undyed and longer—but he could still stand to watch the woman's hips swing: she wore a tight skirt and boots. If it was Ana, miraculously transformed, he'd cover her eyes with his hands from behind and make her guess the surpriser. But when the woman turned and exposed all her incontestable dissimilarities, Joshua, like an experienced stalker, slipped into the Coffee Shoppe. He needed some coffee, he decided retroactively.

Coffee in hand, he tried to sneak past Stagger's door, emblazoned with a *Cubs Fans Only* parking sign. But it flew open the moment the first stair creaked; a soundslide of Guns N' Roses washed over Joshua. Stagger emerged bare-chested, with sinews, bones, and muscles on full and elaborate display; his was the body of a junkie marathon runner. His ponytail was loosened so that his face was parenthesized by hair, streaked with gray here and there. He sported two shiny studs through his nipples, and, between them, a tattoo of a snake whose tail's tip touched his navel. No doubt somewhere within his domain he had a treasure chest full of cock rings and handcuffs, and many more things unimaginable.

Joshua unhurriedly ascended onto the next creaking step. He was scared of Stagger and his nipple-studded intensity, but he didn't want to look like a coward and run up.

"Would you care to come in?" Stagger said, in a voice that only he could've thought alluring. "We could hang out, suck on, you know, some beer."

"Come on, Stagger," Joshua said, not looking at Stagger. "Jesus!"

"Leave Jesus out of this," Stagger said. "I ask you respectfully." He stepped back heels first into his dark den and closed the door. Relieved, Joshua proceeded upstairs through a tide of creaks, listening to what sounded like bottles being smashed to the beat of "Paradise City." What was troubling was not so much the noise as that Stagger kept going. How many bottles for smashing could he possibly have in that place? Every little castle in the kingdom of Chicagoland includes a TV, fridge, and stacked crates of refined insanity.

Joshua's back was tense, his loins elongated to the point of pain, his shoulders painful from the burden of the last couple of days. A sensation of a noose around his neck, stretching it, providing relief as he hung from the ceiling, emerged in his mind. He looked up to see if there was a hook above the stairs where a belt could be attached, but there was none.

His place was exactly as he'd left it: mouse-gray dust clumps patrolling the corners; the piss-sticky bathroom floor; the hunt picture slanted, the fox heading downhill. The books stood on the shelves; the two chairs facing the table like reprimanded children; the unwashed cereal bowls still unwashed; the oriental chimes not orientally chiming. How stable everything was when he wasn't there! Everything remained in its place until he moved it. Unless, that is, Stagger haunted it in his absence, pawing his stuff, then returning it exactly where it had been.

Kimiko had visited his place (home?) only once or twice. She couldn't abide the moldy shower curtain, the cockroach families vacationing in the kitchen, the flatulent reek of singlehood infusing everything. She may have initially found it exotic—an endearing symptom of Jo's prolonged youth, perhaps; a recognizable point on this little patient's trajectory, something she could work with. It had become obvious quickly that she couldn't be turned on within the walls of this dystopic dorm-room replica. Joshua hadn't insisted; he'd been pretty content to spend nights (and many long days) at her place. That way he'd practice being fully adult while retaining an escape tunnel into his prolonged adolescence; that way everything here could enjoy its comfortable stasis. Man reaches a point in his life when unchanging becomes a matter of pride; the habits and remnants of youth are thereafter kept in the museum of the self.

When Kimmy was gone for a conference in Orlando or some such hotel-and-Enrique-friendly place, Joshua would spend days writing at his abode, leaving it only for work and movie rentals. Back when he'd been a true adolescent, with Janet acing it in college and his still-married parents frequently absconding to Michigan for a weekend with the Blunts, he'd liked to stay at home by himself. He wouldn't go out, wouldn't invite his friends over, wouldn't wash dishes or shower—he'd just read, drink, watch movies, and masturbate. It was bachelor-pad communism: producing according to one's abilities, consuming according to one's needs, but no commune to get on your nerves. Come Saturday night, he'd reach a utopia of abandon, a delightful blankness of mind that eradicated the outside world in all its unrewarding complications. He'd clean up the place only a couple of hours before his parents' return. At least once, the outside world had barged in unexpectedly, Bernie returning too soon, catching him naked and deeply invested in porn. Months of indulgent therapy would follow.

He should call Bernie again, he recognized. If he called him now, he wouldn't mention his prostate; he would simply tell him he was moving in with Kimmy; that would make him happy, maybe help him forget his cancer for a little bit. Then again, Bernie was long-winded, even when he was not terrified of dying. Besides, what could Joshua actually tell him? Everything will be okay? Maybe it would be better if he called Connie to tell her about his father's prostate *goyter*, maybe she'd take enough pity on Bernie to take care of him. Or he could call Janet, she'd know what to do.

Joshua put his coffee down and straightened the fox-hunt picture. There was no sense in cleaning this mess up. A better man would say goodbye to this disarray, to this life of entropy. It was time perhaps to fully join the adult world, take responsibilities, assist his father in need, be worthy of a grown-up woman. The fact was, there was little he wanted from this place (home? nah!), except maybe some clean underwear. If somehow all this were to burn down, he'd experience no feeling of loss whatsoever; on the contrary, it would be a kind of purging. The great American cycle: catastrophe prompting reinvention; reinvention resulting in further catastrophe, and on we roll toward apocalypse and redemption. Script Idea #99: *A foxhunt from the fox's point of view*.

In his bedroom, his underwear was washed and folded on his bed in a neat, unfamiliar stack. And there, next to it, was Ana, her legs crossed, her fingers entangled on her knee, wagging impatiently her shoe on the tip of her foot. She looked like she'd been waiting for him for a long time, ripening.

"I brought your wallet," she said. "Mr. Stagger opened door for me. He is funny."

"Funny is not the right word," Joshua said.

She wore a white shirt with leg-of-mutton sleeves; there were chocolate smudges on her collar and her chest, even on her cuffs. The hem of her skirt cut across the globes of her knees; he could smell her, her *anabashed* arousal. She unzipped her purse and dug through it until she excavated his wallet. It was different, as if it had aged and become archaeological; Joshua remembered his wallet being light, but now it emitted darkness in the bedroom's gloom. He took it and held it, deliberating whether to check if all of his cards were there. He could now prove again he was his legal self, so he decided to show that he trusted her. Stagger was still destroying "Paradise City" downstairs, but she either didn't hear or didn't care. Or it wasn't happening at all. What if he were the only one hearing it, if it were all taking place in his head?

"See if wallet is okay," she said. "I never trust Esko."

The card catalogue of his life: library card, video-store card, credit cards, long over limit and now canceled; wineshoppe punch card; driver's license—the face on it appeared only vaguely familiar, as if belonging to a younger distant cousin with an overbite suggesting learning disabilities. There was no confusion, no sign of interiority in that face, nothing he could connect with the intricacies of his present self. I skip like a pebble across the surface of time, until I reach the first Tuesday of my new life.

"He don't know I'm here," Ana said. "Don't worry."

"Worry about what?" Joshua asked. It was an inane

question, both insufficient and redundant. Ana smiled and bit her upper lip, as if preventing herself from answering. The flesh of her lips, the shimmering softness in the creases. It was too dark to see, yet he saw it all. His penis stirred and then began transmogrifying into a full-fledged cock.

"We would be making a terrible mistake," Joshua said.

"Passion is never mistake," she said. Here he was at a crossroads: he could follow this living woman, let his body respond to all the stimuli she emitted; or he could honorably go the other way and return to Kimmy, who had done things to him last night he'd want done again.

"Passion is a fragrance brand," Joshua said. He squeezed by Ana to get to the closet. He dug out a New Balance duffel bag he used to use when he used to go to the gym.

"You will be going somewhere?" she asked.

"I'm moving in with my girlfriend." *My girlfriend.* There had been a time—many times—when he'd lied about having a girlfriend. He'd lied to Jessica in college, claiming that Jennifer had been his girlfriend, and then he'd lied the other way around. He'd bragged to a number of fellow guys about the outrageous things his nonexistent girlfriend would happily do for him in bed. In pursuit of his parents' respect, he'd misrepresented his relationship situation. Even when he'd had actual girlfriends he felt he'd been lying. It could well be that no man can say *my girlfriend* or—come to think of it—*my wife* without lying through his teeth. Still, after last night's heart-to-heart and the subsequent genitals-to-genitals, it was hard to deny that Kimmy had unimpeachably acquired the status of his official girlfriend.

"Very nice," Ana said. He could detect no sarcasm or sadness in her voice. "I will have been happy for you."

"Thank you," Joshua said, cleaning out his socks drawer.

He felt Ana's hand on his thigh, tugging him back with the slightest of forces. He dropped the duffel bag and sat back on the bed next to her. There was surely a way out of this, but she took his hand and examined the moons of his nails, caressing the underside of his knuckles. The bottle-smashing downstairs stopped, and then Axl Rose shut up; Joshua pricked up his ears in expectation of more, but it remained quiet, as if Stagger was waiting to see what would happen upstairs.

"My father has prostate cancer," Joshua wanted to say, but didn't. Now everything mattered less, but also more. *By the time I'm sixty-five, I'll have lived for a very long time.* She slid her leg over his and pulled him in toward her. Her dimples had a penchant for appearing at exactly the right moment. Too distraught to look her in the eye, he put his hand on her knee, then pushed her skirt up. It turned out she wore no underwear. He who provides food to all flesh, everlasting is His loving kindness.

When she was on top of him, the immobile ceiling fan distracted him. There was a hook next to it, as if conveniently installed for his hanging. He closed his eyes and heard thuds coming from below, either Stagger hitting his ceiling to let them know he was privy to it all or playing drums on his furniture. *I don't want anything to change. I just want more of it.* He felt weighty, his muscles laden with arousal; he did what he had to do. Ana whispered obscenely Bosnian words into his ear, pushing him deeper in, and deeper in he went until his cock's forehead was slamming against her interior walls. A very small man hunched in the crawl space of his mind, itemizing the moment, as if collecting evidence of his commitment to this experience: her wetness; the mutual thrust of their hips; the underwear scattered on the floor;

her coat hanging in his closet; the bedside lamp tottering to the edge; the adult ecstasy of it all. She sneezed as she was coming and he actually said: "Bless you." And blessed she was.

They shared a pair of his clean anchor-patterned shorts to wipe themselves off. Ana sat up to deposit her breasts in her bra, locking it skillfully in the back. Naked and cold under the sheet, Joshua watched the care and ease with which she resumed her shape, rubbing her back idiotically as if to encourage her. The lust always exceeds the act it leads to, as does the memory of it. Her breasts seemed larger when packed than when she was naked. Now what?

"We have to stop doing this," he said. "You have a husband."

"I don't care about husband. He is wild," she said, putting on her chocolate-smudged shirt.

"I have a girlfriend," he said. "Who wants to live with me."

"I have my daughter," she said. He pushed her sleeves up, because there was nothing else to do, and caressed her forearm with his knuckles. He liked her, he realized. Pity this was the only thing they could do. She leaned in to kiss him. Her lips had a Bosnian taste, like some food he'd had at her party. Lamb, perhaps? For a moment, he couldn't recognize his room or remember what was just outside it. Everything outside the limelight of now is swallowed by the darkness of elsewhere.

"I don't want to be responsible for your child's unhappiness," he said. In truth, he didn't care all that much. He hadn't really cared when Rachel had discovered that Bernie had had a titty mistress for years—by that time it had become too late to give a damn. When he'd eventually met

Connie, he could see why Bernie wanted to screw her every day, all day long.

"Everybody has unhappiness," Ana said. "What is life without no unhappiness?"

"A life without unhappiness is a happy life. It's a warm blanket," Joshua said. "That's what it is. What we all want."

"There is no such life like that," Ana said. Her eyes were crazy green; and there was the way her lips worked together and lightly parted to produce a soft consonant (suCH). "Nobody has life like that."

"Somebody, somewhere has such a life, even if it's not you. You've got to believe that. That's what the pursuit of happiness is all about."

She didn't understand, but she was used to not understanding what was said in English. She stood up to loom over him. She was a brave woman. It took courage to sail over here from some fucked-up elsewhere. It took courage to have sex with your English teacher, to follow through with your desires, wherever they might take you. Joshua had desired often, but seldom followed through. He'd always waited for the first move to come from the lusted-after. Ana fixed her hair, raking it with her fingers. Joshua loved that it was hennaed, that it wasn't real, that he didn't know what the real color of her hair was. She was true to herself by being different from herself.

"What's your real hair color?" he asked.

"White."

"Gray."

"No. White."

"We say gray hair. Not white hair. Even if it's white."

"We. Who is this we? You and your girlfriend?"

"Americans."

All of Joshua's sex fantasies were about that first move: young women spreading legs on the El to exhibit the shimmer of their moist vaginas; married women moving their manicured hands along the inside of his thigh, from his knee to his dick, while sitting across the dinner table from their innocent husbands; tipsy best girlfriends in the elevator offering a threesome between the fifth and tenth floors. The aphrodisiac of someone else's courage.

"We can't do this, Ana. I can't do it. I have a girlfriend. I've got problems. I've got happiness to pursue."

"What does it mean *pursue?*"

"Chase."

She grabbed her coat out of his closet. The hanger swung and then fell; she picked it up. He wanted to tell her it didn't matter: things land where they fall; things eventually take care of themselves.

"Teacher Josh, don't be afraid. I will not have tell to your girlfriend. I understand."

"Thank you," Joshua said. He waited for her to say something else, to blame him or to shrug this whole thing off as merely sex. But she put her high-heel shoes on and thus fully resumed the shape he'd known from the classroom. There was no noise downstairs and a bubble of hope floated to the surface of the present: what if Stagger was gone, from his apartment, from this building, from Joshua's life?

"Do you know my last name?" Ana asked.

"Of course I do. You're in my class," Joshua said. "It's difficult to pronounce, though."

"But that's from my husband. Do you know my real last name?"

"No," Joshua said. It had never occurred to him that she'd had a life before what she was now.

"It is Osim," she said. "It means: 'except.' "

"Except?"

"Yes. Like, everybody except me. *Svi osim mene.*"

She bent over to kiss him on the forehead. "I will not go to your class no more. By the time you forget Ana Osim, you will have had good life. With everybody except me."

She walked out without looking back and closed the door. It surprised him that he felt no regret, no loss. The stasis was instantly restored, even with Joshua there, the ceiling fan perfectly motionless. The hook was still there, but he was now relaxed. He picked up a pair of clean underwear from the floor and put it on. My soul, return to your resting place, because the Lord has rewarded you.

The moment he stepped off the last creaking step, before he could even touch the front lock, Stagger's door opened. This time, Stagger donned an untied bathrobe, tiny spectacles on the bridge of his nose, as if he'd just been reading small-print poetry. In his hand, however, there was a long samurai sword. There were shards on the floor as far as Joshua could see inside his apartment. He glanced at Stagger's feet expecting them to be shredded, but he wore a pair of frog-green Crocs.

"How was it?" Stagger asked.

"How was what?"

"Rolling in the hay with Ana. How was it? Good? Sounds like you've got some techniques, Jonjo."

"None of your business."

Stagger poked Joshua's duffel bag with the tip of the

sword, as if to inspect it. Joshua pressed his back against the
wall, closely monitoring the sword, now between the door
and him. Strangely, he was not afraid—he was, rather, going
through the habitual motions of fear, as if he had yet to
learn to live without it.

"It has to be my business, because you were banging
away up there," Stagger said. "All I was trying to do in my
humble corner was enjoy some relaxing music."

He casually leaned on the sword like Fred Astaire on a
cane.

"You let her up there. You let her into my place without
my permission. That was none of your business."

"I was just being your friend, Jonjo! I'm the kind of guy
who'd do anything for his buddies."

"Could you put that sword away, please?" Joshua asked.
"It looks ridiculous."

Stagger looked at the sword in his hand as if he'd just
discovered it was there and liked it too.

"Would you like to step in?" Stagger said. "Hang out?"

"You're a fucking freak, Stagger! I need to go now."

"I'm a freak? Look who's talking! Don't you have a girlfriend? One Kimiko Motherfucking Home? Would she be
familiar with your techniques?"

Stagger now started throwing the sword up and then
catching it by the blade. Joshua foresaw his hand being cut,
but evidently Stagger had practiced, making a face as if to
say: "How about this?"

"I'm moving out," Joshua said.

"When?"

"This instant."

"Your lease is not up yet."

"I don't care. I'm out."

"I'm gonna have to keep the deposit."

"Keep the damn deposit. In fact, keep all of my stuff. I'll just send someone for the books."

"Come on, Jonjo," Stagger said, still holding the sword by the blade. "I like having you around."

"I'm out. It was fun while it lasted."

Stagger squeezed the blade and a trickle of blood spread along it.

"Maybe you want to keep a place for screwing your lady friend on the sly? I'll lower the rent. You can tell Kimiko you moved out. It could be your love den. How about that?"

"It's over, Stagger," Joshua said and pushed past him to open the door.

"Let's just have some beer and discuss it like men!" Stagger said. He followed Joshua onto the porch and then down the steps. "Hey! Jonjo! Don't go! I'm your buddy!"

All across the wide world, spring was landing on its fairy feet. Everywhere, trees were budding and coming into leaves, ground thawing and earthworms stirring, dog shit defrosting and releasing the pungent stink that brought back memories of springs past. There was a whiff of awakening even in Chicago, where the April thaw was forever behind schedule, where the relentless winter made everything more sharp-edge real. All the living things on Magnolia—trees, squirrels, people—seemed to be involved in some secret chatter, readying themselves for the demands of rebirth. This is the gate to the Lord, the righteous shall walk through.

Once he'd stepped out of the gloom of the Stagger palace, Joshua felt his chest fill up with new air. Exhaling, he felt no guilt. None. He'd just cheated on his girlfriend, soon to be an official live-in one, for the first time ever; he went beyond his cowardice and crossed the line into a different Joshualand. And many years from now, after the evil cell had perhaps evolved into a mature *goyter*, he would have no regrets about missed chances. Feeling no remorse was a new and powerful sensation: the frigid snap in his lungs, the tingling fingertips on the duffel bag handle, the vapor of his own breath washing over his face. This was real, this Joshua in this aftermath, for whose actualization sex was just a prompt. It was like finding a new, big room in the overfurnished house of his self. This was freedom. The Lord provides food to all flesh, because His kindness is without end.

Buses stopped at stop signs; birds flew overhead without falling down; clouds floated like meringue zeppelins; sirens wailed; people moved on the outskirts of his life as mindlessly and reliably as movie extras. Leave when at the top, Michael Jordan taught us, retire while winning. Joshua had an urge to call Bernie to talk man to man, or even Bega, to brag, to assert himself. And what about me? Am I not entitled to this presence in the world, to myself as I am? May the conqueror conquer if capable of conquest. This was, he understood, why men cheat, why all mankind are liars—the power of acting without regret, the destruction of remorse. It wasn't the sex: it was the freedom to take or do what you want. The presence of death, the gaping void, afforded entitlement. This was what wars were for.

Ana was gone, leaving no traces or demands. He went in, he went out, no harm done. And there was more: he was now someone with secrets, someone simultaneously operating in the inner and the outer world, like an actor or a spy. He was now possessed of shamelessness, like Ulysses responding "Nobody" to a Cyclops asking for his name. He

acquired the unknowable, variable depths; he could be anyone he wanted to be, and if he didn't like who he became, he
could switch again, going in, going out. And who the fuck
are you? he wanted to ask the random passersby. Who the
fuck do you think you are? You are nothing but your lousy
self! He walked up Magnolia with a determination he anticipated would look sexy to Kimmy. Tonight might be her
turn to be handcuffed and beg a little. *Oh, Jo!* she'd say. Jo's
gone, baby, he'd say: I'm Levin. Joshua Levin.

EXT. LAKE SHORE DRIVE — DAY

The waves roll against the shore, disintegrating
bodies sloshing in the shallows, bobbing on the
lake as far as the eye can see. Major Klopstock,
Woman, and Boy track along Lake Shore Drive,
clogged with abandoned vehicles. Major K has a samurai sword in his hand. Boy moves slowly and whimpers, as he's overweight. Woman picks him up with
some effort, puts him on her back, and continues.
A black helicopter emerges menacingly from behind
tall buildings. Major K quickly makes Woman and
Boy duck. They slip under an incinerated truck at
the wheel of which is a charred corpse. The helicopter hovers over Lake Shore Drive, then creeps
along it, as if looking for someone.

                    MAJOR K
        Make no move.

Boy whimpers suddenly, slips out of Major K's grasp,
and runs out from under the truck.

                    WOMAN
        No!

She tries to get up, but Major K pulls her back
down. The helicopter descends very slowly until it
hovers over the boy, who waves frantically at it.

                    MAJOR K
        Fuck! There is nothing we can do now.

The very night after his tryst with Ana, Kimmy crowned
Joshua with the silver cock ring. She must have recognized
the new quality in him, the depths and the exponentially in-
creased fuckability factor; he was happy to let her bestow
his well-deserved reward. He changed, but, boy, so did she.
In the middle of the furious coitus, his cock vibrating with
pleasure at the previously unthinkable frequency, he could
not recognize Kimmy at all—what was supposed to be routine intrarelationship intercourse appeared like an insane
one-night stand. She bit his cock's root; she screamed gib-
berish like a magic incantation; she growled: "Fuck me,
Levin." I must be dreaming! Levin thought. Just before his
climax, she grabbed him by the throat, cutting off his air
supply, and looked into his eyes with a fury that scorched
the inside of his skull. For a long, ecstatic minute he was dying and coming at the same time.

Kimmy took a day off and they spent their Thursday
morning splitting and parsing the newspapers, a commodi-
ous couple interrupting the earned silence only to brief each
other on what they were reading: *The Vagina Monologues*
had been successfully performed in Islamabad; a twenty-
pound carp had shouted apocalyptic warnings in Hebrew
to a Hasidic fish cutter in New York; Saddam Hussein was

undergoing major ass destruction. He could see himself in her eyes: funny, smart, handsome, and deep. He liked that guy.

Then they went out to Ann Sather's for brunch. Brunch was an abominably monstrous compound noun, Teacher Josh insisted, but they still shared poached eggs and Swedish sausage and cinnamon rolls. He performed for her the John Wayne joke. Standing up in the narrow passage between the tables to act out the punch line, he was fully aware of the danger of appearing crass, but did it anyway, and she nearly pissed herself laughing. Not once did he think of Ana, not once. Kimmy suggested they invite his family for dinner, Janet included ("*Even* Janet") and he had to tell her that, on top of the acrimony between his parents, Bernie also had "prostate problems." She didn't quite understand whether that meant Bernie should or shouldn't be invited, but she deferred the question, so a day was provisionally chosen and she was going to call them. They watched *Dawn of the Dead* in the bedroom—required research for his script, he claimed, even if he'd seen the movie a thousand times. He outlined *Zombie Wars* for her as if pitching it to some big shot in LA: the virus and the apocalypse, Major K, the loyal cadet and the rogue soldiers, the woman and the boy. He heard the confidence in his own voice; she couldn't wait to read the script; he enjoyed the weight of her body against his. I will walk with the Lord in the lands of the living, and the rest of yous can go fuck yourselves. He was so far beyond feeling guilty: having sex with Ana may have been the best thing he'd ever done; it definitely made him a better man. Farewell, Ana Except, thank you for everything! May you have a kind trip back to elsewhere. And I shall always cherish your dimples. Before the movie ended, Joshua and

Kimmy had more furious intercourse and then passed out intertwined, Bushy snug as a bug between them.

On Friday, he kissed Kimmy's still-wet hair at the door, waved at her in loving slow motion as she drove off to work, and scooped Bushy off the porch. It was a bright, balmy morning. The spring had hit the ground running: the sunlight bent at an angle more favorable to all the warm colors, the shadows were sharper and leaner, the trees were taking their leaves seriously. He was going to call Bernie, see how he was doing, maybe set up another lunch; he was now capable of dealing with that particular situation. Then he was going to call Mr. Strauss and resign from his teaching job at the PRT Institute, and, thus relieved, write *Zombie Wars* at least part of the day, and then spend the rest of his life writing what he was meant to write. He could see an open, straight path stretching all the way to his horizon; he could see the horseman coming.

Before all that, he needed to undergo proper cleansing— metaphorical and real—and have a shower. Undressing, he inhaled the residual smells of last night's copulation. He had Kimmy-inflicted battle wounds all over his thoroughly fucked body: two parallel scratches across his thigh; a ring mark on his dick and balls; his throat still sore from strangulation.

He examined his face in the mirror and appreciated the relaxed maturity, the conspicuous new peace, the overbite retreated to a mere bite. Janet had once confessed to him that she'd had a dream in which she'd shot up heroin. She'd been so overcome by the tranquil well-being that, when she'd woken up, she'd tracked down a drug dealer. She'd bought a little pouch of heroin—*the starter kit*, the dealer called it. But Janet had never shot it up. The needle aspect had been too unsettling, while snorting was too cocaine-eighties, which she despised. She might well still be hoarding the heroin in her drawer. The episode had provided him with Script Idea #87: *A woman scientist develops an experimental sex-changing drug she tests on herself; she transforms into a violent man who exacts revenge on all the assholes who disrespected her, including her lecherous ex-husband. Title:* Mrs. Jekyll and Mr. Hyde. Well, here were Mr. Levin and Mr. Sexy, joined in a happy union, looking at each other through the mirror.

He heard the phone twittering downstairs and a rush of unexpected terror surged through him: what if it was her? He was very proud of not having thought of her. And he was certainly not going to talk to her. But the phone rang again and the thought of her—of Ana Except saying, *I will have been happy for you*, of her tug on his thigh, of her body—the thought of her could not be abolished now, even if the phone eventually shut up. He stepped under the stream of water with a hard-on, which happened to come in handy for excising the thought.

Pissing in the shower afterward, he decided he needed to put some funny stuff in *Zombie Wars*. The undead are always so damn dour, and the global cataclysm is a super-downer, to say the least. How about zombies at a disco club, dressed for *Saturday Night Fever*, tottering about to "Stayin' Alive"? He also didn't know how to end it, whether Major K's vaccine would save humanity or provide the hope for survival of a small unit of humans. Hope sold, of course, and well; it was the corn syrup of existence, fast burning and addictive. On the other hand, it was cheap and everywhere. Hope and war: the ping and the pong of America.

He consulted the mirror again: time to shave, even if he liked the weary-warrior scruffiness. The thing was that Kimmy would always get a rash from his facial hair, even on the inside of her thighs after he ate her. Wouldn't zombies have long hair and nails, given that these keep growing for a while after death? Perhaps there could be degrees in the state of undeadness. Some zombies could be more conscious, so that the vaccine could work differently for them. He put a towel around his waist—it made him feel porny and husbandly at the same time—and went down to the kitchen to get some coffee. Kimmy had turned on the coffee machine this morning while he was sleeping, and now it was ready. She also left a Post-it with a smiling little sun; *Have a lovely day!* it simply read. With Kimmy there was no stasis. She made sure his life flowed in his absence, an intimation of immortality.

At the kitchen table, there sat a huge, large-headed man, with a barbed-wire tattoo going around his neck, Bushy purring on top of his crossed legs. The man's feet were not only large but enormously wide, like snorkeling fins. Before Joshua recognized him as Esko, the man appeared—for a split, foolish second—as a cable guy with some kind of an emblem on his chest. Next to him, in a T-shirt that read, "If there's no God, who pops up the next Kleenex?" there was Bega, complete with an unkempt smile on his swollen, undershaven face, his blue eyes bright and watery, a cigarette in one hand, the other one on Esko's shoulder, as if trying to keep him down. They shouldn't have been there, the two of them, yet they were right there.

"Translate," Esko ordered Bega and continued to mutter a relentless stream of lippy Bosnian consonants, spit particles catching morning sunlight as they hovered above the table. When he stopped, Bega uttered: "Me and my wife had face-to-face conversation."

He stopped as if waiting for Joshua to say or acknowledge something, which was beyond Joshua's abilities at the moment. The two of them looked horribly at home in Kimmy's kitchen. Think, thought, thoughtful, thoughtless, thinker—the scattered ashes of the entire family.

"Maybe better to say heart-to-heart conversation," Bega went on. "I believe it is very unacceptable that you"—he pointed at Joshua—"are putting your dick inside my woman. We were in the war together." Confusingly, Bega pointed at Esko and himself. "We survived together in hell."

He enunciated the words with little emotion, as though he translated threats every day of his life, as though he'd never drunk with or seen Joshua. Esko produced another bunch of consonants, stroking the cat all along. He didn't look upset; his face was serene; occasionally, he sucked on his teeth, as if bored. There was a dime-shaped scar on his forehead Joshua hadn't noticed before, right above his left eyebrow. Bushy was revving his little pleasure engine, apparently in the middle of an extended orgasm. When Esko stopped talking, Bega nodded and smiled, as if content that he already possessed the exact words. Joshua stared at him in disbelief, unable to utter the obvious question. Idea: he could charge out of the kitchen, through the living room, then shout for help from the porch. What would he say to the neighborhood, though? Help! The husband of the woman I slept with wants to punish me!?

"I am considering slicing your"—Bega paused to relish the precision of his translation—"prick off and putting it in your mouth until you choke."

The minuscule portion of Joshua's mind that was not

paralyzed with mortal fear thought that that was a rather powerful translation. Bega shrugged and grinned, as though to suggest that one day they would all be laughing it up when recollecting in tranquillity this comic scene. Clearly, he did not see his trespassing presence as a betrayal. Speaking of betrayal: Bushy was kneading the top of Esko's knee, his eyes slits of pleasure. Right over there, by the coffee machine, there was a collection of very sharp knives of all sizes. The big one was top-of-the-line *Psycho* quality. Joshua couldn't move; his body had deserted him.

"However," Bega continued, "in this country to do such things is not very acceptable."

Without letting go of Bushy, the man put his enormously large hand gently on the table, shaping it as a gun pointed in Joshua's direction. Oh Lord, don't chasten me and make me a disposable character in your spec script!

"Maybe I will just shoot your knees," Bega went on, "so that you must never walk again and touch my wife or any other woman."

That was not me. That was not me at all. It was someone else. Saying it would increase his chances, even if infinitesimally. But there was no way for Joshua to actually utter anything. He wasn't able to open his mouth, even if an incipient word gurgled in his throat. All of his inner passageways were crumbling like mine shafts in one of those Indiana Jones movies.

"Understand?" Esko asked.

"Understand?" Bega repeated.

"Understand," Joshua finally spoke up.

"Very good," Bega said and sighed—there was nothing else that could be done about any of this. Esko lifted Bushy to face him and smiled at his friend the fluffy cat. He grasped

Bushy's head with his enormous thick-fingered hand and wrung his neck in one swift move. Bushy attempted a yelp but then went perfectly limp within a blink. Esko laid him down on the table, stroked his head one more time, and stood up.

"Ay!" Bega said, nodding, as if now everything made sense.

Only then did Joshua realize that his towel had dropped to the floor and he was naked. Good news: his penis was still there, as were his knees, if trembling.

"He was in Special Police. Little crazy," Bega said. "Sorry about that."

He flicked his cigarette into the sink where it hissed, and he followed Esko out, glancing back at Josh before failing to close the door behind him. No sound was available for hearing. No rewind for comprehending.

The Lord had installed a huge hook for a light fixture right above the table—Joshua could climb on the table, attach the belt, and jump off, thereby stretching to the point of snapping his neck. He leaned against the counter and poured himself coffee with his violently trembling hands, spilling it and burning his navel area. All the knives had black handles; knives always had black handles: why is that? He couldn't sit down; in fact, he couldn't make it to the chair, as his legs were so drained of blood that there was no way to control them, even if his knees were somewhat operational. The kitchen smelled of the man's homicidal perspiration, of Bega's smoke and cologne, of Bushy's death, of Kimmy's lavender-and-papaya conditioner in Joshua's hair. He tried to put the cup on the counter but missed by some distance and it exploded against the floor. Bushy's eyes were glassy with mortal surprise, his neck perpendicular to his spine. There had been life there, and now there wasn't. Everything in this house belonged to Kimmy; everything now perished. As the coffee spread into a puddle, Joshua looked outside: perhaps everything in the world was about to be taken down as well, like a spent stage set.

Out on the sidewalk, Bega was caught mid-step in watching something with a concerned frown. Joshua wanted to see; he moved shakily along the counter, along the wall, then stepped out on the porch.

Bare-chested and barefoot, indifferent to the cold, his hair in two pigtails, all the nipple studs and tattoos in place, wearing Joshua's stars-and-stripes shorts, there stood Stagger. There stood Stagger, pressing the tip of his long samurai sword against the spot between Esko's eyes. The Bosnian had his hands at his thighs, the right one still gun-shaped. There stood Stagger facing him.

"Want me to cut him, Jonjo?" Stagger hollered. "Say a word, I'll slice the motherfucker!"

Esko was ninja-still, his muscles tight as violin strings, staring Stagger down. The barbed-wire choker on Esko's neck looked much thicker now. He said something to Bega, giving him some sort of order, so Bega moved gingerly toward his red Honda, keeping an eye on Stagger and Esko all along, as if loath to miss anything. All the movement within Joshua's frame of vision was perfectly coordinated, as if they'd all rehearsed it before. Esko spread his feet a bit, finding a better position for some inescapably forthcoming move. Everything was rushing forward, except for Joshua, who stood still, like a rock in a stream.

"Don't move or I'll cut you, motherfucker! Jonjo, just say a word! I'm here for you, baby!"

Bega got into the car, turned it on, and opened the passenger door. Two plush dice dangled from the rearview mirror. Joshua, stark naked, leaned against the wall, feeling the cold on his buttocks. There was a yellow rocking chair on the porch he hadn't noticed before. The obese mailman was waddling along Magnolia, happily protected by his earphones from the Lord's wrath and the myriad evils of the world. A man attached to a Great Dane progressed toward a vanishing point. The car engine was roaring, Bega now brandishing sunglasses. Some kind of a wan bird hovered obliviously at the empty feeder Joshua had never seen before. Please, Lord, let my soul slip free!

"Say cut him, Josh, and I'll cut him!" Stagger bellowed.

But before Joshua could choose what to say, he said: "Don't."

"Just say it, Joshua! Say the word!"

"Don't," Joshua said, a breath louder.

"What? Can't hear you!"

"Don't cut him," Joshua said again.

Stagger looked at him as if it had never occurred to him that Joshua might not want Esko cut.

"You don't want me to cut him?" he asked, glancing at Joshua in disbelief. "Jonjo?"

And then, as if snapping his fingers, Esko hits Stagger's hands at the hilt with the blade of his left palm, the sword dropping with a clang like a fork. Stagger looks perfectly surprised, even a bit offended, as if their play suddenly turned serious. Esko grabs Stagger's right arm and keeps it stretched, pushing its wrist backward, until Stagger is bent downward on his knees. It all looks rehearsed, even when Esko thrusts the wrist farther and Joshua hears it crack, and then still farther until Stagger shrieks like a hanged dog. At which moment Bega winces. Esko releases the arm for Stagger to fall on the ground and gather it against his stomach.

No word is said. A long time ago, Joshua had a voice and a throat it came from, but now it's all gone, which he knows because nothing comes out as he, again, says: "Don't." Esko squats to punch Stagger in the nose, which commences bleeding. Stagger shuts his eyes in pain then opens them defiantly to stare at him, the pain converted on his face into hatred. Bega honks. Esko stands up. Stagger, his nose an exploded red sun, moves with his unbroken hand toward the sword. Esko stomps on his forearm. Stagger thrashes like a severed tentacle. Esko kicks him in the head. Bega honks again. The Great Dane and its man are watching it all as if it were happening on the screen. It's a lovely April day.

Joshua drops down into the rocking chair, sitting on his testicles in the process, but unable to adjust his position for comfort.

"Don't," he says. "Please."

INT. BASEMENT LAB — NIGHT

A naked, wriggling zombie is tied to an operating table, belts around his neck, wrists, and legs. His eyes roll back and his ROAR is ear-piercing. Major Klopstock and Cadet stand above him, both in surgical gowns and gloves, an array of shining scalpels on a tray within their reach.

MAJOR KLOPSTOCK
You sure you're ready for this?

Cadet nods without a word. Major K pulls up his surgical mask, as does Cadet. Only their worried eyes are visible now. Major K grabs the biggest scalpel, looks at Cadet one more time — he nods — and then makes a deep cut down the middle of the zombie's abdomen. A mass of rot and pus erupts from the incision. Cadet retches. Major K puts the scalpel away, then plunges his hands inside the zombie, who is oblivious to the undertaking, steadily roaring and eye-rolling as his intestines SLOSH in his rotten abdomen.

                        MAJOR K
        Come on, Mr. Liver, talk to me.

Major K moves his hand inside the zombie and then
finally pulls out the liver and shows it to Cadet:
the liver is a very sickly yellow, but it somehow
looks alive. Cadet cuts around it until it is detached from the body. Major K pulls down his mask.
Cadet shakes his head. Major K nods.

                        MAJOR K
        All right, then. No kissing for me today.

He bites into the liver.

As we unshuffle our mortal coils, each and every one of us will sooner or later reach the point of looking back at our lives to appreciate the few good decisions we might have made, small as they seemed at the time. Indeed, a sperm of future pride was already swimming toward the egg of Joshua's ego, for—as the mailman waddled away shaking his sizable rump to the rhythm of his inner music, as Stagger squirmed in pain on the pavement—Joshua unexpectedly gained a presence of mind and did everything as if he'd been drilled for such a contingency. He cleaned up the mess, hid the sword behind the washing machine, slipped on a (clean) pair of underwear, stuffed Bushy in the New Balance duffel bag, improvised a sling for Stagger's broken arm and took him in a cab to the hospital—all before anyone could get around to calling the police. Stagger didn't want to deal with the law, let alone the order, and neither did Joshua. Without belief, no good thing could ever happen; Joshua did believe there was a way to conceal this morning's shenanigans from Kimmy.

In the ER waiting room, Joshua put the cat-heavy duffel bag on the floor and tucked it under a chair. It felt disrespectful, but Bushy was too dead to incur respect. Last night's residual drunks were sleeping off their alcohol poisoning in impossible postures on seats so uncomfortable they must've been designed to discourage sitting. A rail-thin guy in full Bulls regalia was interrogating the water cooler ("Whaddya want? What da fuck ya want? Whaddya want?"), which refused to cooperate. It was too difficult for Stagger to sit with Joshua's sling, so he stood, cradling his arm against his chest. Still in his green Crocs and Joshua's shorts, he shot threatening glances at the interrogator, his pigtails like ropes over his ears. The damaged areas of his face merged into one enormous bruise centered around his mouth, like makeup gone terribly wrong. Joshua could tell that Stagger wouldn't mind fighting the stick man, who was focused on the cooler releasing defiantly an occasional bubble. He tried to kick the blue water bottle as if it were a head, but the Bulls sweatpants fallen halfway down his ass prevented him from connecting with it.

"What happened to my sword?" Stagger asked. His lips were swollen, as big as slugs, and he was slurring his words.

"Don't worry about it right now," Joshua said. "I put it away."

"You should've let me cut him."

"I'm sorry."

Stagger leaned over a trash bin and released a string of bloody saliva into it.

"I'll need my sword back," Stagger said.

"First get your arm back."

"I'll be fine. I just feel naked without my sword."

"You'll get your sword back. You'd still be naked with it, though."

"You should've been strong, Jonjo. You should've let me cut him."

An elderly, well-dressed couple sat on the edge of their seats, ready to be attended to. The woman's left foot was broken, as evidenced by a baroque hematoma, with which her navy blue blazer perfectly rhymed. The man was calmly reading *The New York Times*, while the woman, holding one of her shoes like a Cinderella, was transfixed with the endless replay of Saddam's statue being pulled down on the silent TV. The way the man and woman occupied their space together conjured up for Joshua their—most probably—Gold Coast living room: the exorbitantly expensive third-rate Cubist paintings on the walls; the exotic thingies on the mantelpiece; the crystal decanters on a silver tray: sherry for the ladies, scotch for the gentlemen. Script Idea #135: *A terminally ill woman goes on a road trip to California with her husband, who suffers from Alzheimer's. They took the trip fifty years before for their honeymoon. She remembers everything, he remembers nothing. Halfway there, she realizes that he thinks she is his mistress. Title:* The End of the Past.

"I used to be married, you know," Stagger said. A security guard with hams for arms and a dildoid baton moved in to caution the Bulls guy, who was not high enough to ignore him, so he promptly sat down and shut up.

"Did you?" Joshua said. The security guard stood over the Bulls guy, his hand on the dildo. Joshua would've enjoyed bearing witness to a beating; more bone breaking would've certainly complied with the spirit of the day. The Saddam loop was interrupted by insanely happy people in bright-colored clothes jumping up and down in slow motion against a blindingly white background. Such unabated joy could be available only to those who deemed themselves indestructible and immortal. No slow-motion jumping for Bernie, or the woman with a broken foot.

"Cindy now vegetates somewhere in Naperville. Married

to her high school sweetheart. Which she was banging through Desert Storm."

"She was in Desert Storm?"

"No, man. I was. Pay attention."

"Right," Joshua said. "I knew that."

A poster on the wall of the triage room pictured the skeleton and muscles of a skinless human being. You could never see deposits of fat on those perfect specimens, let alone goiters. No one had yet provided painkillers for Stagger, so each time he moved, he winced in excruciating pain. Yet he couldn't lie still on the gurney: the currents of his enormous energy ran through his body; his wiry landscape positively vibrated with it. A skinned Stagger would look much like the skeleton-and-muscle boy on the wall.

"So what was your ex-wife like?" Joshua asked. After he let Stagger down in the trenches, he was obliged to show interest in his bizarre life. If Joshua had let him cut Esko, it'd be the Bosnian who'd be here now staring at the edited cadaver on the wall.

"Cindy was a fruitcake. She had nightmares about vampires. Vampires sucking her blood." With his beaten lips he pronounced *fruitcake* as *furcakh*.

"Vampires? Why vampires?"

"Fuck me if I know. She read some book and it messed her up. She wrote to me, almost every day. First page, worried about hubby being blown to bits. Second page, gossip. The rest, vampires."

It was hard to imagine what Cindy would've been like, what kind of person would've married Stagger. It was hard to imagine Stagger in any form or shape other than what he was at this moment, whatever the moment. In that respect he was not unlike a vampire.

A leather-faced male nurse came in with the New Balance duffel bag.

"Is this yours?" he asked.

The nurse wore short-sleeved scrubs, exposing hairy forearms and chest, a stethoscope around his neck like a pet snake. In the olden, John Wayne days, before the democratic joys of painkilling, nurses used to hold the patients down for surgery, pouring whiskey into their throats when not providing hardwood sticks to gnaw on and stave off pain. Joshua took the bag from him and thanked him with a nod. There was no place to put it, other than at the foot of Stagger's gurney. A Zen master was once asked what the most valuable thing in the world was and he said: "A dead cat's head." Because you couldn't put a price on it.

The same nurse had cleaned up Stagger's face not so long ago, but he looked at it again with an expression of concerned expertise. "You okay?" he asked Stagger, who nodded. The nurse nodded too and left. Women never nodded like that. Joshua had never seen Kimiko nod wordlessly. She smiled, she glared, she rolled her eyes and sucked in her lips, she raised her chin and contracted her nostrils, but nod she did not.

"I'm writing a movie script about zombies," Joshua said.

"What's it called?"

"*Zombie Wars.*"

"You gonna make a movie?"

"Highly unlikely at this time," Joshua said. "Or ever."

"You ever made any movies?"

"Do I look like someone who's made movies?"

"Why are you doing it, then?"

"It's what I do. I don't know what else to do."

"If you need any help with the wars part, I'd be happy to help. Or if you need a stuntman."

Joshua picked up a loose stethoscope to listen to his own heart. What would a heartbreak sound like? His heart was working all right, but there was the noise of the stethoscope scraping against his clothes and the hum of his blood. There were living layers to him, the body always the last one to quit.

"Zombies are cool, but if I had to choose my undead, I'd still go for vampires," Stagger said. "For one thing, they can have sex, and a lot of it too. I think that's what Cindy liked."

"There's that," Joshua said. "Sex is one reason not to go all undead."

Stagger groaned and adjusted his position, nearly kicking the duffel bag off the gurney, so Joshua put the stethoscope away and picked the bag up.

"Why aren't they giving you some painkillers?" Joshua said. "We should ask for some."

"This is nothing," Stagger said.

"You have a broken arm. It's quite something."

"It's nothing, believe me. I knew this maggot, the only one who ever stepped on a land mine in the entire Operation Desert Storm. Lost his legs, his hard one too. Wheels himself around these days like a welfare pro. Lemme tell you: that's something."

Desert Swarm, Stagger slurred. Joshua could feel Bushy's rigor mortis in the duffel bag; the weight was distributed differently. He couldn't find a place to put him down.

"Probably no push-ups for a while," Stagger said. "That's the worst thing for me."

A young resident walked in through the triage room curtain. The name tag said Dr. Ehlimana K, as if she'd been named after a homeopathic remedy. She wore a head scarf and looked unhealthy, thoroughly pallid and drained from dealing with other people's injuries and complaints. Could she recognize and diagnose her own illness? The ability to imagine all the worst outcomes, always calculating the probabilities of your own suffering and death—that would be terrifying. To monitor yourself as you die, to understand what is happening. The Lord is the guardian of the innocent; I was brought low and he provided me with oodles of oblivion.

"What does K stand for?" Joshua asked.

"It's a Bosnian last name," she said. "You could never pronounce it."

"Are you Muslim?" Stagger asked.

"I'm a doctor," she said. "That's all that should matter to you."

"I had a Bosnian friend once," Joshua said. "A long time ago."

Dr. Ehlimana K put the X-rays up on the light board and turned it on. Stagger's arm looked demolished, so badly broken that Joshua gasped in shock. You could pulp a body with a crowbar and it would still live. Bega's drunken war joke: a mortar shell hit his unit, fell at the feet of the sergeant and took him apart. Nothing was left of him except the asshole, and now he's a captain.

"Good news. Clean break! No surgery needed, so putting the cast on should be nice and easy," Dr. Ehlimana K said. "How did you do this to yourself?"

"Fell off my bicycle," Stagger said. Dr. Ehlimana K ignored the sarcasm. She kept looking at the pictures, as if recovering some lost beauty from them.

"I bet you were not wearing a helmet," she said.

"Do I look like my brain is not damaged?" Stagger said.

She touched his face to look at the superbruise, then pressed against his cheekbones and temples. He tightened his grin into a grimace of enduring pain.

"Is this from the tricycle fall too? A CT scan might be a good idea."

"You don't wanna know what's inside that head," Joshua said.

"It's nothing," Stagger said.

Dr. Ehlimana K pointed at the duffel bag.

"What's that? Were you planning to stay in the hospital? It might not be necessary."

"It's the most valuable thing in the world," Joshua said.

"It's a dead cat," Stagger said.

Once Joshua took responsibility for Stagger, it became difficult to be rid of him. And it didn't help that Joshua felt that if he hadn't distracted Stagger, the standoff with Esko would've ended up in a stalemate, or, at worst, Esko being cut up. What could've been is what never happened, Nana Elsa used to say. She never wanted to talk about her experience of the Holocaust. What should've happened would've never happened. Only what happened happened. Everything else is drek.

Joshua was tired of lugging the Bushy bag, but he couldn't leave it behind either. His mind refused to engage with the future in which he'd have to confront Kimmy. Right now, he was hungry and cranky. Stagger had finally calmed down only after he'd been given some strong painkillers, but all they'd had to eat while waiting interminably for the CT scan had been bags of animal crackers the nurse provided. After forty-five minutes of convincing the claustrophobic Stagger to lie down and slide into the CT tunnel, his brain looked surprisingly undamaged and sane.

The cabbie's neck was not unlike a tree trunk with hair vines crawling toward the bald crown. The hospital made Stagger wear a gown, lest he be arrested in Joshua's shorts for public indecency. His right arm was in a cast extending to his biceps, bending at his elbow. The cab crawled to a stop along Lake Shore Drive, stuck in the Cubs-game traffic. It was evening already, the lights were on, the city sparkling with despair.

"Jonjo!" Stagger said. "I gotta say something."

"Please, don't," Joshua said. "And stop calling me Jonjo."

"It wasn't your fault."

"What wasn't my fault?"

"That guy busting my balls."

"Was it my fault?"

"No, it wasn't. Even if you should've let me cut him."

In an obscure language the cabbie spoke to someone who could have been anywhere on Earth, or—why not?—another planet. Suddenly, everywhere around him, everyone around him—other than Stagger—was a foreigner. Script Idea #142: *Space aliens undercover as cabbies abduct the fiancée of the main character and he has to find a way to a remote planet to save her. Title:* Love Trek.

"Also," Stagger said. "I've never been married. I was just fucking with you."

"Were you this nuts before Desert Storm?"

"Desert Storm was a holiday in the sand," Stagger said. "But there did use to be a life before it."

"You need help, Stagger."

Stagger shrugged, as if it all had already been tried.

His cast was on top of the duffel bag between them, no doubt crushing Bushy's stiff body. Joshua was bothered by it, but couldn't formulate anything to justify a complaint. Stagger was pitiful in the stinking hospital gown, his fingers swollen and white from the cast.

"Where's my sword?" Stagger suddenly asked, and Joshua groaned with annoyance.

"It is behind the fucking washing machine. Did you want to take it to the hospital and discuss the incident with the police? We'll get you your sword in due time, I promise. Let's just get out of this situation safe and unharmed."

"Washing machine? Why washing machine?"

"Why the hell not? It's where it is and I'll get it when I can. Right now, I'm exhausted. God! Take another pill!"

Stagger opened the pill bottle with his teeth and tipped it back to suck in another dose of painkillers. They sat in heavy-breathing silence as the cab crept up Lake Shore Drive. Joshua watched the waves spurred on by a northwest wind, crashing into the concrete ramparts, foaming in fury. As a kid, he'd liked to see ice cover the lake all the way to the horizon. On insanely cold, sunny days, when flesh fell off the bone and there was no bird in sight, the frozen lake surface would blaze with perfect iciness. Even if it didn't really freeze all the way to Michigan, the lake somehow managed to complete itself, to reach its outermost possibilities and then stop there. When the cold grip was released, the ice would start cracking and floes would be pushed against the shore, forming ice mountain ranges. And then it would all thaw and return to its routine grayness. Any given point is the end point of something. Nothing is ever a beginning.

"I'd like to say something," Stagger said, but Joshua's cell phone rang just then. Joshua checked the phone screen:

Kimiko M. Home. He ignored it, but something inside him—his prostate, maybe—cramped.

"I like the way you smell," Stagger said. "There, I've said it."

"Okay, you've said it," Joshua said. "Could we not talk about it, please?"

"Okay. Not a word. I've shut up."

Kimiko M. Home. Script Idea #144: *A man saves the life of his comrade, which impresses his girlfriend so much that she suggests a threesome.*

"I just want you to know that I'm not a homo," Stagger said.

"I didn't ask, so you don't have to tell," Joshua said. "That's something you'll have to sort out all by yourself."

There was a runner on the bike path along Lake Shore Drive, trudging along with obvious effort as if it were his twenty-sixth mile, throwing his head to one side to pull his body forth. A homeless man stumbled—not unlike a zombie—toward the runner to bum something, but the runner just sped by. Joshua turned to look at the runner's face as they passed him and he could see the pain. *My soul, return to your resting place.*

"Do you think we could find another cat like this?" Stagger said, tapping on the duffel bag with his cast.

"Where? It's not like I can go to a cat shop. He's not a vacuum cleaner. She would know," Joshua said. "And Bushy would know."

Stagger unzipped the bag to look at the stiff Bushy, whose eyes were wide open.

"He was a fine cat," Stagger said.

"He was a slut," Joshua said. "Please zip up the bag. He's looking at me."

"My arm is broken," Stagger said.

Joshua's cell phone rang again and it was, again, "Kimiko M. Home."

"Oh, man!" Joshua said and took the call.

Kimmy waited at the top of the porch stairs, her position and pose promising nothing good. Kimmy in her sharp work clothes: the narrow skirt, the wide-shouldered blazer, her arms akimbo, her hair in a tight ponytail. Joshua had always liked the smoothness of her jawline, but now it looked like she was concealing razors under her skin. He stood at the foot of the stairs, the duffel bag in hand, unsure whether to dare going up as if everything were as usual. At the center of him, where his modest guts used to be, there was now a vacant, overheated chamber.

"And who's your wounded friend?" she asked. A step behind Joshua, like a bodyguard, Stagger attempted to stretch his tumescent lips into a grin.

"That's Stagger," Joshua said. "My landlord."

Kimmy stared at Stagger the helpless martyr: damaged face, broken arm, bare feet, snotgreen gown, ridiculous pigtails. She had a lot of questions, but she didn't ask any of them.

"I've heard so much about you, Mr. Stagger," she said.

"Pleasure to meet you, Ms. Home," Stagger responded.

"I can't find Bushy," Kimmy announced. This was the moment to come clean and face the consequences, not least because Kimmy glanced at the New Balance bag. Rather than come clean and face the consequences, however, Joshua stepped up to the first stair without going farther. He was close enough to smell her: her lavender-scented perfume could not conceal a wet-cloth smell of anxiety and frustration, as when she was menstruating.

"He must have run after a squirrel or something," Stagger said.

"Please stay out of this, Mr. Stagger," Kimmy said. "This is between my partner and me."

Partner, as if they were a law firm. Joshua moved up a couple more stairs and reached Kimmy's eye level. He foolishly considered kissing her cheek.

"Howdy, pardner," she said, the ice in her voice stretching all the way to her own private Michigan. Her eyes were dark and—as they'd say in a novel—foreboding. "Your friends have stopped by to see you."

INT. UNDERGROUND LAB — DAY

A desk lamp casts a narrow circle of light on the
desk, where there is a syringe and a notebook. Major
K is hunched at the desk, his head in his hands. He
sits up, punches himself in the face.

                    MAJOR K
          Do it, goddamn it! Be a man! You gotta do it!

Finally, he grabs the syringe and stares at it. He
cleans with a wipe a spot on his forearm and plunges
the needle into it, emptying the syringe. He pulls
it out, carefully dismantles it, and disposes of
it. He sits back and closes his eyes. His jaw is
clenched to the point of breaking.

MOMENTS LATER

Major K opens his eyes, takes a pen, and opens his
notebook. He writes the date at the top of the
page.

INSERT

Major K's handwriting.

> MAJOR K
> (v.o.)
> Muscular tension. Irregular breathing.
> Despair. Suicidal thoughts.

Joshua stepped into Kimmy's living room as into a fur-
nished nightmare. Everything was overwhelmingly familiar
yet disturbingly misarranged—the flowers in the vase appeared positively aggressive, the books on the coffee table
growled at him—not least because Ana and her daughter
were seated on Kimmy's sofa. Her face ashen and devoid of
dimples, Ana kneaded her hands, wearing the white shirt
with leg-of-mutton sleeves, minus the chocolate smudges. Her
daughter (what was her name?) stood up to offer her hand
to Joshua, as if welcoming him to a scheduled appointment.

"We have met once before, but you might not remember
me," she said. "My name is Alma."

Joshua shook her hand—firm and confident—but he
couldn't muster any words. *You kids have fun*, she'd said to
him at Ana's place before prancing off. Stagger extended his
encased hand and they exchanged warm, nearly conspiratorial smiles. Perhaps they knew each other. Nothing was beyond Stagger, or this day, or this nightmare. The Lord is a
great plotter, the clever tormentor of the innocent. Ana didn't
look up or say anything to Joshua, who was grateful for her
restraint.

"Perhaps you'd care to tell Teacher Josh what brings you
here," Kimmy said. Ana rose and took a deep breath, Alma

looking up at her, eager to hear her next line. Joshua set the New Balance bag on the table with a flower vase, as if preparing to be slapped around. Ana's eyes were a different, darker shade of green in the diffuse light of Kimmy's living room. Perhaps if they all remained silent for as long as possible, they'd slip out of this moment into the next one, and then the next one, until all the preceding moments were erased from memory and everything could start all over again. The ultimate American dream: the eternal present, where nothing has ever happened before what is happening now.

"This is what I've learned, Teacher Josh, while we were waiting for you to enrich us with your presence," Kimmy said. "Her husband threw them out of their house. He said he no longer cared. He's done with being a stepfather and a spouse."

Alma nodded, confirming the general outline of the unfolding catastrophe.

"A most complicated family situation, this. A plot worthy of a fat Russian novel," Kimmy went on. "The trouble is I can't stand Russian novels."

"They're not Russian," Joshua offered. "They're Bosnian."

"Whatever. They're strangers," Kimmy said. "In my living room. In my home."

A centrifuge of terror spun in his stomach. He couldn't have imagined that the fear booth could offer services like this. Neither the vase nor the flowers moved, nor were the coffee-table books in any way affected by what was transpiring. Joshua's mind was burning to reach a perfect state of blankness—he could be approaching satori, if it weren't for the mean little man in the crawl space, making notes, gloating: one day, when we're all dead and gone, this will be a page in a script.

He didn't like it that Kimmy's arms were crossed at her chest. It rendered her determined to inflict the most brutal punishment in abeyance of any forgiveness. Meanwhile, Stagger drifted toward the bookshelf and bent his neck to browse through the book spines. Joshua could learn a lot about the art of psychotic detachment from Stagger, who was rubbing his forehead presently, as if to stimulate a dormant thought. Kimmy was too self-possessed to be forgiving; ever confident she could tell right from wrong, she hated the wrong. Joshua really needed to sit down. Perhaps he could escape and join the marines, go to Iraq, lose his mind honorably. Become like Stagger, a man inoculated against suffering and sanity. Where was the samurai sword? In the laundry room, yes, he left it there. It might come in handy for a future hara-kiri.

"What do you think you should do here, Jo?" Kimmy asked. "'Coz I'm plain flummoxed."

Everyone waited for him to say something. Everyone could see he was clean out of explanations or ideas. Whereas Kimmy was flummoxed. He did think that *flummoxed* was an odd word to use in this particular context.

"Why don't we all just sit down and talk it over," Joshua said. "I'll try to explain."

"Esko also said that we were now free to go and live with Teacher Josh," Alma said. Somehow, she seemed blithely untroubled by all this. How early can you learn to stay out of your own life? To watch it as if it were taking place on the screen? Ana barked something in Bosnian at Alma but she ignored her with ease. Stagger grinned at some sinister book on the psychology-of-sex shelf. *Flummoxed.* What the fuck? Joshua clawed at his head, aware that his paralysis combined with his anxious gestures indicted him. When I find myself bound by death's ties, I call upon the Lord to make me completely catatonic. Coppola had once faked an epileptic seizure in a meeting with rapacious film executives. Joshua's mouth, however, was much too dry for foaming. Ana leapt up from the sofa toward Alma, as if to slap her, but the girl stepped back, disobediently and dexterously, to continue her testimony.

"He said that Teacher Josh can now feed and fuck us," Alma said. "I beg your pardon: feed us and fuck *her*."

"Please, stop!" Ana said.

"I'm just saying what your husband said."

There was still a way to explain this into some acceptable shape: pathologically jealous husband plus excessively devout teacher equals terrible, *terrible* misunderstanding. Kimmy panned from Ana to him and back—like guilty children, the two of them conspicuously avoided eye contact. Why was it so difficult to dissemble? The one thing that parents need to give their children to increase their survival chances in this punishing world is the skill to lie blatantly and unflinchingly. Bernie was good at lying, like many a man of his age and generation; yet he failed to teach Joshua how to look a woman in the eye and deceive.

"I see," Kimmy said. "Teacher Josh. Yes."

"All I'm saying is I'm just saying," Alma said. She sat down, evidently relieved to have contributed to the comprehensive unmasking. Teenagers should be rounded up and forcibly trained in lying; it should be part of the high school curriculum. We must learn to be concerned with the meaning of utterances, not with their truth. Script Idea #151: *Subterfuge Summer Camp, where everyone's a liar, except for one boy, who keeps getting punished for his suicidal honesty, providing a lesson for the rest. Title:* The Lies of Others.

Ana sat down on the sofa to fully dedicate herself to weeping. Joshua had never heard her crying; he'd never even imagined her crying—she was suddenly someone else, someone whose throat was convulsing as she emitted high-pitched yelps that couldn't be construed as anything other than hurt. Even Stagger looked up from the book he was flipping through—*Female Perversions* it was, too fittingly.

"Is there something you would like to say to me, Jo?" Kimmy asked. There was a time when Joshua's mother had often delivered the very same line, expecting little Josh to grovel apologetically. One day he'd had nothing to say, and he'd said it and it was poetry.

"That was not me," Joshua said.

"What's that?"

"That wasn't me."

"Try again."

"Her husband was in the war in Bosnia," Joshua tried again.

"Let's first agree on some facts: you had sex with his wife, who is also your student. Yes?"

"He was in Special Police."

"Did you or did you not?"

The ice in her voice started cracking. Joshua wanted to grab her hands and bathe them in kisses, but he knew it wouldn't have been a prudent move. He said:

"I was trying to help."

"Did you or did you not?"

"He did," Alma said, and Ana, tears streaming down her cheeks, swung from the sofa to backhand Alma's biceps. There was going to be a bruise there.

"He's an extremely dangerous man," Joshua said.

"Well, shall we call the police, then?" Kimmy said.

"No police!" Ana yelped.

"The police would deport us," Alma said, holding her biceps. She had an Abercrombie and Fitch shirt, her hair gelled into a cool misshape. You could tell high school boys followed her around like lemmings.

"No worries. I'm not going to be the one to call the police," Kimmy said. "You are now Teacher Josh's responsibility. He can now feed and fuck whoever he wants. Except for me. I'm out."

Uninterested in the drama, what with all the pain murdered inside him, Stagger kept operating on the fringes: now he was reading postcards and notes on the fridge, including the smiley-sun Post-it Kimmy had left for Joshua. Stagger struggled to open the fridge with the hand in the cast, eschewing for some reason doing it with his left one.

"Actually, you know what? You, Teacher Josh, are out," Kimmy said. "Yes. Get out."

It was utterly amazing to Joshua that he was still standing and speaking, while his true and only self curled up on the filthy floor of his being to writhe like a fetus in a frying pan. The little man at the desk noted that down as well. Also, the beckoning hook above the table.

"Out!" Kimmy said.

Stagger finally succeeded in opening the fridge and clasping a bottle of beer. He was as indifferent as the vase and the flowers and the Lord.

"Do you have a bottle opener somewhere?" Stagger shouted from the kitchen.

Were this taking place in a movie, here would be a nice cut: all of them winced simultaneously as Kimiko ferociously slammed the door behind them. "This is crazy," Stagger said, the beer bottle between his hands. He attempted to bite off the cap, but Alma took it from him and opened it with a cigarette lighter she magically pulled out of her pocket. Stagger high-fived her, impressed. They bonded in disengagement, in their absence from the moment.

"I'm sorry," Ana said. There were many questions Joshua could have thought of asking her: Why in the world did you come to Kimiko's? Did you not understand that consensual sex is a completed transaction? Why didn't you mind your own business, stay away from mine? In this country everyone is constitutionally required to mind their own goddamn business. The way we do business here is mind our own. Otherwise, the social contract is as good as toilet paper.

"It's okay," he said, disingenuously.

CUT TO: A fortress-sized SUV rolling into the frame.

It parked right in front of the house and Rachel and Janet emerged from it. Mom stopped in her tracks to stare at her son, unable to parse the foreign presences around him. Janet opened the trunk to get out a large pie, but before she closed it, she noticed Joshua and the incongruous others: half-naked Stagger with one hand in a cast and a beer in the other; a woman with smeared mascara; an Abercrombie-and-Fitched teenager.

"Rhubarb," Janet proclaimed, pie in hand.

All stood motionless, contemplating the rhubarb pie. When I find myself flummoxed and bound by death's ties, and the agonies of the abyss something something, when I am wound up in misery and grief, please, Lord, let my ass slip free without serious repercussions.

"Are we not supposed to have dinner tonight with Kimiko

and you?" Janet asked. "Did you not invite us? It was to-night, right, Rachel?"

"Tonight," Mom confirmed.

"Fuck me," Joshua said.

"Joshua!" Mom said.

"Where is your duffel bag?" Stagger asked.

"Please explain," Janet said.

Joshua trawled his mind for something to say, something that would allow him to avoid explaining, but nothing came up.

"Now is not a good time," he said.

"Now is the only time," Janet insisted.

"You left your duffel bag back there, Jonjo," Stagger said.

"We should probably get out of here," Joshua suggested.

"What duffel bag?" Janet asked. "Who are these people? Why don't I know what's going on? I don't like this one bit."

They all packed into the car but went nowhere, sitting in silence until the windows fogged up. Janet started the car and the heat, and turned to face Joshua and Ana in the backseat. *The Abasement of Joshua Levin*, by Yahweh Asshole.

"Okay, Jackie," Janet said. Mom was facing him too. "What's up?"

"Jan . . ." Joshua whimpered. Why was it so hard to speak? Stagger was in the far backseat with Alma, who was eating the pie with her fingers, feeding some to him. She must be high, Joshua reckoned. That must be the bond.

"Don't Jan me! Talk!"

And he talked, necessarily omitting certain salacious de-tails. But he let the story come out of him as it was, relating in spurts and *umm*s its confusion and twists and the absence of a comprehensible narrative arc. He did own up to the fact that Ana's husband—as well as Kimmy—was justified in being severely pissed. "Acts were committed," he admitted. "Feelings were hurt." His honesty made him want to vomit. If he lived through this, he would never stop lying. He rolled the window down, then rolled it up. Rolled it down, rolled it up. Down, up. Seven times up, eight times down.

"You haven't been my little brother since you were my little brother, Jackie, but it seems to me you're fucking it up big time here," Janet said.

"Janet! Language!" Mom said. She used to have a swear jar: Janet and Joshua had had to put in a quarter each time they'd uttered a curse word. They'd never found out how she spent it. The heyday of Janet's teenagehood would've paid for a vacation in France.

"Shut the fuck up, Rachel!"

Mom rolled her eyes at the language. It was her default gesture of helplessness—she rolled her eyes through her marriage and divorce; she'd probably roll them at the Messiah.

"Listen, Janet—" Joshua interjected.

"No, you listen, Joshua. I know what I said about Ms. Mitsubishi—"

"Matsushita," Joshua said.

"Okay, Matsushita. The point is: she's good for you. She's a serious person."

It had never been clear to Joshua why Janet disliked Kimmy. He used to think they'd get along splendidly, being professional successful women and all, but something had gone very wrong at some point, which point Joshua had entirely missed.

"This is a great pie, ma'am," Stagger said from the back.

"Thank you," Janet said, not bothering to look at him. Ana was looking out at Magnolia: the barely budding brown trees, the somber tendrils of April grass, Kimmy's orderly porch. Stagger and Alma kept eating the pie, as if it were a wedding cake.

"It is not his fault—" Ana said.

"Please stay out of this," Janet said.

"We had passion," Ana said.

"Passion?" Janet scoffed. "Passion is a fragrance brand."

"What's done cannot be undone," Joshua said.

"Yes it can!" Janet shouted. "It can be undone. Everything can be undone. Go back in there and fall on your knees and undo it. Tell her that this woman"—she pointed at Ana—"drugged you and raped you. Tell her it wasn't you who did it. Tell her you'll never do it again. Show some leadership. Un-fucking-do it!"

"The cat is dead," Stagger said, his mouth full of rhubarb pie.

"Excuse me?" Janet said.

"The cat is dead," Stagger repeated, having swallowed.

"What cat?"

"Kimiko's cat. It's in the duffel bag. Which is in the house," Stagger said. "I reckon the cat is a huge problem for Jonjo. In this particular situation."

"The cat?" Janet turned to look out the windshield at a winter-exhausted squirrel that froze halfway up a tree.

"Curiosity didn't kill the cat. It was Ana's crazy husband," Stagger said, and Alma giggled. She was a little patient, Joshua thought, growing up to be a very big one.

The squirrel spiraled speedily around the tree trunk, first down, then up, as if remembering something important—it must have been the absence of the cat, the gratuitous freedom. Janet started slamming the steering wheel with the palms of her hands. Many years ago, during an apocalyptic teenage tantrum, she'd smacked Joshua's aquarium with a soup ladle, then proceeded to crush with her foot the tropical little fish flapping on the floor.

"What is it with you people!?" she hollered. "Why is every single man in my life a fucking idiot? Why can't you just quietly go about ruining your life without getting me involved? I don't want to deal with your dead goddamn cat in the middle of my fucking separation!"

She pounded at the steering wheel with terrifying fury, the SUV shaking. When she stopped, the soundless aftermath was even more terrifying.

"Okay," Janet whispered. "Everybody out."

Alma opened the door and stepped out instantly, as if she'd been waiting for the command all along. Stagger had a hard time getting out, what with his broken arm, but Alma helped him. Joshua stored away the weirdness of their quickie friendship for a future better understanding.

"Thank you for the pie, ma'am!" Stagger said.

"You're welcome," Janet said. "Should've poisoned it."

The backseat was covered with pie debris. Joshua was reluctant to leave the car, because he didn't want to be outside, exposed. At some point in human history, someone somewhere thought of making rhubarb pie. How does humanity arrive at such decisions? If there is no God, who made the first rhubarb pie? Mom nodded understandingly, approving of Janet's instructions. Back in their adolescence, Janet and Joshua had conducted long debates trying to determine which one of them had been better loved and understood by their mother. In the end, they split the difference: Joshua had been better loved and Janet better understood.

"Out. All of you. Get out," Janet repeated.

"Janet!" Mom pleaded. Ana opened the door and stepped out.

"Enjoy rest of your day," Ana said, unsarcastically. She was hard to hurt, Joshua realized, because she must've been hurt hard. It was then that he recognized that what happened between them couldn't just be about sex. She was right: the transaction had not been completed. There was more.

"You too, Rachel! Get the hell out," Janet barked.

Joshua still could not move, but Ana held on to the door handle, keeping it open for him, and he followed her out.

"Out, Rachel!"

Mom got out, grunting. Stagger offered his broken hand to help her descend from the SUV's high step. The moment she landed back on earth, Mom turned to Joshua and gave him a scolding look—many years ago, that look would've meant no movies for the rest of the school year. Janet shifted into gear and drove away.

"Janet did it again," Joshua said.

"Oh no, Joshua Levin, you did it again," Mom said. "And it's the best one so far."

"Fuck off, Mom," Joshua said.

She was just about to roll her eyes when Kimmy's screams arrived from the house to bang on everyone's eardrums. She must have discovered the most valuable thing in the world.

INT. BASEMENT LAB — NIGHT

Woman, wearing latex gloves, prepares a syringe.
She sucks something out of a petri dish with it. She
pushes the air out of the syringe, taps on it.
She turns around to face a cage, with Boy in it,
obviously zombified, MOANING with hunger. Major
Klopstock sleeps in the other cage, but its door
is open. Woman approaches Boy's cage. When he
reaches for her between the bars, she grabs his
hand at the wrist to avoid his long nails and
plunges the needle into his forearm. Boy HOWLS as
she empties the syringe, thrashing around in hor-
rible pain. Then he stops. Woman watches him. The
undead Boy looks pretty dead, his overgrown hair
spread around his head like a halo. Woman closes
her eyes in defeat and takes off her latex gloves.
She looks over to Major K's cage. His sleep is so
deep it looks like he might never wake up.

Joshua was in the dark at the bottom of the stairs; up at the top there was light. He needed to climb toward it, but Bushy dug his claws in his calf, clinging to it as he stepped on the next stair. Joshua smacked him to shake him off, but Bushy kept clawing up his leg, progressing toward his eyes with the intention of scratching them out. If Joshua could reach the light, Bushy would be burned by it like a louse with a cigarette, and Joshua would be safe. But he also didn't want to kill Bushy. The only thing he could do, scared and angry, was ascend in the hope that the situation would resolve itself. Before it did, he woke up.

His first fully conscious thought was of Kimmy, and the plain truth presented itself to him: he hurt her, callously. She put her love and trust in him, and he wagged his dick at it all, betraying her. From here on in, whenever she thought or spoke of him she'd have a gut-tearing feeling in her stomach; like a memory of food poisoning, he'd be to her. Where there had been love, now there would be hatred, and hideous stomach cramps. She would have no compunction telling all of their friends—her friends, really—about the sordid magnitude of Joshua's assholeness. For as long as she lived, there would be at least one person in the world—and likely many more—considering Joshua lesser than a salmonella bug. It was a problem: the *goyter* of her judgment would forever bulge out of his neck, forcing his head to bow.

Then he thought of Bernie and his evil cells; but then, he couldn't think about that right now. There was nothing he could do now; not even call Janet. Bernie was a big boy, able to fend for himself until Joshua recovered.

He heard the bedroom door opening; the toes on the floor, the pee twinkle in the toilet. He could tell it was Ana: the self-effacing care not to wake him up; the discomfort in her step; the grace. She was hurt too. With how many layers of hurt has the Lord encrusted us?

In one of Joshua's half-ass scripts a scientist, Dr. Oldenburg, discovered gateways between many parallel universes, where the same events took place, only with slight delays. Dr. Oldenburg figured out how to transport himself between the universes, effectively traveling in time, which came in handy when he had to prevent the death of the woman he loved. But then he discovered that the number of universes was infinite, as was the number of differences among them. Dr. Oldenburg was a superhero in one universe and helpless in another—to save his beloved he had to find the right universe. *The Right Life*, the script was called. It didn't work because all of the worlds were tediously confusing, the differences among them obsessively minimal and thus boring. Also, he never got anywhere near finishing it. But now, who knows?

He pretended to be sleeping as she was making her way back to the bedroom.

He heard her stop and he knew she was looking at him, perhaps hoping he'd be awake. What did she see? A salmonella man in his thirties, sleeping on a sofa in a T-shirt and underwear. There was at least one way to measure the quality of a life: if you slept on a sofa in your own apartment at the age of thirty-three, things were not going well. She stood there (where, exactly?) for a while and Joshua made himself stay so still that he endured a beastly itch spreading all over his scalp down to his spine, or whatever was left of it. Just as he gave in and decided to scratch his dandruff off to the point of bleeding, she slipped back into the bedroom. He'd once seen a hair-care commercial in which one of the ecstatic shampoo users was identified as a dandruff survivor.

An hour later he attempted to open the bathroom door but it was locked. He tried again, baffled by the resistance. For a moment, it seemed he was inside one of his dream traps, but then he heard gasps and yelps and thought it was Ana crying. He removed his hand from the knob, because he didn't want to deal with her tears. Ana, however, came out of the bedroom wearing his blue button-up linen shirt. Where did she find it? It was a summer shirt, displaced deep in the back of his closet.

"I was cold," Ana said, holding her elbow like John Wayne.

"It's okay," Joshua said. Her short hair was all messed up and stood up in spikes. For the first time he noticed its stubborn thickness, rhyming with the fat dark lines of her eyebrows. "I think your daughter is in the bathroom."

"She will have been there whole day," Ana said.

Joshua knocked on the door, just to make sure Alma knew they were outside, that her mother could now hear her crying. How exactly have I ended up here, he thought, outside a bathroom of tears? Alma came out, wearing only a skimpy top and panties, her puppy breasts protruding. He could smell her: she reeked of morning adolescence, of glands and hormones, of nascent adult loneliness. She skipped by him, flashing a smile that he would have thought effortless had he not heard her sobs. Maybe she wasn't crying but moaning with pleasure. He discarded the thought as obscene and double-locked the door behind him.

He peed facing the foxhunt painting. There was a bird perched in the crown of one of the trees, watching with indifference the fox's struggle. Joshua had never seen the bird before, even if scanning the picture had been part of his pissing ritual since he'd been in this apartment. What kind of bird was it anyway? A nightingale? He had no idea what nightingales looked like. Because they live at night, obviously—no one ever sees birds at night. The bird was brownish and hard to see, small and separate from the busyness of the hunt. Why would the painter hide a nightingale in the painting? There were worlds of living creatures Joshua would never see, still trusting blindly that they actually existed. He heard Ana and Alma argue in Bosnian outside. Maybe it wasn't a nightingale. Maybe it was a buzzard waiting for the fox to go down. He had seen a buzzard, in Arizona, once: an ugly, filthy, bald bird. Maybe this was a British buzzard: restrained, classy, bland, like the queen or the dead what's-her-name's prince husband. Script Idea #163: *The princess leaves Whatever Palace for some night fun—say, to meet her youngish lover—but then she finds him dead. Muslim terrorists tortured him to get the info that would allow them to get to her. Now they're after her. Meanwhile, a ruthless tabloid reporter follows the scent of the royal rat. The princess's only help: a handsome London cabbie, whose name is Will. Title:* Will of the People.

Joshua shook off his willy and studied his face in the mirror. There was a subcutaneous pimple developing in

the corner where his nostril met his face—highly unsqueez-
able. Yet he bent his nose and pressed his sharpest nail against
the minuscule protuberance. Willy and the princess fall in
temporary love. But once she's back in the palace, there is no
way Willy could replace the jug-eared, dull prince. Miraculously, the pimple popped. Willy now knows far too much—he
has seen her sitting on the toilet, which few mortals ever have.
MI5+2, a supersecret agency, dispatches assassins after him.
His only hope: the princess herself. The sequel title: *Tri-
umph of the Willy*.

Fuck me, Joshua thought. This is all hopeless. I'll die
an amateur, a dandruff survivor.

Ana made Bosnian coffee in a sauce pot. It was thick and
strong; she took it black, while Joshua had to add milk and
a lot of sugar to make it palatable. They drank it by the window, above which the silent chimes hung in a tangle. She
rolled up her sleeves, quietly, looking out at the wasteland of
back alleys and garage roofs. So much of Chicago consisted
of what nobody cared to look at.

"I lose my dreams," Ana eventually said.

"Your dreams?"

"When I wake up I forget my dreams. Lot of things happen then I can't remember," she said. "Like I live then lose
life."

"Me too," Joshua said. "Except I lose them before they
even happen."

He was assembling a sentence to explain his perpetual
struggle with his inconclusive dreams, when Alma came out
of the bedroom, ready for the day. Her hair combed and pony-
tailed, she appeared bright and happy. She kissed Ana on

the forehead, then surprised Joshua by doing the same to him. It was possible that she was humming some song as she left, closing the door softly behind her. Where might she be going so early on a Saturday morning?

"Is she happy?" Joshua asked. "What could she possibly be happy about?"

"She is living," Ana said. "She is happy."

"I'm living and I'm not happy."

"She has future."

"Are you happy?"

"No. But I am not misery."

"Miserable."

"I am not miserable."

Alma ran back in, returning to the bedroom to fetch something. On her way out, she was putting a headband on, scuttling along. The confidence of her movements, the nimbleness of her body, the random smile she shot at them without saying a word. What's wrong with teenagers? Joshua wondered. Indestructible, they come into and out of hell as they see fit. The little patients have so much of themselves and they know more is always coming, so they can afford to keep wasting it. One day, sooner or later, they run out of themselves and enter punitive adulthood. Once you mature, you start spending your limited life, every day one fewer to live.

"You ever read *Anna Karenina*?" Ana asked.

"Never finished it," Joshua said. "Too drawn out for me. I could never remember all those names."

"You must read it. It is beautiful. It is about real life."

"Right, real life. I have no interest in that at this time. Real life kind of makes me sick."

"What do you write?"

"In my screenplays?" The plural was both misleading and humiliating. "All kinds of stuff."

"About what?"

"Oh I don't know . . . What I'm writing now is called *Zombie Wars.*"

"What is it about?"

"About zombies. And wars."

He felt embarrassed talking about it. She would know wars. She would know what was really real and legitimate. She would know death.

"It's just, you know, commercial stuff. Except nobody's buying it. Weird stuff."

"It is probably good," she said, and seemed to believe it.

"My father has prostate cancer," Joshua said without thinking. "I don't know what to do."

He regretted saying it as soon as it came out: now a response was required; now empathy was necessary. But he didn't want response or empathy; he wanted Bernie's prostate cancer not to be. He wanted not to think about it. He stirred his coffee, then focused on the beige whirlpool in his cup.

"Most men get prostate cancer. Most live," Ana said. "Best cancer."

"There is no good cancer. All cancer fucks up your body and your mind."

She stroked his cheek.

"Many men survive from prostate cancer."

He was tempted to escape her touch, to show he didn't need anything, but her hand was warm and soft, comforting.

"You know what is good thing about you?" she asked.

"Do please tell me one good thing."

"You are good."

"There's a cultural gap right there. One thing I am not is good. I am selfish salmonella."

"Your face gets red."

"I blush? I don't think so."

"For Tolstoy, people are good and they blush."

Ana grabbed Joshua's hand and pressed his palm against her cheek, as if to make him touch her *blushness*, or, maybe, to show she was not afraid of salmonella contamination. It was warm, her cheek, its texture familiar to him by now.

"You make me blush," she said.

He pulled his hand out of her grasp. The coffee in his mug was still revolving, if slowly, around some imaginary center. There must've been the first person who put milk in coffee. Who was the first person to stir it?

"I find you very attractive, Ana, and sweet," he said, "but this is not the kind of arrangement we could sustain for a long time. It's kind of wrong."

"What does it mean: *sustain*?"

"Maintain. Keep going. Whatever. I'm no longer your teacher."

Ana put her own hand on her cheek, as if to remember what Joshua's touch felt like.

"There is no place where I can go."

"I know. But we cannot live like this."

"We have to live. Like this or like something else."

"Let's think about something else, then."

She sat with her legs crossed, Joshua's shirt barely covering her ass. He could see the soft gossamer shimmering on her thighs; he could perceive the beauty of her body as expressed in that particular detail, as he could perceive her evanescent dimples and the imperfect moles scattered along her neck and the fact that, if her morning-alert nipples were her eyes, she would be slightly cross-eyed. He could perceive that it was those imperfections that somehow made her more authentic, more real within the space he shared with her. From this distance, Kimmy looked like a commercial for a girlfriend, bereft of imperfections—now that he was gone, she was definitely a completed person, every bit of the scaffolding finally removed. Ana applied her lips to the brim of her cup and he watched as the coffee in small sips flowed into her mouth. He wanted to kiss her, but a kiss at that moment would've confirmed an unspoken agreement he was unwilling to sign, promising a future. He took a sip of his coffee, its bitterness completely vanquished by milk and sugar. She moved her tongue behind her lips, as though to spread the taste all over her gums, the dimples dancing all over her cheeks. Was there a Bosnian way of drinking coffee, whereby they rub it into their gums like heroin? How would she drink her wine? She'd probably look even more beautiful.

"Why?" he suddenly asked.

"What: why?"

"Why did we do it? Why did you sleep with me?"

Ana drank more coffee and chortled, looking at Joshua.

"I like you," she said. "I wanted."

"Come on, Ana. You risked—and lost—everything because you like *me*?"

She took another sip of coffee, rubbed it into her gums with her tongue.

"What can I lose that I didn't lose before?" she said. "I lost my youth in the war. I lost my life. I lost my job because I came to America. I lost my husband."

"You have your daughter."

"My daughter," Ana said. "She is super old for her life.

She was three when her real father was killed in the war. She didn't go out for walk until she was six. She couldn't play on street, because snipers like to kill children."

She was mad now, her eyes tearing up.

"Last week she watched on television how somebody killed some dogs with poison gas. It was on television, just like that, and she watched it. She could not sleep. She could not eat."

"Why?"

"Why? Because dogs didn't do nothing to nobody. How can you ask why?"

Her anger was beautiful: her eyes gleamed in the morning light, greener than ever, and she licked her lips between thoughts. Her tongue never stopped moving.

"You think I have something now? I find Esko in the war, and I lose him in the war too. Good man, but he comes from the front and hates me because I don't understand what is happening on the front. He hates me because I am woman. He hates me because I am doctor and I see people die every day in hospital, so I don't cry over him. He doesn't know how to play with Alma, how to talk with her. He is not her father. She sees him crazy every day. He screams and breaks things. He can't wait to go back to the front. He wants to die. Always I have to say: one day, after the war, everything will be good. I tell him, I tell Alma, I tell myself: one day will be good."

She stopped to pour more coffee in Joshua's cup, making it darker. She topped off hers too and took a sip.

"You know when I decide to come to America? One day, I was driving. I see truck coming to me. I don't want to stop. I don't care. Who cares? If truck cares, he will stop. He stop, in the last moment. It was like I wake up. I was very scared. I decide: I must go from here or I die. I don't want to die."

A tear rolled past her lips, and Joshua couldn't bear to watch it reach her chin. He added sugar and milk and stirred his coffee well beyond what was necessary. The dread of life: that there is always far more to people than what the commercials claim. Nobody really lived all that happiness you could see on television, in magazines, everywhere around you. Who was the first person to declare happiness? They should've shot the bastard, right then and there. Or just let him slowly succumb to the evil cells.

"Good day is today. And today they poison dogs who did nothing to nobody. Where is good? Where is me? Me?" Ana implored him. She touched his forearm, and a current went through his body. He'd had no idea that such things could be inside women.

"You ever seen dead person?" Ana asked.

"No," Joshua said, but it was not true, strictly speaking.

"Like day with no light. Like ball with no air. They just empty."

Joshua had cracked his head and, when Bernie had taken him to the ER for stitching, he'd seen the bloated purple feet of a corpse on its way to the morgue, where, perhaps, it would've been deflated. He, and everybody, always imagined zombies as bloated and heavy with rotten flesh. But what if they were empty, like sacs, like camp inmates, the only remnant of life their insatiable hunger? That would allow for some empathy with them, an urge to save them, rather than just blow them up.

"I am not old. I love life. Maybe too hard, but I love it," Ana continued her monologue. "I have soul. I have passion. I don't want to be victim. I am strong."

"Each thing, as far as it can by its own power, strives to persevere in its being," Joshua said.

"What is that mean?" Ana said. "I am not thing."

"That's Spinoza."

"What's Spinoza?"

"Spinoza, the philosopher."

"I don't like philosophy," Ana said. "I don't like talking about nothing."

Her body had a smell that made Joshua want to lick her skin like ice cream. He returned to stirring his coffee.

"You are like that truck," she said. "I don't care."

"Okay, but why would you want me? You deserve better than me, better than a fucking truck. I'm not handsome. I have dandruff. And look at this place"—he pointed in the general direction of everything around them—"this is a garage for failure. There is nothing here you'd want to want. If you risk everything, you should risk it for a better man, flattering as it all is to me."

"I want to take what I want," Ana said and stroked his cheek. "Every man think he must be best. Man think people love you when you attack. But when you attack you don't believe that people like you at all. Because you don't like when other people attack. You lie to make people like you, and when they like you you don't trust them because you lie."

"I don't attack," Joshua said. "I do lie, though, if not very well."

"You think that man is job. In the morning you go to work to be man. You think that job is everything. But it is nothing. It is just job."

"What job? I don't know what you're talking about."

Ana shook her head, forgiving of his thickness.

"You are not strong."

"Thank you!" Joshua said. "Finally! Thank you for your honesty!"

He instantly realized, of course, that he would've preferred if she'd thought him strong. She grabbed both of his hands and held them in hers, as if about to propose. Baruch was wrong about one thing: desire that arises from sadness is much stronger, other things equal, than that which arises from joy. It could be, in fact, that desire arises only from sadness, the daily devastation of constant dying. Ana was much larger than him, or anything he would ever be. On his way through the desert, he was passing through her as through a memory of a verdant forest.

"You are better," Ana said. "You are sad. You blush. You are warm."

"Warm? It's probably stress."

She put his hands on her hips and drew closer to him to press her coffee-flavored lips upon his.

He felt like a guest in his own bed, which made it more comfortable. This time, he wasn't cheating on Kimmy, technically, so Ana's body felt different. For one thing, there was more of it: she was dripping wet and he licked her cross-eyed nipples in concentric circles, until the shape of her breasts led him toward her armpits and then he went down her sides and across to her belly button and she was spreading her legs as his tongue inched down toward her picture-perfect clitoris. Deflated she was not. His cheeks were smeared with her wetness, so much of it that he had to swallow it, and his tongue was burning with it. He thrust his tongue inside her, as she lifted and twisted her hips, and slid it up to her clit and back, and put two fingers inside her, and she came, hitting his back with her heels, reciting something in Bosnian, speaking in rhymes and tongues.

Then he slid up her body and his cock was inside her, and he was kissing her, the same whetted tongue now inside her mouth. Far in the back of whatever was left of his mind, the light of reason was struggling against being finally extinguished and he was aware that wearing a condom would've been a good idea, but there was no way that he was getting out of her, because she took him in and he was with her in every move, in every gasp, kiss, and lick—she let him in so deep he didn't have to think about her, and therefore he didn't have to think about himself, but of course he was thinking about not thinking about himself and he was about to start thinking about himself when she bit his cheek, as if eager to spread the pain, and it hurt and he loved it and he could feel the skin was broken and he started coming and so did she.

EXT. ROAD — DAY

Major Klopstock, Ruth, Cadet, and Boy walk with ex-
haustion and hunger evident in their strides. Here
and there, a burnt vehicle is in a ditch. A huge
plume of smoke hovers on the horizon. The waddling
shadows of zombies climb up a distant hill toward a
lonely house on its top.

Major K's crew come upon a cistern truck. The
driver's body at the wheel has clearly been devoured
by the ravenous undead, his rib cage wide open and
devoid of organs. Major K rummages around the cabin,
checks the glove compartment, finding nothing use-
ful. He breaks open the box on the truck's underside to discover two jerry cans, both empty. He
thinks quickly, takes out the jerry cans and gives
one to Cadet. First he, then Cadet, climbs the ladder on the cistern toward the hatch at the top, but
Cadet's jerry can CLANGS against the cistern. Everyone freezes: they can clearly hear CLANGING in
response from the inside — they exchange glances.
Major K clangs again: TWO TIMES LONG, TWO TIMES

SHORT. The response: TWO TIMES LONG, TWO TIMES SHORT. Cadet descends, puts the jerry can down and cocks his weapon. Major K pulls out his gun and goes all the way to the hatch.

                    MAJOR K
          Hello! Any humans inside?

He can hear VOICES, but no words. He calls again. Now he distinctly hears words spoken back to him. He reloads the gun.

                    MAJOR K
                  (to his crew)
          Step back!

Ruth takes a few steps back, but Cadet gestures toward her to tell her to get as far from the truck as she can and take Boy with her. They move to stand at a distance. Cadet points his weapon at the hatch. Major K unlocks it cautiously, jumps off the cistern, and runs to stand by Cadet. They watch, their weapons ready.

The hatch opens. One by one, living, filthy people crawl out to be blinded by the sun. It is clear they do not know where they are or what has been happening. The refugees look around, flummoxed. They seem to be a family. PADRE (50) climbs down the ladder.

                    PADRE
          ¿Qué está pasando?

His cheek still hurt; there were still Ana's teeth marks on it. The shameless complicatedness of it all made him feel exhausted yet mature, as if he'd been initiated into a brutally authentic domain—not a commercial for an idiotically happy one—where people were lost but still managed to struggle and live. Now he had a wound to show for entering the real world. Now he was ready to step in front of the truck named Billy Cooperman.

Billy was on the up, even if his name seemed to belong to the realm of chintzy porn. Graham had known him for years and sometimes sent students his way, because Billy seemed to have figured out the ways to sign up good local creative talent before they ended up in California to have their souls crushed by the Morlocks of Hollywood. He placed his bets early, he lost some, he won some, but overall, Graham was convinced, he was bound to be a winner, for one simple reason: he believed in himself like a motherfucker. *Zombie Wars* looked pretty promising, Graham thought, and it was time Joshua should meet the people and learn the skill of being in the room. Of course, he could go crazy and fly out to LA to meet the people (Who were *the people,* actually? Joshua had wondered. What's a *real* room?), but that meant hotels and plane tickets, bling and fancy dinners, all the dazzling shit required for minimum respect, never actually provided. Or he could begin at home, before Billy hit it out of the park. The worst-case scenario: Joshua would learn a thing or two about pitching his stories.

The whole thing, smallish as it was, had a kind of movie-business orchestration about it: Graham connected them; Joshua sent pages from *Zombie Wars*; Billy agreed to meet him. But as soon as a lunch meeting had been scheduled, Joshua became overwhelmed with embarrassment, as if he'd gotten drunk and naked in front of his grandparents (which had indeed happened at least once upon a time). By now it all was as if it had been arranged decades ago, in those happy times before the Bosnian wrecking crew had entered his life and Kimmy escaped, before Ana had laid a claim on him, before Bernie sent him his cancerous text message. The intents and purposes neither of his life nor of *Zombie Wars* were easy to recall, but he was just too fatigued not to go with the flow. And the little man clamored in the crawl space, hungry for notable experiences.

Billy was waiting for Joshua at Sushi Samurai, at least one baby bottle of sake already consumed. He reminded Joshua of someone else, yet someone irretrievable from memory: short and taut, like a ballet dancer, with a pointy nose, small mouth, and playboy pompadour. He wore a slick navy jacket, as if he'd just parked his yacht around the corner, his white shirt unbuttoned to reveal a wedge of hoary chest. He said nothing as he spread his arms for an embrace Joshua walked right into. Billy rubbed his back and squeezed him, as if checking for wires under his clothes. In the limelight of Billy's Botox-survivor grin, Joshua placed his ass in the chair.

"So?" Billy asked, still standing.

"So?"

"So what does your gut tell you?"

"About what?" Joshua asked.

"About me!" Billy's smile was unchanged, his eyebrows curled up a little in what ought to have been surprise. How does one learn to move different parts of one's face independently? Joshua's gut was growling with hunger and regret, telling him he should be having a cheeseburger elsewhere. He considered getting up and leaving, but then he would have to confront Graham and explain everything. You gotta grab an opportunity by the balls, Graham had said. Why would an opportunity have balls? was the unanswerable question. Why not, say, breasts? Or some other kind of opportunistic protuberance? Why not grab an opportunity by the nose? And how would an opportunity react, if it indeed had a body, to having one of its parts grabbed? The human mind does not involve adequate knowledge of the parts composing the human body.

"You gotta go by your gut," Billy said. "Brains is for amateurs."

The waiter, too large and slow to be a professional—casily cast as the laziest sibling in the family, the prodigal son who came back from college as a stoned failure—approached them gingerly, his pen at attention. Billy adjusted his smile to garble something at him.

"Excuse me?" the waiter said.

"It's Japanese," Billy said. "It means: 'My Japanese is bad.'"

"I'm Korean."

"My Japanese is still bad!" Billy laughed, the loyal soldier of the ever-growing army of people who laugh at their own jokes. They laugh because they feel no one else would or should. A symptom of injurious loneliness, the little man noted. One day there might be only solo laughter, the streets ringing with the roars of abysmal solitude. Joshua spread his napkin, tucking a corner into the shallows of his chest, if only to avoid being witness to the embarrassing exchange. The waiter looked toward the bar, as if asking for help. There was no one at the bar; no help was forthcoming.

"Anything to drink?" he asked Joshua.

"What kind of green tea do you have?"

"Green. And greener," the waiter said. He already disliked Joshua, because of his affiliation with Billy.

"Green, then," Joshua said. He was going to buy some expensive green tea in Chinatown and deliver it to Bernie. The waiter abandoned them for the comfort of the empty bar, where he reread the order with a confounded expression on his face. Joshua could tell his escape paths were just as foreclosed.

Billy was an expert on sushi, ate it with his fingers, the way it was done in Japan. He'd spent a summer in Tokyo, where he'd picked up the language. Food in Tokyo was incredibly expensive. An avocado cost a hundred dollars, Billy said, unless it was cubical, which cost even more. The Japanese grew vegetables in boxes to save space. He disliked avocado because it was the only vegetable with fat in it, a lot of it. Fat was his primary enemy. Fat was the devil himself.

Dexterously, he deposited in his mouth one piece of sushi after another, talking all along, rice grains fluttering down to his napkin. You could tell Billy knew and liked himself well; he'd sail with himself to the end of the world and back. Joshua listened without even touching his seaweed salad, thinking without thinking: there was a refugee woman back at home (home?) waiting for him to share her pain; there was a father filling up with evil cells; everything else was, well, kelp. He sipped the green tea occasionally, impatiently. Had Billy even read the *Zombie Wars* pages? Joshua considered for a moment that, first, he'd never sent the pages and, second, that he'd never in fact written them and that everything had taken place solely in his head. Script Idea #168: *A desperate writer runs into a producer at a bar and pitches his movie idea. The producer loves it and wants to start shooting immediately. The writer subsequently discovers he is losing his mind. His career, including the producer, turns out to be entirely imaginary.* Title: Head Shots.

Green tea had a lot of antioxidants, Billy said, and they were good against cancer. He cleaned off his plank of sushi, pulled the napkin off his chest, releasing a flock of rice, and dabbed his mouth. He was now ready to talk business. Momentary confusion compelled Joshua to take the last piece of sushi from his plate. He wondered all of a sudden what Kimmy would think of Billy and his macho projections, of his need to dominate with grins.

"Let's pretend we don't know each other at all," Billy said. "Let's pretend we're at a party. Everybody's drunk out of their minds. There's an orgy with a rotating cast in the spare bedroom. You have exactly five seconds for your pitch. Sell me *Zombie Wars.*"

His mouth loaded with unagi, Joshua slowed down his chewing to think of the way either to avoid this test or, if that proved difficult, to get up and walk away. The waiter would understand. Ana would understand. Even Kimmy would understand. Joshua swallowed.

"*Zombie Wars* is a story of an ordinary man trying to survive in difficult circumstances," he ventured.

"Not bad. Not bad at all. But let me give you some advice. Never, ever use the word *ordinary* when you pitch. Ever.

Another thing: *trying*. Heroes don't try. They either do it or they don't. Mainly they do it. *Survive*: *verboten*! Unless it's a Holocaust story. And *circumstances* has too many syllables, easy to fumble."

"You know what?" Joshua said, standing up, fumbling the napkin. "I don't think this is a good idea."

"Sit down," Billy said.

"I'm sorry. There's been a misunderstanding. I'm not ready for this."

"Sit down! Right now."

Joshua sat down. Billy was glaring at him so intensely it seemed possible to Joshua that he might smack him. Nervously, he took a sip of his green tea.

"I know what you're thinking: you think I don't know shit. Fine! I don't know shit," Billy said. "But let me tell you something: I'm so sick of people like you, Joshua, who think they know what life is and they have no experience of it. None. Zero. Nada. They think they can bullshit me, like I know nothing. What did you expect when you came here? What do you think I do? What do I do? Do you know? Tell me: what do I do?"

Billy maintained his Botox grin waiting for a response, and it was its unchanging aspect that compelled Joshua to say something.

"You're an agent. You represent clients."

"Wrong! That is wrong! Try again."

"I really can't do this."

"I make my people look good so I can sell their goods. I can sell a phone book page as a treatment for *The Return of Titanic*. I get things done. That's what I do. I am an agent because I have agency. I know you don't have an agent, but do you have agency, Joshua?"

As Joshua comprehended the question, Billy signaled to the waiter with a little twirl of his index finger as if demanding a pirouette. Instead, the waiter moved at deliberately slow speed between the vacant tables, pushing the chairs aside.

"No, you don't," Billy said. "Which is why you need an agent."

The waiter arrived, visibly exhausted by his slow-motion slalom. Billy ordered a selection of mochi balls without consulting Joshua, shaking his head as if astonished at the perfection of his choices. This man's energy was so abundant as to be desperate and therefore pathetic.

"You gotta figure out what to do with all that potential you have, because potential can fuck you up big time," Billy said as the waiter retreated. "Yes, zombies could be killed all day long and no sane person would ever root for them. Yes, God made them for boys and video games. Yes, there are loads of redemption, and killer units, and heads exploding, and cultural references up your backside. Yes, the main guy is a doctor. Yes, there should be a lady. And yes, I can get someone real nice for the female lead, Gwyneth or someone like that."

"Gwyneth? Gwyneth Paltrow? You know Gwyneth Paltrow?"

"Are you kidding me? Of course I don't. Fuck Gwyneth Paltrow, she's done for. I was thinking of Gwyneth Szpika. A star in the making. Brilliant in *Improv Hamlet*," Billy said. "This is Chicago. We win big only if we place our bets early."

The waiter spilled water all over the table while topping up Billy's glass and then dropped a bundle of dirty chopsticks, which danced on the floor. Billy and Joshua were the only patrons in the restaurant, perhaps the last ones before it closed its doors for good and released its indentured staff to pursue greener tea pastures. The waiter kicked the chopsticks out of sight, under some other table, into some undetermined future.

"I'll be honest with you, Joshie: I need you like I need a broken broom handle up my ass. I got so many clients I'm gonna have to start offing them. Why? Because nobody believes in my people more than I do. Every artist has to believe in himself. Yes, of course! It's a cliché. But what happens when it feels like all your belief is drained away? When there's nothing left in the tank? This is where I come in: I believe in you! I'm like a Swiss bank of belief. I keep it forever."

He was mopping the water around his glass with a napkin.

"See that waiter? He'll never make it in the world of waiting. Why? Because nobody believes in him. Do you think his boss believes in him? Do you believe in him? I don't."

Joshua looked at the waiter. He was there, so he was believable. To Joshua it seemed that the waiter's biggest problem was plain, mind-crushing low-wage boredom: the pain in the calves, the same demanding assholes, the same Muzak loop, the same orders, over and over again. Meanwhile, elsewhere, everywhere, the world unfurled like a flag. The basic task in everyone's life was pretending it was more than mere survival.

"I know what you're thinking, Josh: Why would George believe in me—in me, in this fledgling novice? Why would George want to waste his resources on a client with another zombie idea when all the film crews in the world could spend the next bazillion years shooting only the optioned zombie scripts? Well, Josh, I'll be honest with you."

Billy deferred being honest for a long moment, his gaze fixated on Joshua, who asked the obvious question: "Who's George?"

"I'm George," Billy said.

"I thought you were Billy."

"George for clients, Billy for friends."

"Why?"

"This business, Josh, is a bitch. Let me worry about all that. There is no I in *team*."

"But there is *am*," Joshua observed.

"What's that?"

"There is *am*. As in I *am*. T-E-*am*. The subject is implied in the verb."

If it hadn't been for the Muzak molasses dripping from the speakers at the bar, they would've been sunk in uncomfortable silence.

"Joshie, I like you," Billy/George said, his face clouding, "but you don't even know that you don't know what you're talking about."

It was clear there was no hope available here. The pitching practice was now over, it was time to return to the dugout. And for the first time, Joshua thought of himself as a man who knew something others didn't: he knew Ana; he knew his father's cancer; he knew the little man in the crawl space. What he knew about all that exactly he didn't know, but he felt the weight of knowledge in his head and muscles; the door opened, and he was stepping in.

"I tell you what: this is obviously not gonna work out," Billy/George said. "But I like you, and Graham is a buddy of mine, so I'll give you some free advice. First, get yourself in the writers' room, work your way up from there. They're shooting shitloads of TV in Chicago now, because we're far more real than LA. Send around some samples, after you clean them up first. There's lot of passive in there, a lot of college-level wrylies. And a lot of expensive set pieces. You amateurs shoot the movie in your head. An extra shot of espresso and galaxies collide. But get your first job, then get another one, and then a worse one, and before you know it, you'll be writing for Michael Bay."

"Who's Michael Bay?"

"Who's Michael Bay!? Did you really just ask me that?"

Billy/George put his hand on his chest to affect surprise. He had an amethyst pinky ring. Joshua should've felt disappointment, but he felt instead like having won a contest: Billy/George was more desperate/deluded than him; Joshua's experience now equipped him to see it clearly. The waiter put the check in front of Billy/George, who pushed it over to Joshua without looking at it.

"He just asked me who Michael Bay was," he said to the waiter, or to himself, or to anyone willing to be appalled at the ignorance.

"Who's Michael Bay?" the waiter asked.

"Who's Michael Bay!?" Billy/George clutched his head in exhibitionist disbelief. "Let's just say he owns an island."

I know what I know, Joshua thought. I can do it, whatever *it* is. He had the weight; he was acquainted with the real people; he had things to say and impart. He was a screenwriter, even if he had nothing to show for it. Fuck Billy and George and the whole lot of them! And more than anyone else, fuck Bega!

There was no way he wasn't going to the workshop tonight.

———

Hence he took up an afternoon residency at the Coffee Shoppe and, fueled by a sequence of galactic-collision-grade cappuccinos, cranked out an entirely new scene, and then another one, and, then, another one. For the first time in a long while, he could perceive the far beacon of a finished script, the end of *Zombie Wars*, beyond which the lights of his better self shyly flickered.

He advanced to Graham's straight from the Coffee Shoppe and landed on the futon not even glancing at Bega, who was the only one already in the living room, reading the newspapers spread on the desk. His ensemble today featured a T-shirt reading *Sarajevo* in the shape of the Coca-Cola logo. He had an orange in his hands, which he, for some reason, kept kissing. The smacking sound annoyed Joshua so much that he kept moving his tongue along his teeth, like a gum-bleeding boxer, which consequently invoked Ana's lips and all that followed. But he managed to get invested in setting up his computer and be conspicuously busy with appearing to be busy.

"I am very sorry about whole thing," Bega said, without looking up from the papers.

"What thing is that?" Joshua snapped.

"Cat."

"Fuck you!"

"What can I tell you? Sorry."

"It was my girlfriend's cat. She loved him. He was her best friend."

Kimmy was no longer his girlfriend, nor would she ever again be one, but the lie gave him no pleasure. Bega kissed the orange once more, then started peeling it with his teeth, spitting the fragments onto the unread page. What was he going to do with the peel? Joshua hoped he'd drop it on the floor for Graham to see and then dress him down for foreign littering.

"How did you explain cat to her? Just curious," Bega said, dropping the peel into a bin at his feet. There was even a box of tissues on the desk, so that he broke the orange up into wedges and lined them up on the paper. "You can tell her he attacked you and you had to kill him."

"Go to hell," Joshua said.

"I'm joking. I'm really sorry about cat."

"And what about Stagger?"

"Who's Stagger?"

"Your killer friend broke Stagger's arm, kicked him in the head. I had to take him to the hospital. He'll never be the same again."

It was hard to imagine Stagger's life being any different than it was—it was somehow unruinable, his insanity its armor. The phone in Joshua's pocket, pressed serendipitously against his testicles, buzzed and vibrated pleasantly, indicating a text message.

"That Stagger. Well, it was fair fight."

"Fair? Please don't talk to me anymore."

"Okay. No talking."

Wedge by wedge, Bega devoured the orange, then dropped the peel in the bin. Motherfucker! Joshua thought.

"Hey, listen to what your friend Rumsfeld said," Bega offered, but Joshua showed no sign he'd heard him. Instead he pulled up the *Zombie Wars* file and it came up to conceal his screen wallpaper: a shot of the newscaster in *Night of the Living Dead* failing to explain the cataclysmic developments. He set out to read through one of his freshly written scenes, scanning for wrylies, wondering where Graham was.

His cheek hurt, feeling swollen. The room smelled of Bega's orange as he read from the papers:

" 'There is among the Iraqi people a respect for the care and the precision that went into that bombing campaign. It was not a long air campaign. It didn't last for weeks. And there was minimal collateral damage—unintended damage.' That is beautiful! Rumsfeld is genius! You should be thankful too, Joshua. Just one fat cat is minimal collateral damage."

Bega's pronouncing words with his Bosnian accent— *bombing* as "bomBing," *damage* as "damach"—made Joshua even more annoyed.

"Fuck you," Joshua said. "You know nothing. Not about the cat, not about me, not about this fucking country."

"What I know is that you had sex with Esko's wife."

"I thought you were my friend. You brought a killer into my home."

"It's Kimmy's home."

"We split the rent. And it's none of your business anyway."

"Nobody was killed. You must have respect for care and precision."

"Go fuck yourself!"

"I thought that I must be there to protect you if Esko goes real crazy. You don't know him. He could've break your neck just like that."

"Could've broken my neck," Joshua said gleefully.

"Broken your neck," Bega said. "You don't want to be alone with Esko, believe you me."

"Thanks for saving my life, then!" Joshua said. His phone buzzed, but he ignored it, immersed in a vision of punching Bega's face in, complete with the sound of his cheekbones cracking. Unleashing a few extra voracious zombies to rip the flesh off his bones could be pretty enjoyable too.

"Are Ana and Alma with Kimmy now?" Bega asked.

"Even if they were, I wouldn't tell you. And they're not at my place either."

"Esko's taking the whole thing hard. Drinking, a lot, talking to himself. He can get ideas, you know."

"Why don't you just leave me alone and take care of your terrorist friend instead?"

"I understand you're angry. I'm there for you."

"I'm here for you."

"What?"

"You say: I'm here for you. Not: I'm there for you."

"I'm here for you," Bega said.

"Well, get the fuck out of here," Joshua said.

Dillon walked in and took the far end of the sofa, inserting his presence between the two of them. "I just saw the craziest thing," he pronounced.

But neither Joshua nor Bega showed any interest in the craziest thing. Graham entered, threw down his papers, and dropped in his chair. All of the splotches on his forehead stood united in one solidly red front.

"If any of you utter the words *weapons of mass destruction*," Graham said, "I am going to projectile vomit directly in your face."

"I just saw the craziest thing," Dillon repeated for Graham's benefit, but he ignored him as well. Joshua's phone vibrated, yet again. There was a time when the phone was not embedded in you, the time when you could be alone with the people you were with. And when there was no one around, you could be by yourself, with yourself. Now your spiderweb was always being tugged.

Alice emerged from the bathroom and smiled angelically at everyone, her hairdo perfectly blown dry. It'd been a while since she'd been at the workshop. She was in her pudgy forties, with a moony face and saucer eyes, which Joshua did not find pretty but, rather, comforting to look at, like a cloud in a perfectly blue sky. Last time he'd seen her, he'd imagined himself curling up in her arms.

"Good evening, gentlemen!" she said.

"I just saw the craziest thing," Dillon tried again, and, mercifully, Alice said: "And what did you see, Dillon?"

"I saw this dog with like wheels instead of his hind legs."

"That's amazing," Alice said and smiled at Dillon, who fidgeted with the pleasure of her attention.

"It was like half dog, half skateboard," he said.

Joshua read from his computer screen, enunciating every word carefully, as if auditioning:

"Ruth opens the cage door and walks in. The boy lies still, facedown. She kneels next to him and rolls him over. His eyes are closed, he looks peaceful, as opposed to the tormented zombie face he wore before. Suddenly, his eyes open."

Alice gasped.

She was in the middle of a spiritual self-liberation journey, working on a script about an Idaho woman who lived in the same shack for forty-seven years, communing with angels every day. "True story," she'd said. "She once even went to heaven and sat at God's throne." Alice could see this scene in her head: the throne of gold; the divine light around it; angels prancing everywhere; and there was Candy, fresh from the shack to rub elbows with the Lord. "That's going to be expensive," Graham had said. "A godless set is considerably cheaper."

"Ruth takes the boy in her arms and strokes his long hair lovingly," Joshua continued. "Feebly, he smiles. Wounds on his face are now slowly bleeding. He raises his hand with some effort and touches the woman's hair. She smiles at him. Boy groans. She sits him up. Boy: 'I'm hungry.'"

Joshua looked up. No one said anything. Graham gestured toward the others to suggest an offering of comments. Bega conspicuously sucked on an unlit cigarette.

"That's pretty good," Bega said. "Better than before."

"I really like that she like risks her life by like going into the cage," Dillon said.

"I think that's beautiful," Alice said.

"But the boy was dead, no?" Graham said.

"Undead, strictly speaking," Joshua said.

"I know, but his brain was dead, right?" Graham said and pressed his forefinger against his mandibular cleavage. He never used any other finger to help his chin climax. "Don't know much about history, or zombie physiology, but humans can't live without the brain. If he was dead, or undead, then his brain was dead. Am I getting this wrong?"

"Zombie brains are infected by a virus that makes them undead," Joshua said.

"It's like it's shut off, like in deep-sleep mode," Dillon said.

"My point is that the boy's brain might well be beyond repair," Graham said. "He can't just wake up and ask for a fucking sandwich."

"Suspension of disbelief," Bega said. "There are no zombies unless you believe they are there."

"It's the power of love," Alice said.

"The power of love?" Graham looked at Joshua, then at Bega, then back at Joshua, like a lawyer before a jury. Saint Pacino gloomily observed the scene. Then Graham exploded in snickers, and Bega joined in and even Dillon chuckled. Alice did not laugh, but she did doodle. I'd fold up in her like a foal, Joshua thought. Graham wiped away his tears of laughter.

"The power of love!" he said. "I'll be damned."

Heroically, Alice ignored the insult and asked Joshua: "What happens next?"

"The boy recovers, but they have to escape because the soldiers find the lab. They all go looking for his father."

"Are they going to find him?" Bega asked.

Joshua didn't even bother to look in his direction.

"They might. They'll have to make it out first," Joshua said.

"Well, let us know what happens," Graham said. "Nearly everything in the world hinges on it."

"I think they should find him," Alice said.

Graham slipped out without asking about the lunch with Billy/George; he must have received a full report and was pissed for wasting his influence. Joshua took his time packing his computer and his notes. Dillon lingered too, pretending he was browsing through Graham's paperbacks, until he abruptly turned to Joshua and said:

"Can I like ask you a question?"

Joshua looked up and Dillon was blushing to his ears, biting his lips compulsively.

"Would you like to have like a drink? Maybe?" he asked,

grinding his teeth in a grin of awkwardness. His trucker hat was at an angle; there was a visible smudge on his thick-rimmed glasses; he was sweating.

"I don't think so," Joshua said. "I don't think we can go on a date or even be friends, Dillon. Because I think you're an idiot."

His phone buzzed and he finally took it out of his pocket to read the goddamn message. Dillon sat back down on the futon, looked up at Joshua, and said:

"You know what, Joshua? You're an asshole."

EXT. WOODS — DAY

Major K, Ruth, Boy, and Cadet leap over rocks and
logs, branches whipping their faces. The refugees
stumble forth in their wake, all pursued by zombies who, extremely skinny and slow as they are,
come from all directions. We can recognize Goiter
among them, as well as Cancer Patient. Boy trips,
slams his head against a rock and goes out. Cadet
stops to help him, as Major K and Ruth hesitate,
then turn around to rush back. The zombies begin
to close in on them, which allows the refugees to
keep running and escape. Cadet looks at Major K,
who understands instantly what needs to be done.
As Cadet takes his rifle off his shoulder, Major K
picks up Boy and runs on, followed by Ruth. Cadet
faces the advancing zombies, picking them off one
at a time with precise shots that blow off their
heads. Many zombies drop, but more keep coming. In
no time they are too close for him to shoot. He
swings at them, smashing a few heads with his
rifle, until the undead snatch it out of his hands.

From a distance, Major K and Ruth watch in shock
and trepidation.

                    RUTH
        I didn't even know his name.

                    MAJOR K
        Angel. Angel Rodriguez.

Major K puts Boy down and takes the rocket launcher
off his back. The ravenous zombies pile on Cadet
Rodriguez, who HOLLERS in terror. Major K loads
his launcher with the only grenade he has and
rushes back. The zombies are unperturbed, too busy
tearing into the fidgeting flesh, Goiter the most
voracious of all. Cadet Rodriguez keeps SCREAMING
as Major K comes close enough to be able to aim at
the heap. In the mayhem, for a brief moment, Major
K's and Cadet's eyes meet. Major K launches the
grenade. Cadet Angel Rodriguez and the zombies are
all swallowed by apocalyptic flames.

Bernie was on his back beetle-like, his left leg immobilized, his arm attached to a despondent drip, the rest of him tucked under a blanket like a shameful secret. Something somewhere beeped occasionally, petulantly. The hospital window looked out at roofs strewn with air-conditioning behemoths, at all the unreal estate and other windows, at solid, reflective, downtown nothingness. Bernie's eyes were half-closed; still, he smiled when Noah attempted to break into the red medical-waste box on the wall. A TV set in the upper corner showed Saddam's statue coming down like a lost erection. This year we are slaves. Next year, may we all be free. And the year after that we'll probably be slaves again.

"Leave it. Noah! Leave it," Janet barked and pressed, impatiently, the call button on the bed remote.

"You're too young to fall in the shower," she said to Bernie. "The minimum age for that is seventy-nine." Then, without even looking at Noah: "Leave it, I said!"

The boy finally abandoned his attempt, only to turn his attention to the bathroom, into which he troublingly disappeared. Bernie's smile remained unchanged, even if he closed his eyes to indicate that he heard her.

"Yes!" the screeching voice of the nurse came through the speaker.

"Could I talk to Dr. Hashmi again?" Janet said. "This is the third time I'm asking. Did he go back to Pakistan or something?"

"He'll be there as soon as he can," the nurse said. "He has many other patients, you know."

"I just need to talk to him about my elderly father. Are his other patients elderly?"

"His other patients need his attention right now," the nurse said. "He'll be there as soon as possible. Thank you!"

Bernie was thoroughly out now, loaded with painkillers to his contented gills. Despite all their philosophical differences, the Levins had always been firmly united in their faith in pain management. The consensus was that pain was no gain, whereas absence of pain was a great gain. There was the sound of the shower coming from the bathroom and Janet hurried to limit the damage, which, this time, was only Noah's Northwestern University sweatshirt becoming soaking wet. Janet ordered her firstborn to sit down in the chair under the TV and not move. He did sit down, still eyeing the red box with a mixture of mischief and malice, plots ever hatching in his head. As his not moving was obviously of a very temporary nature, Janet excavated a Spider-Man comic book from her purse and shoved it into his hands. When could she find time to simply love him, always so busy with getting him under control?

"Dr. Osama says Bernie's hip is bruised but not broken. He will need replacement down the road, though," Janet whispered, as Joshua provided a requisite brotherly squeeze. "Whereas I need a martini drip presently."

She was taller than Joshua, so that she had to bend down to put her head on his shoulder. They were both uncomfortable in that position, but the rules of sibling consolation demanded that they stay attached for a while. An old man, thin as a stick, regressed down the hallway, pushing very slowly the walker on which his half-full colostomy bag hung. His hospital gown was not closed in the back, so his withered, doughy ass was there for all to behold. Noah's face lit up with the joy of bearing indecent witness. Script Idea #185: *A teenager discovers that his girlfriend's beloved grandfather was a guard in a Nazi death camp. The boy's grandparents are survivors, but he's tantalizingly close to achieving deflowerment, so when a Nazi hunter arrives in town in pursuit of Grandpa, he has to distract him long enough to get laid. A riotous Holocaust comedy. Title:* Righteous Lust.

"It will be okay," Joshua said.

"Don't tell me it will be okay," Janet said, pulling away. "I can't even remember what okay looks like."

"It's just a bruise," Joshua said. "He looks good."

"He looks good? This is not a beach pageant. He almost smashed his hip to pieces. And, soon to come to a life near you, dementia and diapers and daily guilt trips to the nursing home."

Bernie was blazingly pale, which allowed his age spots and moles to multiply. He was drooling on the pillow, a wet spot growing under his cheek. Everything in Joshua wanted to call Kimmy to tell her about his father having stepped into his dotage as on a land mine. She'd had to take care of her parents as they slipped out of life, breaking their half-desiccated bones along the way. She was the kind of person who could talk him through all this—in her wise therapist voice, she could tell him what to do, how to do it. But he'd never dare to ask her for advice or succor, or call her again, as a matter of fact. And then he also wanted to watch Ana's lips telling him life was not misery. In a perfect universe, he could talk Kimmy and Ana into a permanent ménage à trois and be forever snug as the meat in the comfort sandwich. This was not a perfect universe, however; it was barely a world.

"We'll figure something out," Joshua said. He knew he should be brave enough to tell Janet about Bernie's prostate, but the doctors were surely going to find the diagnosis in his file and tell her all that needed to be told.

"Jackie, I love you. I'd give you my liver if you needed it," Janet said. "But don't tell me we'll figure something out. You do not figure things out. That's not what you do."

The old man stopped by at the door of Bernie's room and looked in. He was akin to an emaciated buzzard, complete with long fingers and uncut nails. He just stood quietly, observing, smelling death. Bernie's neck was thin, his earlobes meaty and big, his ears enormous. The body laid down on this hospital bed should not belong to the father that Joshua knew. Where did the real Bernie go? He'd actually been born as a Shmuel, but back in his high school days his shtetl name had practically served as a contraceptive device, so he'd introduced himself as Bernie to his first goy girlfriend. In the beginning, and steadily thereafter, our fathers worshipped idols.

"Where I live, it's all figuring out, all day long. It never stops, not for a moment," Janet said. "There's so much more to figure out and I'm so damn tired."

The old man turned to walk away at a mortally slow pace. There was a dried streak of blood on the inside of his thigh. Noah stood up to follow him, but Janet glared at him until he sat back down and returned to the comforts of Spider-Man.

"You know what Noah asked me the other day?" Janet whispered.

" 'Where do tits come from?' "

"Oh, shut up! No! Shut up! Come on! He's sweet. No! He asked: 'Who made the first person?' And then: 'Was the first person a boy or girl?' "

"What did you say?"

"I said it was complicated. And he said: 'I think every person is the first person.' "

"You should be saving money for his therapy," Joshua said. "It's going to be very costly."

"Don't you think that's sweet, though?" Janet said. A tear in the corner of her eye twinkled and then evaporated. "Every person is the first person."

"He can be sweet," Joshua said. He'd never seen Noah being sweet, not since he'd been a cooing baby, and even then describing him as sweet would've been a stretch of imagination.

"Did you talk to Constance?" Janet asked.

"I don't think they're together anymore," Joshua said. Bernie was grinning and drooling in his sleep, rehearsing for a future life in pain-free oblivion.

"When it rains, it pisses," Janet said. "Poor guy."

She pushed her hair behind her ear to lean over and kiss Bernie. The heavy earring stretched the hole in her lobe and it appeared enormous—she had Bernie's ears. She'd been Father's girl; he'd taken her to baseball games, even fishing; he'd interrogated and vetted her boyfriends, none ever worthy of her. When Doug had salsa-ed his way into her life, the brawny ass first, Bernie had thought him unworthy but had failed to share his opinion with Janet, because she'd seemed so happy. Now she couldn't remember what okay looked like, and Bernie was out like a light.

"There's another thing," Janet said. "His prostate is rotten."

Joshua turned to stare at her in disbelief.

"I know," he finally said.

"You know?"

"He told me."

"Why didn't you tell me?"

"He asked me not to tell you. I thought it was the kind of a secret only men can share."

"Right. Men and their secrets. Where would we be without them. Except he asked me, too, not to tell you."

She sat down on the edge of Father's bed.

"He texted me," Joshua said. "Imagine that. He learned how to text. Constance would be proud."

Bernie began to snore, his breathing achingly even and so loud that they couldn't help but recognize—and confirm it with eye contact—that one day, very soon, Shmuel Levin would end that whole breathing business and withdraw finally from the earthly domain of cruise ships and suffering. Every person is the first person; every death is the first death. Janet's face was suddenly, soblessly, wet with tears. The TV now showed a trailer for a Batman movie and Noah looked up: a grown man who liked to dress as a bat stood facing a clown in some kind of a showdown. Spandex defeats death: those bastards manage never to grow up, let alone die; ridiculous costumes stave off mortality. Janet put her face in her hands to sweep away the tears.

"You coming over for Seder?" she asked.

"Do I have to?"

"Yes."

"Okay, I'll come."

She grabbed the remote and turned the TV off, then pressed the call button, then did it again, but there was no response.

"Could you do me a favor?" she said. Whenever Janet demanded a favor, Joshua would normally cringe in trepidation, but there was no way he could deny her at a time like this.

"Name it," Joshua said.

"Doug is coming to pick Noah up. Can you take him down?"

"Take Doug down?" Joshua asked. "Like, off him?"

"Funny," Janet said, without laughing. "Would you really off him for me? That's so sweet. The only thing is that, as far as I'm concerned, he's already dead."

It must be taking enormous energy to do her Janet-did-it-again shtick every day; no wonder she was so worn out.

"Could you take Noah down, then, so I don't have to lay eyes on that dick?" Janet sat down next to Bernie's bed and commenced pressing furiously on the call button. "Please!"

One day Noah would recall his boyhood in full Technicolor, wherein he would be a thinking, reading, sensitive boy whose parents' painful rift turned him into a lifelong little patient, for which he'd be entitled to resent them to his grave. It was a safe bet that he wouldn't be capable of recalling himself as a selfish little scourge who showed no desire to consider others. He would certainly edit out the long ride down in the hospital elevator with his distraught uncle, made all the longer by his pressing twenty-two buttons before said uncle could intervene to stop him.

What was I really like as a kid? Joshua wondered as, floor after floor, the elevator leapt, sped up, stopped. He routinely recalled himself as a pensive boy, who liked to read in quiet corners, who in the movie theater hid under his grandmother's seat sneaking peeks at *Doctor Zhivago*. But he was also a lonely boy whose wrath at his warring parents was expressed randomly: hiding Bernie's wallet behind the wilted ficus; pissing into the paper shredder; dropping Rachel's car keys into the garbage; reading anything but the Torah at temple; sabotaging Seder by using the Goofy voice when it was his turn to read. It had never occurred to him that he'd done all that simply because he'd always just been himself, a congenital asshole perhaps, that he would've done it all even if his parents' marriage hadn't imploded so ignominiously. The American story: we reinvent ourselves in order to punish others for what we believe has been done to our previous version. For his part, Joshua was sure that the scourge of Noah had nothing to do with Doug and Janet, yet the boy's sinister nature would end up buried under the alternating layers of his self-pity and his parents' guilt. Kimmy would know what to say about all that, as she understood the mysterious ways in which little patients ruthlessly turned into themselves.

"Hey, Noah, let me ask you a question!" Joshua said as they stopped on the twelfth floor. "What are you going to be when you grow up?"

Noah looked at him, not so much surprised by the question as by his uncle asking it at all.

"I don't know," Noah said. "What can I be?"

"You could be a firefighter," Joshua offered.

"Firefighter? Who wants to be a firefighter?"

"Many kids. It's a very noble profession. They fight fire.

They save lives. On nine-eleven, they saved hundreds of people."

"Why aren't you a firefighter?"

When Joshua was Noah's age he wanted to be a speedboat racer, piano tuner, nuclear physicist, monkey wrangler. Never a firefighter. South Side Irish became firefighters. Not North Side Jews.

"When I was your age I wanted to be a firefighter. It was my dream. But then my mom and dad got divorced," Joshua said.

A flash of pain on Noah's face caused a surge of shameful pleasure in Joshua's chest.

"Well," Noah said on the seventh floor. "I don't think I want to be a firefighter."

The boy did indeed have some feelings; he hadn't turned into a sociopath quite yet. They lurched between floors on their way down amid the whooshing and screeching of the machinery.

On the third floor, Noah said: "I'm going to be a doctor."

Doug the former hip-flexing competitive dancer; Doug the manager of some shady money-laundering fund that made him spend months at a time in Dubai; Doug the wiry charmer, the casual prick. Doug the Dougster. What did she ever see in him? What was it she didn't wish to see now? There had been a time when Doug had offered to his young brother-in-law sagely advice on the various means of getting laid; another when he'd shared a line of Wall Street–quality coke. There had been a time when Doug would wink at Joshua randomly across the family dinner table, as if to confirm the feasibility of some conspiratorial plan. "It will be okay," Doug's twitching eyelid would signal. "Don't you worry about any of it." But the conspiracy would never pan out, simply because Joshua could never understand what exactly it was supposed to be.

"How's Bernie?" Doug asked. He wore a snazzy suit, his tie rakishly loose, his sunglasses pushed up above his tanned forehead. It was actually him that Billy/George resembled, Joshua abruptly recognized: he could now see the same subcutaneous wiring, the same energetically deceitful sheen on their respective surfaces. Noah was leaning into Doug's hip, hugging his thigh, eager to get away from his passive-aggressive uncle. A little convoy of overweight people in scooter chairs progressed glacially across the vast foyer.

"Not that good," Joshua said, in the vain hope that Doug might feel guilty, which he most obviously didn't.

"Poor guy," Doug said.

"Let's go, Dad," Noah said.

"I want him to get better soon. I like him," Doug said.

"Me too," Joshua said.

"I'm sure the doctors are taking good care of him," Doug said. "This is a top-shelf hospital."

"And how are you doing?" Joshua asked. Noah was watching the scooter convoy advance toward the elevators, his back now turned to Joshua, Doug absentmindedly stroking his head.

"I'm good," Doug said. He was trying to read Joshua, assuming—correctly—that Joshua didn't really care about his well-being.

"Janet is good too," Joshua said.

Doug nodded faintly wistfully, as if remembering her name from way back. "Good," he said. "I'm glad."

"She'll destroy you," Joshua said. "She'll rip you apart."

Doug laughed. He laughed like someone who had just been told good news, stroking his son's blond hair all along.

"I seriously doubt that," he said. "And it's not something you yourself should worry about."

As the scooter convoy reached the elevators, Noah turned to look at Joshua with what could be interpreted only as bitter contempt. How is this nightmare different from any other nightmare?

"Let's get out of here," Noah said to his father. "Let's go see a movie."

Doug pulled out a wad of dollars, peeled off a twenty, and handed it to Noah. "Go get yourself a little bit of whatever you want," he said. Noah considered the twenty then took off toward a TCBY store, where for his money he could get gallons of high-fructose yogurt.

"Okay," Doug said. "Let's talk to each other like men."

How did men talk? Bare-chested? While arm wrestling? Nodding a lot?

"I know this is hard on the family," Doug said. "But it'll pass."

"Of course it'll pass," Joshua said. "The way a tornado passes, leveling entire communities."

"I don't need a lecture," Doug said.

"What do you need, then?" Joshua said.

"I'm off to Iraq," Doug said.

"You joined the army?" Joshua said. Doug had it in him; it had never before occurred to Joshua, but he did have soldierness in him. Perhaps it was the way he stood before Joshua: straight as an arrow, hands on his hips, feet apart, chin pointing out. He could see him barking at his underlings, in desert camos, the sunglasses under the helmet, the hand gun on his thigh, spitting out the sand. He'd love the smell of napalm in the morning.

"Fuck, no! I'm not that crazy," Doug said. "Don Rumsfeld and his people are setting up a team to get the economy running. I used to do stuff for him when he was in Chicago. We'll be handing out money, pretty much. We'll provide the camelfuckers with a starter kit for market capitalism. It's a dream job. They need people like you wouldn't believe it."

There was Doug, winking at him again, as it were, across the divide, including him even if he didn't have to.

"I suppose you'll need buckets of cash for the divorce," Joshua said.

"Yup. There might be reparations aplenty," Doug said. "You should come along with me, make some dough. Then you can write your scripts for fun."

"Does Noah know you're going?"

"I'm about to tell him," Doug said, looking toward TCBY.

The end of the heavy convoy was filing into the elevator that would take them up to some kind of disinfected heaven. Noah was on his way back, digging yogurt out of a tub, licking his lips before and after he deposited a lump in his mouth.

"I'll be coming and going, but looks like I'll be gone a lot. I was going to ask you to watch out for Noah. Jan can be a little, you know, overwhelming. He needs a man in his life."

"Sure," said Joshua, the man.

"It's not like I'm gonna shoot at the towelheads and sleep in a tent. It shouldn't be too hard."

"Don't get too killed."

"Nah!" Doug said. "It should be a cakewalk."

EXT. CORNFIELD — DAY

A vast field. Ruth parts the jungle-like greenness
of corn, while Major Klopstock has Jack firmly
strapped to his back. They move fast. Ruth occasionally checks if Young Woman follows in their
wake. Young Woman drops to her knees, then rises to
go on walking. She glares at Ruth to indicate that
she is determined to make it.

A choir of zombie GROANS AND HOWLS somewhere in
the distance. An overhead shot shows that Major K,
the women, and the boy are in the center of the
cornfield, while stick-thin zombies are all around,
wandering aimlessly. Neither Major K and his group
nor the zombies are aware of a well-armed unit
surrounding all of them. Two concentric circles,
at the center of which is Major K.

What do you do after you see your very own father fallen and helpless, after you find yourself caught up between your sister and her Iraq-bound spouse, after you've been promoted against your secret wishes to the rank of a responsible uncle? What do you do? What do you do instead of going home (home?), where a refugee and her daughter are squatting, taking their time to figure out what to do next? What do you do if there are decisions to be made, penitence and rebuilding to be done after you were carpet-bombed by life? What do you do? You do what you must: you have a drink at a fount of manhood, because that's what you know, because that's where the central fear booth is located.

The Westmoreland was more crowded than usual, which is to say that there were two tables taken, and there was Bega at the bar, reading the newspaper again. Paco was still behind it, apparently unmoved from his posture of TV-watching, except the TV was off. The *goyter* looked a bit bigger, the new head evidently ready to hatch.

Spitefully, in Bega's full and derisive sight, Joshua sat at the far end of the bar. Bega didn't bother talking to him, not even when Paco walked over to take a double-bourbon order from Joshua.

"Hey, Paco," Bega said, "did you know that Homeland

Security tells you what to do in case of terrorism if you call them?"

Paco shook his head for Joshua to see, and it was hard to know whether that meant *No, I didn't know* or *I can't believe that guy's trying to talk to me.*

"Listen." Bega read, " 'The time to prepare is now. The fight against terror begins at home . . . Store heavyweight garbage bags and duct tape to seal windows, doors, and air vents from outside contamination. While there is no way to predict what will happen or what your personal circumstances will be, there are things you can do now.' "

Kontamneyshn is the way Bega pronounced it. Paco returned to deliver Joshua's drink, shaking his head again, a motion no doubt limited by the growth—if it wasn't for his *goyter*, he'd probably be swinging his head around like a mace. This time he seemed to be expressing some kind of disbelief. Bega was looking at both of them to detect their respective reactions, but Joshua avoided eye contact.

" 'We can be afraid or we can be ready,' " Bega finished, chuckling mirthfully.

He stood up and limped along the bar to sit on the stool next to Joshua.

"Be afraid or be ready, Josh!"

"Consider yourself nonexistent," Joshua said.

Bega shrugged, lit a cigarette, and inhaled deeply, leaning on the bar.

"Why is the TV off?" Joshua asked Paco.

"Cubs already lost," Bega said. How did Paco decide when to speak out?

"I can see you're limping," Joshua said. "I hope it's horribly painful."

"War injury," Bega said, letting the smoke out of his

mouth and nose. It floated past Paco, toward the dark TV, like a half thought. "Leg gets dead after I sit for long time. I have to keep moving. Like shark."

Joshua downed his bourbon and coughed as the alcohol burned its way through his gullet to his stomach. He considered getting up to finish his drink at one of the empty tables, but that would've been a statement involving too much drama, attracting too much attention. He wished he had a knife; he'd pin Bega's hand to the bar. And then they would talk through the torture, Joshua slicing off Bega's fingers until he understood what needed to be understood.

"What are you going to do?" Bega asked as Joshua was experiencing a flash of déjà vu.

"About what? What exactly do you want from me, Bega?"

"I don't want nothing from you. I just like to watch how you don't know shit."

"Shit about what?"

"About people. About world. About everything."

"And how do you know all that shit?"

"I watch. I pay attention. I know."

"Should I be scared of you? Is that what you're saying? 'Coz I'm not."

"You should be scared of yourself."

"I'm not scared of anything. I don't give a fuck," Joshua said, and called for another bourbon. *Kontam* fucking *neyshn*. Bega raised his hand with two fingers to indicate he'd have one too.

"I'm not buying you a drink," Joshua said.

"It's okay," Bega said. "I'm buying you."

Paco delivered the bourbons and returned to his spot, picking up Bega's *Sun-Times* along the way, immediately flipping to the sports pages.

"So," Bega said. "A Bosnian, we call him Mujo, hates his wife's cat, wants to get rid of it. He puts cat in the bag. He drives to country, to forest outside his town, lets cat out of the bag, drives back home, cat is sitting on the stairs waiting for him. Tomorrow, his wife goes to work, Mujo does it again: cat in the bag, to country, deeper into forest, lets cat out, back home. Cat is sitting on the stairs waiting for him."

Why would he bring up the cat again? Joshua would fight him, if he had to. He'd headbutt him, and kick at his knees, and then stomp on his fucking face. Paco looked up from the papers to listen to Bega. He never paid any attention to his patrons, but here he was, enamored with Bega.

"Tomorrow, again: cat in the bag, to country, even deeper in forest, cat out. But then Mujo gets lost in forest, can't find way out. So he calls his wife at home. 'How ya doin'?' 'Fine,' she says. 'Is cat at home?' Mujo asks. 'Yes,' she says. He says: 'Can you put him on the phone?'"

Bega slapped the bar with his open hand, exhorting Joshua and Paco to laugh. Joshua suppressed a feeble chuckle to maintain his mask of anger, but Paco chortled exactly once, which, in the gloomy world of the Westmoreland, was the equivalent of roaring laughter. The chortle turned out to be worth two shots on the house.

"I slept with Ana once too," Bega said suddenly. "It was okay."

The confession coincided with the return of the burning sensation from Joshua's stomach to his throat.

"Back in Sarajevo. She was widow before Esko. We were tired." Bega sipped his bourbon, smacking his lips. "We take it as it comes. We swim in catastrophe."

"What is wrong with you people?" Joshua wheezed, his throat still burning but now accompanied by the pain in his lungs. Shed your wrath upon the assholes that do not recognize you, and on the kingdoms that will not proclaim your name! His eyes were now tearing up. He didn't want Bega to think that he was going to cry. The way it should work: every day of your life you wake up knowing a little more. The way it ends up working: the less you know, the less you care, the less you're scared, the better it is.

"*You people?* You think you are special?" Bega said. "You think you are her hero?"

"I don't think anything," Joshua said. "I just can't get back to where I was before."

"Nobody ever can," Bega said. "Welcome to world."

"Does Esko know that you slept with Ana?" Joshua asked.

"What happens in the war, stays in the war," Bega said. "You can never get to where you was before. The war destroys all before."

Joshua called for another round. There was a part of him—mainly abdominal—that wanted to elbow Bega's nose and break it, that would enjoy a river of blood advancing along the filthy bar, coloring the beer puddles, soaking the coasters. But there was another part of him for whom merely lifting the elbow off the bar demanded effort and conviction he no longer possessed. Where did his *konviksheyn* go?

"What are you going to do with Ana?" Bega asked.

"What am *I* going to do? Nothing. What can I do? It's up to her," Joshua said. "She's the battered woman."

"Battered woman? Esko never touched her."

"How do you know?"

"I'm their friend. I live close. I know."

You people, he wanted to say again, but it hit him, with all the force of the bourbon, that he was turning into one of the *you people* too. Everyone at the Westmoreland was a foreigner, Bega the foremost of them; everyone everywhere was foreign and strange, the world equally populated with *you peoples*, here or in Bosnia or in *fukn* Iraq. He was leaving America, Joshua was, the bar stool and Jim Beam the only things tenuously providing *koynekshen*. And once he left, he was going to stay out, never to return. Like John Wayne at the end of *The Searchers*, leaving again, forever heroically outside, holding his elbow, until the door closes in his face.

I'm not going to be afraid. I'm going to be ready, thought Joshua. But ready for what? The night outside was disorderly, with the kind of wind that made him grind his teeth and pinch the skin on his forearms. *I can't even remember what okay looks like.* What would okay actually look like? The only okay Joshua could presently recall was watching *Dawn of the Dead* with Kimmy in his arms. That particular okay was no longer okay and never would be. Ana biting his cheek while coming was almost okay too. He touched his wound as if to confirm that he hadn't been imagining his life up to this point. Magnolia was deserted, not even random car alarms cared to provide evidence of human presence. No nightingales either. Bega had told him tonight he liked his zombies. He'd been well drunk, but he liked the zombies, and Joshua believed him because Bega had been too drunk to lie and Joshua had been too drunk not to believe him.

He stood under his apartment window, watching Ana's shadow moving in and out of the weakly lit frame. He'd never looked from the outside at anyone inside his apartment— when he was not there, nobody was there. How was it that time passed even when you were not there, or when you were asleep? Before all this (what exactly was *all this?*), there had never been anybody in his space to bear witness to the alleged object permanence: it had to have been possible that all the objects inside his place disintegrated when he was not there to look at them, reintegrating into their ineluctable visibility only upon his return, which was why they always seemed so static. And what would happen if one day he didn't return? Nothingness would permanently replace the stasis and reign in the space that once hosted his being. Tonight, Ana's pacing shadow was surely what kept it all together.

The thing with zombies was, Bega had said, the more undead, the fewer living. Moreover, every living person was always a potential zombie. "Bosnians say: we fucked the hedgehog," Bega had said, laughing and slapping the bar like he was insane, beer bottles hopping all over it. Why was that funny? What did it even mean? None of the things he said made much sense.

The warm wind made the branches on the street titter. The buildings, the cars, the city appeared tensely still, as if wound up and ready to spring into a frenzy. Could nightingales survive in Chicago? Are they migrating birds or do they shiver in tree holes all winter long? Darkness was centered around a burning dot on the porch.

"Good evening, sweet prince," Stagger greeted him.

"I'm not in the mood, Stagger," Joshua growled, coming up the stairs. "It hasn't been a good day."

Stagger exhaled an enormous cloud of smoke, infusing the night with the skunky smell of weed. "What's wrong? Tell your landlord," he said.

"Many things are wrong. In fact, almost everything is," Joshua said.

"I happen to got a homemade stress inhibitor right here.

This shit can smooth the wrinkles out of your grandmother's ass," Stagger said, offering him a fat joint. Joshua had already put his hand on the door handle to proceed upstairs, but the little weed light burned before him like a beacon. He took the fattie off the tips of Stagger's fingers and inhaled a veritable storm cloud. The alcohol burn in his chest reactivated, and he started coughing so violently he had to sit down. His landlord rubbed his back, a bit too supportively. Joshua gave him back the weed.

"I dreamed last night I was a Mexican hockey player," Stagger said, sucking in smoke. "I wore the skates and all the padding, but also a sombrero. Man! Why a sombrero? I was beating this dude with my hockey stick, cutting his face open, breaking his teeth. But I had a sombrero. Fuck me!"

Stagger passed back the joint.

"Sombrero's weird," Joshua said, and inhaled without expectoration.

They passed the diminishing joint back and forth for a while, even though a ball of coughing pain was still lodged deep in Joshua's lungs. This child of Israel groans from the toil and cries to God from under the weight of his work. "Joint chiefs of good shit, we are," Stagger announced.

Gradually, the lumps of anxiety in Joshua's mind and body shrank and then began dissipating. He enjoyed the unwinding; he sagged into the wicker chair. The night was strangely warm. Why hadn't he thought of drugs before? Alcohol had certainly helped some, but he should've been smoking or snorting something every day. Drugs were such a pleasantly simple solution and widely available too. There was a good reason why millions of good, decent Americans took drugs every day, legally and illegally, pursuing their happiness stresslessly and successfully. An idea unrolled itself before him like a beach towel: he could get some real shit, or even some real good shit, and share it with Bernie. It would help with every problem, medical and mental. Bernie was drugged up anyway, but with boring shit. Now was the time for Joshua to explore some truly mind-altering shit while bonding at zeppelin-high altitudes with Bernie Levin. And while they were at it: there must be other things too that they could do together, Joshua and his father. Although he couldn't think of any other things right now. Abruptly, scorchingly, it was clear how little time they had left to do anything.

"Fucking sombrero," Stagger said.

Time maybe passes when you're not there, but not when you're *really* not there, because if you're *really* not there, you're dead. Time flows, all right, but it can at any moment just stop. Hence Joshua giggled to himself: life appeared to him exactly like the joint burning inexorably toward his fingertips— once it's smoked it cannot be unsmoked. Stagger extended his arm to place the fattie before Joshua's mouth, so that he only needed to lean forward and suck the smoke, and that was precisely what he did.

"They got no idea what they're dealing with in that fucking desert," Stagger said. "They think we'll fuck them real hard and sooner or later they'll learn to like it. Who wouldn't wanna be fucked by the world's only remaining superdick?"

Joshua had difficulties processing Stagger's claims, so he continued to giggle until tears trickled down his cheeks. He wiped his wet face against his shoulders and inhaled another generous helping of the THC. The Messiah, whenever he decides to stop by, will surely be a supreme drug dealer; the promise of salvation is nothing if not the promise of being eternally high, never coming down. There will be a time of distress such as has not happened from the beginning of nations. But everyone whose name is found written in the book will get a little sack of crack and float like a swallow in the friendly sky. There will be great respect for the care and the precision, so it should all be okay. Giggling made Joshua's cheek hurt.

"If there's pain in every man's heart you gotta shoot them in the head. Bang!" Stagger transformed his hand into a gun, using three fingers for the barrel.

Pain in the heart was right, Joshua thought. In fact, he may even have said it, but there was no way of really knowing, as Stagger failed to react or acknowledge. Every person is the first person, but who will be the last person? Not everyone can be the last person. There'll be a lot of fighting over who gets to be the last person. He felt he was sweating.

"The only thing you can ever rely on are your buddies," Stagger went on. "The jerk-off on the bed above you, from Kansas of all places, like what's-her-name."

Who will be the lucky guy to see everything off? To the last person everything is past. There is no future at the end of the world. How do zombies handle time? He should look it up in the *Zombie Encyclopedia*, under "Time." If the undead could come back, how would they remember anything that happened in their undead pasts? Would they remember chomping on people's intestines? Perhaps that's why they look so spent and exhausted: they can fly to no fucking sky. It wasn't improbable that Stagger had rolled another thick serving of THC and the Lord knew what else, for it appeared considerably fatter when the joint came back to Joshua. It may have been fattened with hashish, because the smell was now different. Although Joshua had never smoked hashish, so he couldn't really know. There was so much more to find out about this life, a fearsome prospect if it wasn't for the fact that life was always almost over. On top of it, he was now hungry like a zombie. And sweating like a human.

"We drank water out of our boots. Man!" Stagger shouted. "Out of our blasted boots! We rolled weed in lettuce. We died standing. We fucked standing. We shat standing."

"What?" Joshua was finally compelled to ask. It wasn't that he wanted to understand—understanding, he understood, wasn't going to happen right now, or anytime soon; in fact, it seemed to be permanently out of his reach. "What are you talking about?" It was that he couldn't afford to be further discombobulated, because discombobulation made him dizzy. Dizzy and voraciously hungry, and giggly, and discombobulated.

"Fucking sombrero," Stagger said.

There were far too many things bombing him presently with care and precision. He needed Stagger to slow down, he was not cool. Stagger was now thrusting the three-finger-barrel gun at Joshua's feet, as if shooting them off.

"Freedom itself was attacked, Jonjo," Stagger said quietly and slowly, so Joshua could comprehend. "We're talking about things that matter."

"What things are we talking about?" Joshua asked, dropping the obese hashish motherfucker on the porch floor. What did matter a lot was the fattie, so he went down on his knees to look under his chair, but only darkness was there and then the light came, everything down there was flashing and moving. He saw a mouse scurrying along the wall, but it was a blue plastic bag with the phone book and coupons. There was a coin, a quarter possibly, shiny. Kimmy, Ana, and Joshua, a happy threesome in a perfect world, the three sides of the same coin. The healthy, happy Body family, living right across the street from the miserable, terminally ill

Thought family. How good would that be? Stagger was barefoot and his toes were misaligned, his feet not symmetrical at all, the whole pedal anatomy completely fucked. He wore Joshua's American flag underwear; the stars on it shone too. Was it summer already? Where was the fattie? And while we're at it, where's everything? The moment you lose sight of it, it vanishes. Where are people when they're not here? Where does time go when it passes? What is the home of death? What is a nightingale? Where is Bernie, where is he going? He needed to find the fat motherfucker.

"Do you even know how huge that Iraq place is? And it keeps growing, like a tapeworm. I'm not kidding." Stagger was back to speaking at the top of his voice, clapping his hands, as if to reduce the mysterious huge place into a patty-cake. "He was the first man I ever cared about. That's God's honest truth."

"Fuck" was all Joshua could say. He still could not find the joint and he decided that giving up and getting up wouldn't be honorable. The Pottery Barn rule: you fuck it up, you're a fucking idiot. Don't fuck it up.

"What's down there?" Stagger asked and, moving his head like a turtle, joined Joshua on his knees to look under the chair, only to roll onto his back with a grunt.

"I can't find the dope," Joshua said. "I lost the fattie. It just disappeared."

"Oh, man!" cried Stagger. "Do you want some of mine?"

Only then did Joshua see that Stagger had in his hand a joint, which in its rewarding overweightness definitely looked familiar. Joshua rolled onto his back as well, took the blessed joint, and inhaled as if his life depended on it, which it did. They were blowing smoke at the undersides of their respective chairs. If someone had been sitting in those chairs, they'd be blowing smoke up their asses. Being alive is nothing if not a bunch of discombobulating possibilities. And sweating.

"What is this?" Joshua asked, exhaling. "This cannot be just pot."

"There's a touch of pot. Some homemade stuff too. Plus some of those head pills, cooked down to very potent chemicals," Stagger said. "Old Desert Storm recipe. It's what got us all through."

The front door opened and they could see a woman's feet: narrow, graceful toes painted in heavenly colors. Mindlessly, Joshua sat up straight and therefore banged his forehead against the chair. There had been a time when the independence of his teenage room was not respected by his mother, who would barge in as his arm was in his crotch. And now he was hungry and his forehead hurt.

"Joshua?" Ana said, softly.

Stagger must not have noticed her, for he kept rambling:

"The sand, man. The fucking sand. Everything you put in your mouth was crunchy. I hate crunchy. I'd rather eat ass than crunchy cereal."

"Alma is not here," Ana said. "Alma is somewhere and I don't know where. I am worry."

Joshua kept stretching his jaw, as if it were out of joint and if he put it back in place everything else would follow, beginning with processing the basic inflow of sensory information. The recollection machinery would soon be working; he could hear the screeching in his head. He couldn't remember where he'd got the pair of underwear Stagger was wearing. Present from Mom? Or an ironic college-era acquisition? Also, Ana's last name. Karenina? I must be dreaming, Bond-James-Bond said.

"Fucking sombrero," Stagger said.

"Give her some time," Joshua said, inhaling adagio and exhaling staccato. "She's probably coming down somewhere. When she comes down, she'll come home."

"It is two in the morning," Ana said. Her level-five English as a Second Language protected her from Joshua's sinister insinuations. Suddenly he remembered the lost fattie and returned to looking for it. It didn't bother him that he was at the same time hiding from Ana and her demands. He didn't want her to know he was high out of his mind. He was going to find the fattie and compose himself under the chair and then reemerge to face Ana in the shape of the man she'd become miraculously attracted to, a steeled dandruff survivor. Except was her last name! Ana Except loves him so much that they'll go together and make a proposition to Kimmy. I am surrounded by all nations and loaded with evil cells, in the name of the Lord, I will crush them like dried leaves.

"All right, let's go find her!" Stagger said. He managed to get out from under his chair without banging his head. He was skilled at this. Pretty good at crawling on the ground intoxicated. Must be his marine training.

"It's two in the morning." Joshua spoke from under the chair. "Who knows where she could be?"

"I go find her," Ana Except said. "You stay here and wait if she comes."

"At two in the morning every creep in the city is out," Stagger said.

The fattie was nowhere to be found and Joshua was now worried that it had rolled under the porch, on a pile of dried leaves or rat bones or whatever was down there, which must've already started smoldering and would soon ignite the porch. They needed to get off the porch, he needed to get off the floor and then down the stairs and then to safety, from where he could watch the spectacular blaze. The Greater Chicago Fire. Once everything burned to the ground, the rebuilding could start. Operation American Freedom.

He looked up to urge Stagger and Ana to run for their lives when he saw the fattie, now diminished to a roach. Stagger was sucking on it as if it were a pacifier. It was flummoxing how Stagger kept pulling out those joints, the resourceful bastard. They would disappear, then reappear in his hand, all part of a magical cycle of being and nonbeing. Fucking sombrero. Joshua got up and plopped into a chair. What was it that Stagger made him smoke? Good shit. The Lord shall always provide the good shit, the things that matter. I will not die so I may live, and recount the deeds of God with care and precision.

"I been calling," Ana Except said. "Esko is not pick up the phone. I worry."

"All right. Let's go!" Stagger said without moving.

"Where?" Joshua asked.

"To find the girl."

"We don't have a car," Joshua said.

"We got a car," Stagger said.

"What car?"

"I got a car."

"When did you get a car?"

"Maybe you can call Bega," Ana Except said. "Maybe he can go to see."

"I've always had a car," Stagger said. "Exactly for situations like this."

"I've never seen you driving a car," Joshua said.

"Bega maybe can see if she is home," Ana pleaded. Why can't she call Bega? Joshua began thinking, but then he stopped. Thinking without producing a thought, that's what he was good at. That and nightingales.

"I've never had a situation like this," Stagger said.

"That's true," Joshua said.

"I am worry," Ana Except said. "I call Esko. I don't have Bega's phone."

"I can call," Joshua said. "But I don't have his number."

"We gotta go. I need my weapon," Stagger said.

"Let's call first," Joshua said. "Let's think straight."

"We gotta go. We can't just sit here and do nothing. We gotta do what's right," Stagger said. "I need my weapon of ass destruction."

"You don't have to go. Joshua can call," Ana Except said.

"Who's he gonna call?" Stagger said. "Who're you gonna call, Jonjo?"

"I don't know," Joshua said. "Bega. I don't have his phone number."

"See?" Stagger said. "We gotta go."

"Fucking sombrero," Joshua said. "I can't think straight."

"Let's roll," Stagger said.

EXT. CORNFIELD — NIGHT

Suddenly, Major K hears a zombie HOWL of a different quality, communicating something. Another HOWL responds. Ruth freezes, as does Young Woman. Major K slowly unties the straps and lets Jack down onto the ground. He makes him lie facedown, then signals to the women to do the same. He listens closely: the RUSTLING of corn, the TRUDGING of the zombies, the HOWLING. Abruptly, everything goes silent except for an obscure NIGHTINGALE. Jack's eyes open wide.

Stagger had quite a bit of trouble getting the car out of the garage, not least because it was buried under a mountain of boxes and crates of beer bottles and Cubs paraphernalia. It was an ancient lily-colored Cadillac, as wide and graceful as a hovercraft, the license plate reading STAG. He then had trouble getting out of the alley, because all the garbage cans had been pushed out to the middle by some local teenage prickster, so Stagger just barged through the cordon of cans, spilling the trash for rats to enjoy. I am surrounded by my enemies, in the name of the Lord, I will spill their guts like alley trash.

"Go straight," Joshua demanded, even if there was no street to turn off to. Stagger was practically levitating above his seat, his chin every now and then hitting his chest, which helped him snap awake. He was going maddeningly slowly, the weight of his forearms, one of them in a cast, pressing the steering wheel and the axle and the wheels and Joshua, who could smell the burning steel. The night was menacingly dark, as if some powerful force had switched off all the street lighting, setting the stage for a hedgehog-fucking invasion of rabid zombies. Script Idea #196: *A rock star high out of his mind freaks out during his show, runs off the stage, and finds himself lost in a city whose name he can't recall, but whose streets are crowded with his hallucinations. A teenage fan discovers him trembling behind a garbage container, begging the Lord to get him out of his trip. The teen decides to keep the rock star for himself for the night. Mishaps and adventures follow. This one could be a musical:* Singin' in the Brain.

Now that they had some kind of a goal to focus on, the buzz was fading, and for the better, except that nausea set in. Ana occupied the backseat in *anabashedly* judgmental silence. Joshua feared turning to look at her, after he'd done it once and her face was obscure; his revolution nearly made him sick. Did she understand how high they were? He received the wavelengths of anxiety Ana's body emitted, her loneliness and angry worry, but did she understand? He should be doing something about all that. He should turn and understandingly squeeze Ana's hand, rub her knee, say something funny. But his cheek hurt, and he was sure she'd have nothing but contempt for his empty gestures. And he couldn't bear moving his head back and forth. His brain must have shrunk and was now rattling around in his cranium like a pea in Tupperware whenever he altered his position.

Nana Elsa had once sat at Seder in absolute silence, except to read her lines from the Haggadah, every one of which had targeted Bernie and sounded as if coming directly from the very pissed Lord himself. All because she'd just learned that Bernie had squandered his family on a mistress. Perhaps he could tell Ana about Nana Elsa, about her being the toughest woman he'd ever known, surviving a camp, losing all her family, trekking across Europe, sailing across the Atlantic, to come to Chicago without a person in the world and work in a button factory. But it wasn't clear how that could be comforting to Ana. Besides, turning back and forth was not a good idea, he was nauseated. He could think of no other thing to do, so he did nothing, and was thus forced to recognize that when seriously stoned he was in no way presenting his best self, even if Ana couldn't see he was high. His best self was way out of town right now, pretty much crouching somewhere in the cornfields of Iowa. His second-best self was helpless, deployed solely to keep the food down. He held on to the dashboard. A speed bump alerted Stagger to the existence of the street and the car he was driving, if ever so slowly. The burst of unexpected consciousness allowed him to put down the hand brake, whence the car lurched forward and sped up.

Somewhere along the way, Stagger and Joshua had come up with a plan: they'd first find out if Alma was abducted by Esko, who was still not picking up the phone. There was no way Ana could say no to that, because they were superdetermined. But their plan was immediately amended, because Stagger wouldn't even consider going on a search mission without his weapon. Ana begged him to forget about it. Stoned as he was, Joshua knew it wasn't a good idea, but Stagger was adamant about his goddamn sword. Adamant! Ana tried to convince him in her heartbroken English that Esko wasn't violent (yeah, right!), that Stagger shouldn't be handling a sharp blade with his broken arm, whereupon Stagger pressed the heels of his palms against the center of his steering wheel and honked furiously, exploding the nocturnal silence. So they were on their way to get the goddamn sword.

"Go forward," Joshua said.

"Always straight, never forward," Stagger said.

Kimmy's house was only a couple of blocks up the street, yet it took them forever to get there, during which time Joshua listened to Ana whimper, redial, and gasp in the backseat. He kept working on a statement of comfort for her, but all that his fattie-addled mind could in the end come up with was: "It will probably be okay."

She wore Joshua's flannel shirt and looked, somehow, Midwestern. *Probably* was the wrong word. *It will be okay* was what he should have said. *It shall be okay* even better. Or: *While there is no way to predict what will happen or what your personal circumstances will be, there are things we can do now.* Kimmy would know what to say, and what to do, but she was the one person he could not call at this time, or ever again in his life. Stagger slammed the brakes and Joshua nearly cracked his nose against the dashboard. As long as the drive took, it wasn't long enough for Joshua to figure out a way to get a samurai sword from behind the washing machine without waking Kimmy up. "Let's think about this," Joshua said. I remember what okay looks like and this is the exact opposite.

Script Idea #200: *A woman is besieged in her house by her demented ex-boyfriend and his insane sidekick. The only weapon she has to defend herself is an ancient samurai sword she inherited from her Japanese father. After much suspense and struggle, she slices the sidekick down the middle, like a dog. In the last scene, she stands over her ex-boyfriend with the sword in her hand, deliberating whether to decapitate or castrate him. Their eyes lock. "Kill me," he says. She kills him. The end. Title:* Assholes Also Die.

"Stagger, I beg you, let's forget about this," Joshua tried again. "I'll come back tomorrow and get your sword. I promise."

They stood in front of Kimmy's house, away from the porch light, close to some unnameable bush, leafless and devastated by the winter, in which something rustled—a fuckable hedgehog, perhaps, or a nightingale. Ana stayed in the car, calling Esko repeatedly, receiving no answer. Stagger took off his Crocs and gave them to Joshua, as if saying farewell. Then he knelt and rubbed dirt all over his face and shirt and body, including his underwear and cast, which happily retained its blazing whiteness. Joshua longingly looked back toward the car, at Ana, who was pressing her phone against her ear, shaking her head at him, mouthing: "No!"

"If you go in there, Stagger, she'll call the police for sure, accuse you of rape. Unless she cuts you in half first. Please, let's just forget about it."

"It's behind the washing machine, correct?" Stagger whispered.

"Correct," Joshua said. "But you don't even know where the laundry room is. I beg you—I'll go get it tomorrow."

"It's my weapon. It's a marine thing to do," Stagger said. "No man other than me should fall for my weapon."

"What are you talking about?" Joshua hissed in lieu of a whisper, grabbing Stagger's cast. "Nobody's going to fall. Come on, man! Let's be grown up here!"

Stagger looked down at the hand on his cast, then at Joshua. Very gently, he removed Joshua's hand. He embraced him firmly and whispered something unintelligible into his ear. Then he slipped up the stairs to the porch, stepped onto the banister, gearing up to climb the downspout under Kimmy's bedroom window. How was he going to do that with the cast?

"Wait!" Joshua hissed. "I have a key!"

"Take your shoes off," Stagger ordered.

"Wait!" Joshua said, and vomited.

It took him a while to find the key in his jacket pocket: movie tickets, coins, and whatnot—a lot of *whatnot*. Joshua pushed the door open without a single creak or crack, Stagger half-naked in his wake. Not so long ago Bushy had rubbed against Joshua's shins; Bushy used to live here, now he's dead, and his spirit could be anywhere, including nowhere. What did Kimmy do with his corpse? What do you do with dead animals? Once upon a time, Mom had put his green parakeet, his first and only pet, in the freezer upon its demise. For months it had remained among the tubs of kosher ice cream, and then, one day, it too had vanished.

The house was lightless, indifferent. On the tip of his ex-marine toes, Stagger crept into the living room, then into the kitchen. Joshua wanted to stop him, but dared not produce a sound, his heart pounding like the drums along the Mohawk. Stagger finally turned around to spread his arms. The gesture should've meant that it was all clear, but with Stagger you never knew. Joshua followed him to the kitchen, where his hunger came back in a rush so powerful that he opened the fridge without thinking. This time, there was no beer. There was, however, a tray of sushi leftovers that looked reasonably edible and he grabbed it, closing the fridge door noiselessly. He placed a piece of California roll in his mouth, crushed it with his teeth, and swallowed, tasting enough of it to know that it was not fresh at all. He offered the tray to Stagger, who shrugged and grabbed a couple of unidentifiable pieces. The two men, one of them half-naked and tattooed, stood in the cold, mute darkness of Kimmy's kitchen and ate leftover sushi—the little man in the crawl space knew this could make a compelling scene in some script. Joshua opened the freezer, and the smell of ice cream and frozen dead animals washed over him. How about a scene in *Zombie Wars*: A morgue worker takes out a tub of ice cream from an empty corpse-fridge compartment. He hears noise coming from the compartment next to it. Foolishly, he opens the noisy one, the pistachio ice cream still in hand.

Chewing the last piece of sushi, Joshua pointed toward the laundry room and Stagger showed him thumbs up. All this wordless communication: it was well nigh troubling that he and Stagger understood each other so well. It would have to end, this buddy-buddy relationship, tonight, right after they got the sword without getting arrested, right after they tracked down Daughter Except, right after they fully descended from their high, as soon as the new day arrived. By the end of Passover, I'll have moved back to my humble abode on Sanity Street.

The dark house was fragrant of Kimmy's life: the industrial smell of the carpet on the stairs, the shop scent of the tchotchkes on the coffee table, the ubiquitous lavender. He missed them all, all those smells, even the rancid sushi, all the meaningless sensory details of a well-governed life. By next Monday, he'll have begged Kimmy to let him back in; he'll have bought her a diamond ring. He'll have said, again and better: That was not me! That was not me at all!

The problem at hand, though, was that the samurai sword was stuck behind the washing machine and it couldn't be retrieved without moving the cumbersome beast, which at three in the morning would surely be heard all the way to the police station. In the gloom of the laundry room they conferred in susurration: Joshua would go upstairs and keep an eye on the sleeping Kimmy and distract her if she woke up; meanwhile, Stagger would figure out a way to get the sword. "Good teamwork," Stagger whispered in Joshua's ear, his breath warm and foul.

Step by slow soundless step, Joshua moved up the stairs, ninja-like. His diminishing high was now compounded by somnolent alertness: he touched the banister so lightly it felt half-existent, as if slow in rematerializing. He could hear the wall cracking infinitesimally; he spotted Bushy's toy mouse— a little rubber monument to his absence—just before it squeaked under his foot. Kimmy must've been disabled with grief, unable to touch anything that belonged to Bushy, unable to remove the remnants of his presence—she surely missed him more than she did Joshua. Script Idea #204: *Mr. Grief comes to your house to clean up after the final departure of your loved ones, providing all kinds of grief-management services. To do this, Mr. Grief has to lock up his own grief deep inside—the loss of his wife. But when he meets a grieving widow, his dead wife's doppelganger, his Box of Grief (the title?) breaks open.*

He reached the top of the stairs. The bathroom was to the right, Kimmy's office before him, her bedroom to the left. As per his orders, Joshua should've stayed there and watched out for any signs of Kimmy's movement, acting to distract her only if she for some reason headed downstairs. But the door of Kimmy's room was invitingly ajar, just enough so he could squeeze through it. His heart was break-dancing in his chest; his memorious dick made the first step toward erection, pointing in the direction of the ring and handcuffs.

There stood Joshua, unpresent in the breathing darkness, taking in the stale lavender air of the slept-in room, the taste of vomit still in his mouth, his cheek burning. He moved along the wall, toward the deeper shadow, closer to her bed. She looked minuscule under the cover, practically bodiless, except for the dark smudge of her head on the pillow. Joshua froze and held his breath when he heard a screech coming from the laundry room. Still, Kimmy's head did not move.

Script Idea #205: *A stalker creeps into the room of the woman he obsesses over, only to find her already dead. She filed a restraining order against him and now he is the prime suspect. Will he be able to find the real killer before the police track him down?*

He missed Kimmy. She was better than him, far too good for him. To be star-crossed, lovers have to belong to the same grade of human quality. Kimmy could love him only out of pity, and he could never believe she wouldn't leave him for the Fourth or the Fifth, or some unnumbered Hummer hunk born into the same rarefied category as herself. Kimmy's grade was honeymoon-in-Tokyo. Joshua's was somewhere between dandruff survivor and leftover sushi.

It was time to say goodbye, even if stealthily. Feeling weightless, closing his eyes—come what may!—he leaned over her to kiss her fragrant shadow. But instead of her silky, thick hair, his lips touched a bag of lavender she kept on her pillow.

She was gone, gone for good.

Tears fogged up his eyes, but he still stumbled through the fog to rummage around her drawer to seek the cock ring and the handcuffs. The cock ring was nowhere to be found; the handcuffs he pocketed like a seasoned burglar.

———

Joshua spent the ride to the Ambassador imagining all the possible consequences of the break-in, the most probable one featuring Kimmy calling the police and having them arrested for aggravated burglary; and if any of her neighbors had seen Stagger prancing along her lawn half-naked, attempted rape might be added to it. But all that was to be dealt with in the future, in the unlikely case it wasn't already foreclosed. If there is never any reason to believe there will be a future, there is only one way to find out if it's coming.

Stagger stood impatiently behind Ana, clutching his sword awkwardly in his unbroken left hand, waiting for her to unlock the Ambassador's door. If ever a man was entitled to a cape and light saber, it was Stagger. Joshua leaned in to read the backlit names next to the buzzers, but they were nothing if not secret words made of consonants. For all he knew, a coded message about the Messiah's coming was inscribed there: the Bosnian Kabbalah. By the end of time, there will have been no future.

Ana presented no plan of action; she somehow trusted them; she took them as they came. Bosnians, Bega had said, take things as they come, they surf the wave of catastrophe. And here was where Stagger and Joshua's mission brought them now, before a wall of unpronounceable names. If there's one thing the Hebrews should be blamed for it is starting all that unpronounceability madness. Hephzibah, for God's sake, the wife of Hezekiah.

Ana walked up the stairs ahead of them, wearing Joshua's shirt and tight leggings, her thighs rather admirably shaped. Not so long ago, Joshua had thrust himself forth between those thighs, but it all now seemed like a wet dream, yet another inconclusive one. Stagger ascended before him, grunting with effort, using his sword as a walking stick, his teeth clenched, tendrils of his ponytail lingering around his ears in disarray.

"I'm good," Stagger said without being asked. How old was he, anyway? If he'd been in his twenties for Desert Storm, he would be in his forties now. It seemed probable, but he was somehow older than that, much older. His body was fit and still young, but the rest of him was, shall we say, excessively mature. Or maybe he was just crashing down from his high. "Proceed," Stagger said, his face ghostly pale. With all the wrinkles and grimaces and madness now bleached from it, Joshua could suddenly perceive the young man Stagger used to be way back before the big party in the desert, before his landlording career and ensuing madness, before all this. Joshua obediently proceeded, but he needed to pee. The body never quits working. The mind goes out, but the body always hums along, proceeding until it stops. The beauty of life is that eventually everybody turns into a zombie, whereupon they die.

Before Ana's door, two large thick-soled shoes with dirty tips stood at an angle, as if turning away in disgust. Ana straightened them with a careful toe poke, out of habit, no doubt. It seemed like a meaningless gesture; yet, Joshua understood, she cared about the way things ought to be; she didn't quite succumb and surf. He, on the other hand, was exhausted as the rococo hopelessness of everything set in. Also, terribly hungry still and in need of urination.

She fumbled for the right key in the batch, and there were a lot of them. What property did she own to have all those keys? The door was unlocked, it turned out, so she walked in. Stagger shuffled sideways in her wake, half squatting like a Jedi, his sword high above his head ready to strike, even if he couldn't fully grip the handle with his cast. Joshua could see the cicatrice stretching between the ridges of Stagger's shoulder blades to reach the base of his neck, where *Semper Fi* was inscribed in blue ink. Joshua had no idea what *Semper Fi* actually meant. How many marines could read Latin anyway? They could've made it more American and vernacular, say: *No quittin'* or *Thrills and Kills* or *Appetite for Destruction*. Everything should be simpler and more American, particularly at this point in time when we must all stand united because we're all falling apart.

Ana switched on the light in the hallway, exposing its emptiness. "Esko!" she called, turning on more lights as she moved deeper in. The vacant sadness of the apartment: they had little, Ana and her family. No pictures on the wall; no carpets on the floor; no heirloom furniture; no framed diplomas; no useless VHS players; no books on the coffee table; no coffee table. They were thrown out of their own past, the *you people*, carrying only their mystical consonants and a weathered catastrophe surfboard. It made Joshua even more queasy, as if he'd just driven over roadkill.

The last light Ana switched on revealed Esko, his left hand under his cheek, lying on the sofa, which was much smaller than him, so his feet hung over its end. One of his tube socks had a huge hole, the ball of his foot bulging out like a peeled potato. He was facing the TV, on which two women, richly oiled and glowing with the soft-core ochre, wrestled in slow motion. Only when Ana moved in front of the TV did his gaze acknowledge her. He glanced over to Stagger in his broken-arm combat posture, and then on to Joshua, who picked that particular moment to gasp for air. Ana said something in Bosnian, something that sounded angry and confrontational, but Esko just shrugged and scratched his nose listlessly. The floor before him was covered with plates and food leftovers and bottles of Corona; it seemed he hadn't left the sofa for a long time. Ana kept talking, the edge in her voice getting sharper. What was she saying to him? Joshua wished he knew, not only because it pertained to the solution of the missing-girl mystery, but also because he really had to relieve the pressure on his prostate and he couldn't leave in the middle of a showdown. Ana pressed her hand against her chest and kept shaking her head dramatically as she spoke, making a poignant point, then offered something to Esko in the cupped palms of her hands. Whatever it was, Esko didn't care much about it. Wincing, as if his nose kept itching, he looked past her at the screen, where one of the women was now arching in what was supposed to be extreme pleasure as the other woman was rimming her navel. Ana stepped forward, excavated the remote from the debris on the floor, and turned off the TV. Her jaw clenched in some form of Balkan fury, as she slapped first her left then her right cheek and then pointed her finger at herself, then at Esko, who finally sat up and nodded resignedly, as if everything had just come together for him, to congeal into an incontestable defeat. Stagger, still as a statue in his samurai pose, stared at Esko with a delirious focus.

"Excuse me," Joshua said. "I don't mean to interrupt your conversation, but could I use the bathroom?"

Ana turned to look at him in what could be adequately described as stupefaction; Esko chuckled as if pleasantly reminded of Joshua's pathetic existence. "You okay?" Stagger asked, not taking his eyes off Esko.

"I really have to pee," Joshua said.

"Go pee," Ana said.

"I got it here, Jonjo," Stagger said. "You go and pee."

As Joshua made his first step toward the bathroom, Esko

leapt off the sofa, over the chaos on the floor, and rushed at Joshua, who froze in place. He would've surely been crushed in a merciless tackle had Stagger not managed to swing the sword and slice Esko with its tip across the curve of his thigh. Ana screamed. Blood gushed instantly out of a gaping crevice, diverting Esko's acceleration. Stagger was about to inflict another cut as Esko put all of his force into the fist whose trajectory terminated at Stagger's nose, which, blinding him, exploded. With another punch to the chin Esko felled Stagger, who crumpled to the floor, on top of the beer bottles, announcing his landing with a painful groan. Ana screamed again and grabbed her head as if to throw it at the men. Esko pried the sword from Stagger's limp hand and turned to point its tip at Joshua, whose bladder miraculously held, even if the air left his lungs rapidly, along with all the words he'd ever learned to utter. Esko said something in Bosnian to him, pressing the tip against his chest. There was already blood at Esko's feet joining with what was coming from Stagger's blown-up nose, but Esko couldn't have cared less. He repeated whatever it was he'd said and now offered the sword handle to Joshua. Stagger looked pretty dead, except for the blood steadily flowing from his nose.

"I don't know," Joshua mumbled with effort. "I don't know what you're saying to me."

"He wants you to kill him," Ana said. "With that thing."

"Oh, no, thank you," Joshua said. "I'm okay. Really."

Esko paid no attention to what Ana was saying to him and pressed the tip of the sword against his own throat. Joshua could see the deep indentation, and the vein it was pushing into. "Please," Joshua said. The tip of the sword now opening the skin on Esko's neck, a trickle of blood emerging; he was glaring at Joshua, but looking into something beyond his face, beyond him. I don't want you to die, so I may live and recount the deeds of God. Ana was talking in Bosnian, sounding calmingly reasonable. Esko was a hairbreadth away from cutting his own throat and Joshua closed his eyes, resigned to a shower of blood. Lord, please save us! Or at least, Lord, save *me*! But then Esko grabbed the handle again, Joshua flinching, and smacked the sword against the floor; it snapped like a bread stick. The blade fell in the blood puddle as Esko tossed the handle away, and fell on his knee, bowing his head like a knight before the king.

It took Joshua an instant to realize that Esko was crying, pressing fingers against his eyeballs as if trying to gouge them out. Ana moved to put her hand on Esko's shoulder, reluctantly, carefully, lest it be interpreted as reconciliation. Esko sobbed louder and louder, forcing Joshua to stumble in retreat, as if his tears were acid that could burn him. Ana knelt down next to Esko and put her arm across his shoulder. "It will be okay," she must've said to him. His wound was agape now that he was kneeling, but Esko in no way showed he was aware of it. The velvet blood bubbled out of the wedge in his denim, darkening instantly. Joshua's knees gave out and he floundered farther backward and dropped onto the sofa. His prostate was painful. Was this how survival was supposed to feel? There was a light hook right above the TV, available for hanging. He needed to pee really bad.

Stagger grunted and sat up. He grabbed a filthy napkin from the floor and pressed it against his nose. Ana kept repeating some Bosnian word, something, Joshua knew, she would never say to him. He wanted her to reconcile with Esko, thereby restoring some semblance of order, thereby allowing him to return from this exile to the land of the before, where there was no humiliation, no blood, no frogs, no lice, no locusts, no clotted darkness or pain, no chaos, let alone the possibility of urine-soaked underwear. Script Idea #1: *Two or more people. Love, life, betrayal, hurt. Title:* God Help Us All.

EXT. OUTSIDE THE PRISON — DAY

Jack is on Major K's back, holding on to his shoulders with some effort. Major K slouches forth under the burden. Ruth stumbles through the mud, occasionally falling down, but still getting up. They're followed by Alicia and a large herd of refugees, a few of them nursing gunshot wounds. Children BAWL. The prison fort is visible on the horizon, its high walls with watchtowers. The people are exhausted, but they know they've almost made it. GUNFIRE in the distance, zombies LOWING.

LATER

Major K BANGS at the steel door, exhausted, intermittently gasping for air. There is no response. He anxiously looks at the crowd behind him, huddled together in hope. Jack and Ruth are fixated on the door, desperate for it to open. Major K

bangs again. The peephole slides open. A pair of
anxious eyes.

                    MAJOR K
        We're all human.

In her demolished living room, her wounded husband in her care, Ana took charge of the entire catastrophe. She extinguished the drama in a most unequivocal way, its meaninglessness now perfectly self-evident. Even Stagger was compelled to comply, although that required his getting the hell out on the stairs to calm down. She then interrogated Esko, who was bleeding soundlessly on the sofa, pressing a towel against his thigh to stop the blood: Alma, she translated for Joshua, was at Bega's. Joshua stood, confused, waiting for further instructions, but all she said was: "Thank you. You can go away now." She pulled her bra straps up, no smile or dimples on her face, no love for Joshua; she had crossed back into the before. He received his order unquestionably, not least because he simply didn't know what else to do.

But there was one last thing he needed before he embarked upon returning to his previous life: a moment to urinate. Releasing the stream, he stared at the water stain on the wall above the toilet: it resembled a werewolf version of a Hasid. Script Idea #300: *Jerusalem is besieged by rapacious vampires* . . . No! Fuck it! Enough of that, he decided.

He had to roll up the bottoms of his pants because they were bloody, which somehow resulted in their being too big at the waist. They hung on him like clown pants; to get into the car he had to pull them up, not unlike Bernie, well past his navel. Swordless, Stagger slid into the driver's seat, failing to buckle up. Dried blood coated his neck and the tattoos on his chest, his jaw tightened into a painful grin of anger. He would've looked like a commercial for a pitiless warrior if it wasn't for the two red-splattered Kleenex pluming out of his nostrils. He had to be in his mid-fifties, at least. The Lord supports me through my allies and so I face my enemies, and my enemies are just ecstatic to see us guys together. The sun emerged from the lake, as if from hiding; finger-fucked dawn crept over the building tops and bare tree crowns and the city in which some kind of violence was always afoot.

Devon Avenue was vacant, as before a zombie assault, except for a sole, inexplicable Lubavitcher, grim under his black fedora, vast as a fucking sombrero, walking speedily toward something, only to make a sudden turn and step onto the pedestrian crossing, just in time to be barely missed by Stagger. Joshua envied the comfort that comes with the Messianic promise, the life of someone whose story had always already been told, the ending the same through eternity, the future vouchsafed.

"Have you ever seen *The Searchers*?" Joshua asked.

"What's that?"

"*The Searchers*, the John Wayne movie."

"No," Stagger said. "I can't stand John Wayne."

"So what's your favorite movie?"

Stagger ripped the bloody tissue plumes out of his nostrils while considering the question, rolled down the window, and threw them out.

"*Star Wars. Attack of the Clones*," he said. "But I don't want to discuss stupid movies."

"Let's go and get the girl," Joshua said without thinking. Stagger turned to look at him: first, in disbelief, and then, fist-pumping in the air. "Fuckin' A!" he shouted and made a U-turn in front of a bus.

Few words were exchanged between them as they drove on. There was no quittin' now. The realization provided joy and relief for Joshua—there was going to be an end to all this. He decided that, come Monday, he was going to write a long e-mail to Kimmy, lay down the whole story honestly and unflinchingly, detail all the undeserved humiliation, explain the exonerating circumstances, accept the responsibility, suggest that he'd been more than sufficiently punished, foreground the fact that he responsibly returned the girl to her mother, and promise he'd change his ways, having learned so much from his recent experiences. She will take him back in; or maybe she won't. Either way all this will have been just a (heroic?) nightmare remembered; and selectively, God willing.

"Buckle up," Joshua said. Stagger was gripping the steering wheel with his unbroken hand, the knuckles white with excitement.

"I don't think so," Stagger said. "I don't think buckling up is something I can stand to do right now."

They soon passed the Ambassador, turned a corner to behold Bega's Honda, complete with the plush dice and a dent in the front right door, sitting in the driveway of a house with a porch—a very small house with a very small porch, but still. An immigrant with so much property? An asshole who constantly berates and complains about this country owns a fancy Japanese car and a cozy little house? Fuck that! They parked on the street, blocking the Honda with the STAGmobile. The street was asleep, except for a couple of sparrows chirping apoplectically at a half-empty birdbath on Bega's lawn.

"I've got to pee again," Joshua said. He didn't, really, but he chased the sparrows away, undug his dick, and urinated into the birdbath. The arbitrary meanness of his act was gratifying: it was a form of freedom. "Fuck you!" he said to no one in particular. The sparrows landed on the skinny tree branches above the bath and watched, fidgeting as dark-yellow urine spread through the clear water like an oil spill.

Stagger rang the doorbell, and it buzzed like a laser in a James Bond movie. On the porch, there were a few cracked, empty pots, and a mound of coupon sheets so sodden they clearly predated the deprivations of the previous winter. Joshua thumbed the buzzer too, but this time there was no sound at all. Stagger pressed his face against the window in the parenthesis of his hands, even if the blinds prevented him from seeing anything. His nose was still bleeding, however; he left a bloody smudge on the pane.

"Probably not home," Joshua said. "We should go."

"I don't think so," Stagger said and banged at the door so vehemently Joshua feared the entire neighborhood would be in no time flattening their noses against their windows. It was fortunate that Esko had broken Stagger's sword; otherwise heads and limbs would be flying.

"He's not at home," Joshua said.

"We'll make him be at home," Stagger said.

Bega opened the door in his boxer shorts, which were

turned to the side at his hips, so it looked like his upper body was twisted at a weird angle. His chest was wispily hairy, cherry-sized nipples looming over his pasty abdominal folds. Joshua hadn't anticipated a wide-faced white cat in Bega's arms.

"Josh," Bega said. "Good morning."

"Is the girl here?" Stagger demanded.

Bega completely ignored him, asking Joshua: "What's up?"

"Is the girl here?" Joshua asked. The cat was watching him intently, as if it knew everything that was to be known about Joshua. It looked like Bushy's sibling: the same fluffy beige fur, the same pink nose, the same gaze, the same self-centeredness.

"Come in," Bega said. "My home is your home."

The cat was purring loudly, which bothered Joshua. Bega had never mentioned his cat. Bushy was dead while Bega had a living, purring cat. He was scratching it between the pricked-up ears, as if nothing had ever happened. *I am considering slicing your prick off and putting it in your mouth until you choke*, Bega had said before Esko wrung Bushy's neck.

"Pretty cat," Joshua said.

"Thanks," Bega said. As if nothing had happened. "Her name is Dolly. She's sweetheart."

Dolly decided to wiggle out of Bega's arms, and, maintaining a deep purr, scratch at the carpet on the floor, on which men in turbans and women in long, ballooning dresses faced each other under intricately woven canopies of leaves, while horses reared and heavenly birds spread their splendorously colorful plumes. The content cat and the carpet stood out in the morning drabness of Bega's living room: a sofa with a blanket-and-pillow mound and three plastic porch chairs huddled around a plastic table, over which a paper-ball light hung from a prominent hook.

"That carpet is the only thing I have from Bosnia," Bega said. "And this." The other thing was a small painting of a closed window on the wall. Joshua studied the painting with exaggerated contempt.

"Where's the girl?" Stagger demanded again, but Bega ignored him, again.

"We came to get Alma," Joshua said.

"She's in the shower," Bega said. "Would you like some coffee?"

"If you laid your hands on her," Stagger growled, "I'm gonna cut them off."

"Who's this?" Bega asked Joshua.

"That's Stagger."

"Yes, okay. But who is he? And what happened to his head?"

Joshua considered Stagger: the demolished ponytail, the bloody nose and tattooed body, the American flag shorts.

"He's . . ." It was too difficult to explain. "He's my buddy."

"What does he want?"

"Where's the girl, motherfucker?" Stagger insisted. He moved deeper into the house to look for her. Dolly abandoned the carpet and slithered away somewhere. What kind of person lets another person kill other people's cats? What kind of person is that kind of person?

"He wants Alma," Joshua said. "We want to take her back home."

Bega should've offered his cat as a replacement, or at

least as retribution. It was only fair. An eye for an eye, a tooth for a tooth, a cat for a cat.

"Okay, no problem," Bega said. "But you and your friend knock at my door at six in the morning. Is that how you do it now?"

"At least we don't kill cats," Joshua said.

Stagger banged at the bathroom door then tried to get in, but it was locked.

"What cats have to do with anything?"

"Cats have a lot to do with everything. You have your pretty little cat and no worry in the world. But what about other people's cats? Do you ever think of other people's cats?"

"You don't say sorry, you don't say good morning, you come and talk about cats and you want to push me around. You can't do that," Bega said.

"Oh yeah? Fuck you! I'm gonna push you all I want," Joshua yelled and stepped closer to Bega, who was unmoved. "We can do whatever we want. You came to my house and killed my cat! And where's the girl?"

"Girl!" Stagger shouted.

"Alma!" Joshua shouted.

"Alma! Come out!" Stagger went on. "You're safe now! We're here to take you home!"

She came out of the bathroom with a towel wrapped around her head and another one around the chest. She now looked like a blooming version of her mother, a lot more of her yet to come, a lot more damage to be done. Alma Except, a debutant at the hurt ball. Her toes were freshly painted pink, pieces of cotton still between her toes. She looked at Stagger in confusion.

"You okay?" Stagger asked. He was concerned; he was a

good guy, a true searcher, if crazy, Stagger was. Caring about people and cats came naturally to him.

"Yeah," she said. "I'm okay. I can take care of myself."

Bega spoke to her in Bosnian and she looked at Joshua, shook her head, and laughed.

"Speak English!" Stagger demanded. "This is America!"

She went into the bedroom, closing the door behind.

"She's fifteen, for God's sake," Joshua said.

"She is almost sixteen. And she is as old as she wants to be," Bega said. "It's not your fucking business anyway. This is not Iraq."

Whereupon Joshua shoved him right between his cherry nipples and Bega head-butted him in return and Joshua stumbled backward, the spot between his eyes throbbing with blinding pain as Stagger charged from across the room and slammed into Bega like a linebacker and took him down, his howl comprised of injury and fury in equal measures. Joshua hit the floor and stayed down, recuperating enough to witness Bega and Stagger grotesquely wrestling on the carpet, until Stagger, howling still, ended up sitting on Bega's chest, as Bega fought to wrangle Stagger's unbroken hand away from his face and throw him off. "Keep his hands down, Jonjo!" Stagger shouted, and Joshua grabbed one of Bega's wrists and pinned it with his knee; then he grabbed the other one and pulled his hand down, releasing Stagger to hit Bega's face with the edge of his cast, and it felt good. Alma stepped out of the bedroom to freeze, framed by the door, naked except for the towel turban. Joshua was now holding down both of Bega's arms, allowing Stagger, groaning with ache and pleasure, to rain mean blows on Bega's face with care and precision, splitting the lip open first, then the brows, then smashing the nose, until the Bosnian was gurgling blood and Alma was jumping on Stagger's back for him to throw her off with one twitch of his shoulders. She moved over to Joshua to scratch his face, so he had to let go of Bega's arms, which were fortunately no longer moving, and sat up to shake her off him, but not before she left a red line across his chin. She flew off and landed hard, her head whiplashing against the floor. Stagger stopped beating Bega and looked in lunatic perplexion toward Alma. She was not moving. They held their breaths. Stagger sat still on top of Bega, his cast completely carmine. Bega looked too peaceful for comfort; his face was pulped, blood running every which way it could, losing itself among his facial hair, treacling toward his ear. When Alma gasped, Stagger punched Bega in the face one more time, presumably to celebrate her return to the world of the living.

"I got handcuffs," Joshua said and whipped them out from his back pocket.

The exotic carpet was stained with blood. Stagger got off Bega and rolled him over, twisting his arms to fit them on his back. Joshua handcuffed him dexterously, as though he'd been doing it all his life, and, before Stagger high-fived him, threw the key across the room. Let Bega crawl on his face to find it.

Sob by little sob, Alma came to. They made her sit, concussed, on the sofa, her hands in her naked lap, a towel over her shoulders. Her little breasts drooped like runny dough. "Get dressed," Joshua said as Stagger kicked Bega in the ribs one last time. "We're taking you home." Alma didn't move or say anything. Joshua stripped a case off one of the pillows.

"I want the cat too," he said. "Let's get the cat."

They turned the place upside down, far more than needed

to find Dolly. Joshua felt his high come back as a feeling of strength and power: he ripped the paper lantern, kicked the table over, threw the window painting down, watched Stagger smash the few plates in the kitchen. Then Joshua dug through the closets, ripping out shirts and bedding and boxes of photos, while Stagger karate-kicked Bega's computer off the stand and then demolished the bathroom, smashing the mirror.

"How's this for a fuck-you!" screamed Stagger, leaning over the unconscious Bega. "You like it? You don't? No? Well: fuck you!"

They found Dolly cowering under the messy bed, the bedroom now reeking of their perspiration. They shut the bedroom door and lifted the bed together to push it up against the wall, exposing aged, strewn socks and unclean underwear. Dolly desperately slipped out between them but then ran into the cul-de-sac at the shut door. Stagger deftly leapt to step on her tail; Joshua grabbed her, screeching like a banshee, by the scruff of her neck. "Hello, Dolly," he said and stuffed her in the pillow case.

He threw at Alma the clothes he'd found in the bedroom. She looked up at him, grinding her teeth, anger bubbling up on her lips, still too dazed to say anything.

"Let's roll," Joshua said.

The T-shirt she wore was Bega's and hung huge on her: IF THERE'S NO GOD, WHO POPS UP THE NEXT KLEENEX? Stagger buckled up this time around and offered his unbroken hand to Joshua for another high five and Joshua slapped it without thinking.

"Man!" Stagger shouted. "A-Team!"

His cast was completely red with blood. What was a wound had become a weapon. Joshua's forehead hurt and he touched the goiterish swelling where he had been head-butted. Bega had come to and rolled up on his back before they left, attempting pathetically to spit in their direction, a glob of bloody saliva landing on his face, to their merriment.

"Mission accomplished! No casualties!" Stagger cried again. "I gotta tell you something, Jonjo. I'd go to combat with you anytime. It's a no-brainer. Afghanistan, Rogers Park, Iraq, you name it. Anytime, anywhere. I'd fight with you by my side."

They could hear the bagged Dolly howling from the car trunk, rolling side to side, back and forth as they made their turns, stopped and started. On their way to the Ambassador they got lost in a maze of one-way streets. Alma looked out the window silently at the kids waiting at a bus stop, at the sunlight reflected in the bagel shop window, at a gas station's neon sign, pale in the morning light. Everything that had happened had happened so long before this moment that it hadn't really happened. The Lord reviewed the whole of what he had done and, behold, he couldn't remember a fucking thing.

"Did you see *that* operation, girl?" Stagger turned to ask Alma, who resolutely refused to look at him.

"Fuck you!" she said instead.

"What do you have to be angry about now?" Stagger said. "You're free."

"I must say," Joshua said, "I understand why you are angry. Honestly, I do."

Alma snorted and sighed; she wasn't going to spend time thinking about what Joshua had to say, now or ever; she was never going to address a word to him again. For her as well, he was forever going to be salmonella. What can you do?

Joshua thought. I can't be liked by everybody. A man must make decisions; people don't like to make decisions, so they don't like deciders.

They stopped as the red eye of the streetlight flashed, cars huddled in the center of the intersection. The Ambassador was down the street. "You know what? Fuck all this," Alma said calmly, opened the door, and slipped out of the car.

"Hey!" Stagger called after her. Joshua turned around in time to see her moving bouncily through the crowd. It would've been classy to deliver her home. Stagger unbuckled to follow, but by the time he got out of the car, she was running, fast and light and alive and unstoppable. She stopped at the Western light to wait for a break in the flow of speeding traffic, then ran across in long strides like an antelope. The young Ms. Except. Nobody was ever going to catch her. She was the first person, and she was going to be the last person. In the plain light of day, he understood it was time to let it all go—he saw that he should never see Ana again, as he saw that it was no longer night. He was now too strong for all that drama anyway. Perhaps even strong enough for Kimiko.

Starting after Alma, Stagger pushed aside an unlucky passerby, an old man in a long dress and a Muslim skullcap, who swirled in a full circle to face Joshua dumbfoundedly.

They got back into the STAGmobile and drove past the cops writing tickets outside burger joints and vegetarian palaces and kebab houses; past the CTA buses huffing and puffing over axle-busting potholes; past the crates of mango and monstrous tubers rotting under green awnings; past the babies in strollers hauling their mothers; past the bike frames rusting anonymously; past the black-coated boys on their way to the yeshiva; past the tired women in saris tottering about in their morning daze; past the angry men scorching their maggot-friendly flesh with coffee in their zombie-mobiles; past everything that could be passed. Whereas Alma flew forward untouched, leaving behind Joshua, Stagger, and all the other zombies, forgetting already everything that needed forgetting. There was nothing to be done, nothing left to do. This is the gate to the Lord, the righteous shall walk through. This is it.

"Let's finish this up," Joshua said. "Let's do the cat."

INT. HOUSE IN WILMETTE — NIGHT

It's Seder. The table is set according to the ancient custom: lamb shank, egg, haroseth, karpas,
maror, matzoth, the whole nine yards. At the head
of the table sits Bernie in a wheelchair, which is
too low, so only his head is visible. He's drooling on his chest, knocked out by painkillers.
At the opposite end is Janet, who actually runs
the whole show. Rachel and Noah sit side by side.
Joshua and Stagger are across the table from them,
their faces disfigured with bruises and scratches
and lumps. Rachel glances at her son with fear and
worry. Stagger nibbles on his matzah. Joshua silently shakes his head and signals he should put
it down, but Stagger doesn't understand. He eats
the last morsel and licks his lips. No one else saw
what he did, so Joshua lets it go.

                    JANET
                  (to Noah)
        All right, Noah: ask!

                    NOAH
I don't want to!

                    RACHEL
Come on, Noah!

                    NOAH
I don't want to do this! I don't care about
this kind of food.

                    JOSHUA
Oh, come on, Jan! Leave the boy alone! I'll
ask the goddamn question.

                    RACHEL
Joshua! Watch your mouth.

                    JANET
Ask the question, Noah, or there'll be
consequences!

                    NOAH
I don't want to ask the goddamn question!

                    RACHEL
See what you've done now, Joshua?

                    JOSHUA
Why is this night different from all other
nights? All right? Pray tell what the big
difference is between this night and all
other nights. Can't wait to find out.

Stagger watches it all in mild amazement, unclear whether this bickering is also part of the bizarre Jewish ritual. He goes for more matzoth.

> BERNIE
> (snapping out of his slumber)
> Chaim? Is that you?

MOMENTS LATER

Stagger pours himself another glass of wine, thereby violating yet again the age-old tradition, but it's too late to care. Somehow, the Levins have granted him a dispensation.

> JANET
> The scriptures dictate the story must be told in ways that will be understood by sages, by the wise and the wicked, by the moron and the mute. And I'm going to tell the story if it's the last thing I do. So, listen up.

Joshua sighs with the impatient anticipation of the same old, same old. Rachel lashes him with a side glance. Noah is off somewhere, having with Joshua's help defeated the pressure from his mother. Bernie is unconscious. Stagger, however, pays attention, sipping his wine.

> JANET
> Long ago, in Egypt, a new pharaoh elected

himself for life. The Jews became slaves,
building pyramids and such. But instead of
dropping dead from all the mortar and brick
production, they bred like immigrants. Being
fairly new to his responsibilities, the
pharaoh freaked out and said, as many of his
ilk would, "Let's wipe out the Jews before
they take over!" Had he been nuclear, it
would've been easy, but his dumb actual plan
was to drown all the baby boys. He didn't
care about the girls, mind you, just the
boys.

Stagger takes another sip of the wine.

                    STAGGER
            (whispering to Joshua)
        This is some good shit.

                    JOSHUA
            (whispering back)
        Prime Bordeaux. Not very kosher.

Stagger fake-punches Joshua's shoulder to show he
got the joke, but Joshua winces in pain.

                    JANET (CONT'D)
            (getting into the story)
        Well, the girls had plans. Luckily for
        Moses, his sister was a strong, smart,
        upstanding woman and she also got along with
        the dictator's daughter. It's always been

about who you know, and Miriam knew that,
deep down inside, the princess had a kind
heart.

                    STAGGER
                (whispering)
Who's Miriam again?

                    JOSHUA
                (also whispering)
The sister.

                    STAGGER
Right! I knew that. It's in the Bible too.

                    JANET (CONT'D)
Well, Jochebed had birthed Moses and hidden
him for three months, but she couldn't
hide him forever. Now, you might wonder
where Moses's father was at this time. He
bailed out, that's where. A full-blown
abandonment of his family. He went about
his own business, probably whoring all
over the Middle East . . .

                    RACHEL
Janet! Calm down. Not the time.

                    JANET
I know. Not the time. Okay.

> JANET (CONT'D)
>
> Moses says: "Let my people go!" And Pharaoh says: "No way in hell!" So Moses's boss unleashes ten weapons of mass destruction, real mean stuff: blood, frogs, lice, wild beasts, pestilence, boils, hail, locusts, clotted darkness, death of the firstborn. Now, what do you think of that, Mr. Pharaoh?

MOMENTS LATER

> JANET (CONT'D)
>
> So Moses puts together the Exodus. Think of it as Operation Hebrew Freedom: an orderly transfer from slavery to the Promised Land, quite a leadership challenge. But that's not where it ends: the pharaoh is an inveterate flip-flopper, so he changes his mind and chases the Jews all the way to the Red Sea.

Stagger appears rapt. He licks his lips and dilates his nostrils, his body taut with attention. Even Noah has come back to listen and manages not to be disruptive. Rachel, whose attention never falters, kneads her hands on the table. Even Bernie seems alert to the story—or at least awake. Joshua watches them all with a mixture of annoyance and love.

                    JANET (CONT'D)
Now water is lapping at their ankles, then
it's at their knees, and then at their very
noses. The Red Sea is big and deep, and they
can't swim for crap. The Egyptians arrive,
raring for the final solution. The Hebrews
appear doomed. But Moses has a boss and
protector who happens to have created the
universe. Turns out the Egyptians can't swim
either. They drown like ants in a kitchen
sink.

MOMENTS LATER

                    JANET (CONT'D)
Well, Miriam perished as the Jews wandered,
an unmarked grave, that kind of thing.
Moses did get a wonderful panoramic view
of the Promised Land, but the boss didn't
let him cross over, God knows why. He died
in the desert, alone too, as everyone
eventually does. It was right there, his
dream, he could see it, yet it was beyond
his reach. After all that leadership, no
dice. There, but not there. Ponder that for
a moment.

Everyone ponders.

                    JANET (CONT'D)
The rest of the Jews did all right, though.

Bernie drops his chin to his chest and starts crying. Rachel reaches across the table to squeeze
his hand and he squeezes hers back.

                    JANET (CONT'D)
        Anyway, drink your wine now. For Elijah.

Joshua gets up to open the door.

                    STAGGER
        Who's coming?

No one responds to him. Everyone sits in silence,
waiting.

The place used to be a high-security prison, with thick, high walls, double gates of reinforced steel, and looming watchtowers at each corner of the hexagon, plus one in the center. The prison yard was now teeming with living humans in all their tragic variety: men, women, children, white, black, blue—all emaciated and exhausted, having lived with constant terror for so long. All of those people had seen their loved ones be torn to pieces or turn undead. The survivors were alive only because they were not dead, but that was subject to change at any moment. They were running out of food, they had little ammo, even less hope.

Jack, still not fully recovered, had a hard time climbing the stairs in Major K's wake. He realized he hadn't gone up stairs in a very long time. When they reached the top of the central watchtower, he was panting and had to sit down to catch his breath on the floor glittering with glass shards. A piece of sky with a sweetbread-shaped cloud was framed, indifferent, by the broken window.

"You all right?" asked Major K. His body seemed unaffected by all the recent peregrinations. He was as strong and wiry as ever, having developed an ability to survive without food and sleep. But Jack could tell that his spirit was well eaten into, and that what used to be a will to fight was now merely an inability to quit. The body keeps doing what it does; the body outlives the soul. Major K maintained a semblance of hope only because there was nothing else left to hang their future on: not on the vaccine, which worked on Jack and himself but could not be reproduced; not on the army, which was now pretty evenly split between the killers and the zombies; not on other humans, as there had been no communication with anyone outside their group for a long time.

Picking shards out of the palms of his hands, Jack finally caught his breath and stood up. From the central tower he could see far beyond the walls. All the way to the horizon, the fields were thick and lousy with zombies stumbling aimlessly, sniffing vague traces of life in the air. They would linger outside the walls, howling and rotting through the end of time, immortal because undead. What the prison protected the people inside from was the knowledge that the world had come to an end. What it provided was a space for hope, which, feeble as it was, would still live on until every last person perished. Even zombies hoped, except they hoped for one thing and one thing alone: fodder for their endless hunger.

Major K looked down on the mass in the yard, the aggregated stench of the apocalypse rising all the way to his nostrils. He bit his lip, as if refraining from saying something that shouldn't be said. He looked at Jack.

"Ready?" he asked.

"Give me a second," Jack said.

"Do take your time, but there's nothing to be afraid of."

"Too late for that," Jack said. "Fuck it! Let's roll."

Jack stepped forth to the broken window and leaned

forward so he could be seen by the people below. He raised his arms and shouted, summoning every particle of energy, his voice booming in the void of the prison yard and beyond:

"People! People!"

Major K could see the mass of zombies outside shifting their random currents to turn toward Jack's voice. The people in the yard groaned and rumbled in surprise and anticipation. Parents shushed their hungry children. Some fell on their knees.

"Last night I had a dream!" Jack lowered his voice, because now everyone listened. "A dream heartbreaking and terrible. But also beautiful."

Major K closed his eyes and passed both of his hands over his face as if washing it. It reappeared devoid of frowns and wrinkles, stripped of despair. Even as Jack was speaking, he recognized that what had just emerged on Major K's face was peace.

"It was a beautiful, big dream. Big enough for all of us," Jack went on. Before he could say anything else, somewhere below, somewhere in the silent human crowd below, a cell phone rang. First once, and then it rang again. The silence between the rings was crushing.

"Pick it up!" someone cried, but nothing happened. The sea of zombies slowly funneled toward the entrance to the prison. The first wave to reach the closed gate simply stopped. They didn't really know what to do, so they just stood there, uneasy, rumbling with hunger.

Acknowledgments

Love and gratitude to:

Etgar Keret (for the immortal cousin story);
Lana and Lilly Wachowski (for reading and laughing when
  needed);
Jasmila Žbanić (for letting me try my hand at comedy);
Velibor Božović (for being himself, indestructible);
Colum McCann (for friendship and loyalty and songs);
Rabih Alameddine (for finding time to read the book despite his
  fantasy-soccer responsibilities);
Vojislav Pejović (for being persnickety);
Catherine Peterson (for research help and the poisoned dogs story);
Duvall Osteen (for the reward of her sunny telephone voice);
Agent Aragi (for many things, but particularly for not moving a
  muscle in her face when I told her I'd written a book she'd
  known nothing about);
Sean McDonald (for patience, friendship, and appreciating the
  funny);
Deborah Treisman (for not allowing me to get by with lesser
  efforts);
Teri Boyd (for everything, but particularly for endless love and
  supportive giggling);
and Ella and Esther (for existing).

A Note About the Author

Aleksandar Hemon is the author of *The Question of Bruno, Nowhere Man, The Lazarus Project, Love and Obstacles,* and *The Book of My Lives.* He has been the recipient of a Guggenheim Fellowship, a "Genius Grant" from the MacArthur Foundation, the Jan Michalski Prize for Literature, the PEN/W. G. Sebald Award, and, most recently, a 2012 USA Fellowship. He lives in Chicago.